PUFFIN BOOKS

PERCY JACKSON

AND THE
SEA OF MONSTERS

Rick Riordan is an award-winning mystery writer. For the past fifteen years he has taught at middle schools in the San Francisco Bay area and in Texas. Rick lives in San Antonio, Texas, with his wife and two sons. *Percy Jackson and the Sea of Monsters* is Rick's second novel featuring the heroic young demigod, following the acclaimed *Percy Jackson and the Lightning Thief*, winner of the Red House Children's Book Award.

Praise for the Percy Jackson series:

'One of the books of the year . . . vastly entertaining' – *Independent*

'A fantastic blend of myth and modern. Rick Riordan takes the reader back to the stories we love, then shakes the cobwebs out of them' – Eoin Colfer, author of *Artemis Fowl*

'Funny, clever and exciting' – *The Times*

'Sure to become a classic' – *Sunday Express*

'Unputdownable' – *Irish Times*

'A fast-paced, entertaining read' – *Guardian*

'It's *Buffy* meets *Artemis Fowl*. Thumbs up' – *Sunday Times*

'Cool, mad and very funny!' – *Flipside*

Books by Rick Riordan

PERCY JACKSON AND THE LIGHTNING THIEF
PERCY JACKSON AND THE SEA OF MONSTERS
PERCY JACKSON AND THE TITAN'S CURSE
PERCY JACKSON AND THE BATTLE OF THE LABYRINTH

percyjackson.co.uk

PERCY JACKSON

AND THE
SEA OF
MONSTERS

RICK RIORDAN

<PUFFIN />

PUFFIN

To Patrick John Riordan,
the best storyteller in the family

PUFFIN BOOKS

Published by the Penguin Group
Penguin Books Ltd, 80 Strand, London WC2R 0RL, England
Penguin Group (USA) Inc., 375 Hudson Street, New York, New York 10014, USA
Penguin Group (Canada), 90 Eglinton Avenue East, Suite 700, Toronto, Ontario, Canada M4P 2Y3
(a division of Pearson Penguin Canada Inc.)
Penguin Ireland, 25 St Stephen's Green, Dublin 2, Ireland (a division of Penguin Books Ltd)
Penguin Group (Australia), 250 Camberwell Road, Camberwell, Victoria 3124, Australia
(a division of Pearson Australia Group Pty Ltd)
Penguin Books India Pvt Ltd, 11 Community Centre, Panchsheel Park, New Delhi – 110 017, India
Penguin Group (NZ), 67 Apollo Drive, Rosedale, North Shore 0632, New Zealand
(a division of Pearson New Zealand Ltd)
Penguin Books (South Africa) (Pty) Ltd, 24 Sturdee Avenue, Rosebank, Johannesburg 2196, South Africa

Penguin Books Ltd, Registered Offices: 80 Strand, London WC2R 0RL, England

puffinbooks.com

First published in the USA by Hyperion Books for Children 2006
First published in Great Britain in Puffin Books 2006
Published in this edition 2007, reissued 2008

18

Text copyright © Rick Riordan, 2006
All rights reserved

The moral right of the author has been asserted

Typeset in Centaur MT
Made and printed in England by Clays Ltd, St Ives plc

British Library Cataloguing in Publication Data
A CIP catalogue record for this book is available from the British Library

ISBN: 978–0–141–31914–8

www.greenpenguin.co.uk

CONTENTS

I MY BEST FRIEND SHOPS FOR A WEDDING DRESS

My nightmare started like this.

I was standing on a deserted street in some little beach town. It was the middle of the night. A storm was blowing. Wind and rain ripped at the palm trees along the sidewalk. Pink and yellow stucco buildings lined the street, their windows boarded up. A block away, past a line of hibiscus bushes, the ocean churned.

Florida, I thought. Though I wasn't sure how I knew that. I'd never been to Florida.

Then I heard hooves clattering against the pavement. I turned and saw my friend Grover running for his life.

Yeah, I said *hooves*.

Grover is a satyr. From the waist up, he looks like a typical gangly teenager with a peach-fuzz goatee and a bad case of acne. He walks with a strange limp, but unless you happen to catch him without his trousers on (which I don't recommend), you'd never know there was anything un-human about him. Baggy jeans and fake feet hide the fact that he's got furry hindquarters and hooves.

Grover had been my best friend in sixth grade. He'd gone on this adventure with me and a girl named Annabeth to save the world, but I hadn't seen him since last July, when he set off alone on a dangerous quest — a quest no satyr had ever returned from.

Anyway, in my dream, Grover was hauling goat tail, holding his human shoes in his hands the way he does when he needs to move fast. He clopped past the little tourist shops and surfboard rental places. The wind bent the palm trees almost to the ground.

Grover was terrified of something behind him. He must've just come from the beach. Wet sand was caked in his fur. He'd escaped from somewhere. He was trying to get away from . . . something.

A bone-rattling growl cut through the storm. Behind Grover, at the far end of the block, a shadowy figure loomed. It swatted aside a street lamp, which burst in a shower of sparks.

Grover stumbled, whimpering in fear. He muttered to himself, *Have to get away. Have to warn them!*

I couldn't see what was chasing him, but I could hear it muttering and cursing. The ground shook as it got closer. Grover dashed around a street corner and faltered. He'd run into a dead-end courtyard full of shops. No time to back up. The nearest door had been blown open by the storm. The sign above the darkened display window read: ST AUGUSTINE BRIDAL BOUTIQUE.

Grover dashed inside. He dived behind a rack of wedding dresses.

The monster's shadow passed in front of the shop. I could smell the thing – a sickening combination of wet sheep wool and rotten meat and that weird sour body odour only monsters have, like a skunk that's been living off Mexican food.

Grover trembled behind the wedding dresses. The monster's shadow passed on.

Silence except for the rain. Grover took a deep breath. Maybe the thing was gone.

Then lightning flashed. The entire front of the store exploded, and a monstrous voice bellowed, 'MIIIIINE!'

I sat bolt upright, shivering in my bed.

There was no storm. No monster.

Morning sunlight filtered through my bedroom window.

I thought I saw a shadow flicker across the glass – a humanlike shape. But then there was a knock on my bedroom door – my mom called, 'Percy, you're going to be late' – and the shadow at the window disappeared.

It must've been my imagination. A fifth-storey window with a rickety old fire escape . . . there couldn't have been anyone out there.

'Come on, dear,' my mother called again. 'Last day of school. You should be excited! You've almost made it!'

'Coming,' I managed.

I felt under my pillow. My fingers closed reassuringly around the ballpoint pen I always slept with. I brought it out, studied the Ancient Greek writing engraved on the side: *Anaklusmos*. Riptide.

I thought about uncapping it, but something held me back. I hadn't used Riptide for so long . . .

Besides, my mom had made me promise not to use deadly weapons in the apartment after I'd swung a javelin the wrong way and taken out her china cabinet. I put Anaklusmos on my nightstand and dragged myself out of bed.

I got dressed as quickly as I could. I tried not to think

about my nightmare or monsters or the shadow at my window.

Have to get away. Have to warn them!

What had Grover meant?

I made a three-fingered claw over my heart and pushed outwards – an ancient gesture Grover had once taught me for warding off evil.

The dream couldn't have been real.

Last day of school. My mom was right, I should have been excited. For the first time in my life, I'd almost made it an entire year without getting expelled. No weird accidents. No fights in the classroom. No teachers turning into monsters and trying to kill me with poisoned cafeteria food or exploding homework. Tomorrow, I'd be on my way to my favourite place in the world – Camp Half-Blood.

Only one more day to go. Surely even I couldn't mess that up.

As usual, I didn't have a clue how wrong I was.

My mom made blue waffles and blue eggs for breakfast. She's funny that way, celebrating special occasions with blue food. I think it's her way of saying anything is possible. Percy can pass seventh grade. Waffles can be blue. Little miracles like that.

I ate at the kitchen table while my mom washed dishes. She was dressed in her work uniform – a starry blue skirt and a red-and-white striped blouse she wore to sell candy at Sweet on America. Her long brown hair was pulled back in a ponytail.

The waffles tasted great, but I guess I wasn't digging

in like I usually did. My mom looked over and frowned. 'Percy, are you all right?'

'Yeah . . . fine.'

But she could always tell when something was bothering me. She dried her hands and sat down across from me. 'School, or . . .'

She didn't need to finish. I knew what she was asking.

'I think Grover's in trouble,' I said, and I told her about my dream.

She pursed her lips. We didn't talk much about the *other* part of my life. We tried to live as normally as possible, but my mom knew all about Grover.

'I wouldn't be too worried, dear,' she said. 'Grover is a big satyr now. If there were a problem, I'm sure we would've heard from . . . from camp . . .' Her shoulders tensed as she said the word *camp*.

'What is it?' I asked.

'Nothing,' she said. 'I'll tell you what. This afternoon we'll celebrate the end of school. I'll take you and Tyson to Rockefeller Center – to that skateboard shop you like.'

Oh, man, that was tempting. We were always struggling with money. Between my mom's night classes and my private school tuition, we could never afford to do special stuff like shop for a skateboard. But something in her voice bothered me.

'Wait a minute,' I said. 'I thought we were packing me up for camp tonight.'

She twisted her dishcloth. 'Ah, dear, about that . . . I got a message from Chiron last night.'

My heart sank. Chiron was the activities director at Camp Half-Blood. He wouldn't contact us unless something serious was going on. 'What did he say?'

'He thinks . . . it might not be safe for you to come to camp just yet. We might have to postpone.'

'*Postpone?* Mom, how could it not be *safe?* I'm a half-blood! It's like the only safe place on earth for me!'

'Usually, dear. But with the problems they're having –'

'*What* problems?'

'Percy . . . I'm very, very sorry. I was hoping to talk to you about it this afternoon. I can't explain it all now. I'm not even sure Chiron can. Everything happened so suddenly.'

My mind was reeling. How could I *not* go to camp? I wanted to ask a million questions, but just then the kitchen clock chimed the half-hour.

My mom looked almost relieved. 'Seven thirty, dear. You should go. Tyson will be waiting.'

'But –'

'Percy, we'll talk this afternoon. Go on to school.'

That was the last thing I wanted to do, but my mom had this fragile look in her eyes – a kind of warning, like if I pushed her too hard she'd start to cry. Besides, she was right about my friend Tyson. I had to meet him at the subway station on time or he'd get upset. He was scared of travelling underground alone.

I gathered up my stuff, but I stopped in the doorway. 'Mom, this problem at camp. Does it . . . could it have anything to do with my dream about Grover?'

She wouldn't meet my eyes. 'We'll talk this afternoon, dear. I'll explain . . . as much as I can.'

Reluctantly, I told her goodbye. I jogged downstairs to catch the Number Two train.

I didn't know it at the time, but my mom and I would never get to have our afternoon talk.

In fact, I wouldn't be seeing home for a long, long time.

As I stepped outside, I glanced at the brownstone building across the street. Just for a second I saw a dark shape in the morning sunlight – a human silhouette against the brick wall, a shadow that belonged to no one.

Then it rippled and vanished.

My day started normal. Or as normal as it ever gets at Meriwether College Prep.

See, it's this 'progressive' school in downtown Manhattan, which means we sit on beanbag chairs instead of at desks, and we don't get grades and the teachers wear jeans and rock concert T-shirts to work.

That's all cool with me. I mean, I'm ADHD and dyslexic, like most half-bloods, so I'd never done that great in regular schools even before they kicked me out. The only bad thing about Meriwether was that the teachers always looked on the bright side of things, and the kids weren't always . . . well, bright.

Take my first class today: English. The whole middle school had read this book called *Lord of the Flies*, where all these kids get marooned on an island and go psycho. So for our final exam, our teachers sent us into the yard to spend an hour with no adult supervision to see what would happen. What happened was a massive wedgie contest between the seventh and eighth graders, two pebble fights and a full-tackle basketball game. The school bully, Matt Sloan, led most of those activities.

Sloan wasn't big or strong, but he acted like he was. He had eyes like a pit bull, and shaggy black hair, and he always dressed in expensive but sloppy clothes, like he wanted everybody to see how little he cared about his family's money. One of his front teeth was chipped from the time he'd taken his daddy's Porsche for a joyride and run into a PLEASE SLOW DOWN FOR CHILDREN sign.

Anyway, Sloan was giving everybody wedgies until he made the mistake of trying it on my friend Tyson.

Tyson was the only homeless kid at Meriwether College Prep. As near as my mom and I could figure, he'd been abandoned by his parents when he was very young, probably because he was so . . . different. He was two metres tall and built like the Abominable Snowman, but he cried a lot and was scared of just about everything, including his own reflection. His face was kind of misshapen and brutal-looking. I couldn't tell you what colour his eyes were, because I could never make myself look higher than his crooked teeth. His voice was deep, but he talked funny, like a much younger kid – I guess because he'd never gone to school before coming to Meriwether. He wore tattered jeans, grimy size-twenty sneakers and a plaid flannel shirt with holes in it. He smelled like a New York City alleyway, because that's where he lived, in a cardboard refrigerator box off 72nd Street.

Meriwether Prep had adopted him as a community service project so all the students could feel good about themselves. Unfortunately, most of them couldn't stand Tyson. Once they discovered he was a big softie, despite his massive strength and his scary looks, they made themselves feel good by picking on him. I was pretty much his only friend, which meant he was *my* only friend.

My mom had complained to the school a million times that they weren't doing enough to help him. She'd called social services, but nothing ever seemed to happen. The social workers claimed Tyson didn't exist. They swore up and down that they'd visited the alley we described and couldn't find him, though how you miss a giant kid living in a refrigerator box, I don't know.

Anyway, Matt Sloan snuck up behind him and tried to give him a wedgie, and Tyson panicked. He swatted Sloan away a little too hard. Sloan flew five metres and got tangled in the little kids' tyre swing.

'You freak!' Sloan yelled. 'Why don't you go back to your cardboard box!'

Tyson started sobbing. He sat down on the jungle gym so hard he bent the bar, and buried his head in his hands.

'Take it back, Sloan!' I shouted.

Sloan just sneered at me. 'Why do you even bother, Jackson? You might have *friends* if you weren't always sticking up for that freak.'

I balled my fists. I hoped my face wasn't as red as it felt. 'He's *not* a freak. He's just . . .'

I tried to think of the right thing to say, but Sloan wasn't listening. He and his big ugly friends were too busy laughing. I wondered if it were my imagination, or if Sloan had more goons hanging around him than usual. I was used to seeing him with two or three, but today he had like, half a dozen more, and I was pretty sure I'd never seen them before.

'Just wait till PE, Jackson,' Sloan called. 'You are *so* dead.'

When first period ended, our English teacher Mr de Milo came outside to inspect the carnage. He pronounced that we'd understood *Lord of the Flies* perfectly. We all passed his course, and we should never, never grow up to be violent people. Matt Sloan nodded earnestly, then gave me a chip-toothed grin.

I had to promise to buy Tyson an extra peanut butter sandwich at lunch to get him to stop sobbing.

'I . . . I am a freak?' he asked me.

'No,' I promised, gritting my teeth. 'Matt Sloan is the freak.'

Tyson sniffled. 'You are a good friend. Miss you next year if . . . if I can't . . .'

His voice trembled. I realized he didn't know if he'd be invited back next year for the community service project. I wondered if the headmaster had even bothered talking to him about it.

'Don't worry, big guy,' I managed. 'Everything's going to be fine.'

Tyson gave me such a grateful look I felt like a big liar. How could I promise a kid like him that *anything* would be fine?

Our next exam was science. Mrs Tesla told us that we had to mix chemicals until we succeeded in making something explode. Tyson was my lab partner. His hands were way too big for the tiny vials we were supposed to use. He accidentally knocked a tray of chemicals off the counter and made an orange mushroom cloud in the trashcan.

After Mrs Tesla evacuated the lab and called the hazardous waste removal squad, she praised Tyson and me for being natural chemists. We were the first ones who'd ever aced her exam in under thirty seconds.

I was glad the morning went fast, because it kept me

from thinking too much about my problems. I couldn't stand the idea that something might be wrong at camp. Even worse, I couldn't shake the memory of my bad dream. I had a terrible feeling that Grover was in danger.

In social studies, while we were drawing latitude/longitude maps, I opened my notebook and stared at the photo inside – my friend Annabeth on vacation in Washington, DC. She was wearing jeans and a denim jacket over her orange Camp Half-Blood T-shirt. Her blonde hair was pulled back in a bandanna. She was standing in front of the Lincoln Memorial with her arms crossed, looking extremely pleased with herself, like she'd personally designed the place. See, Annabeth wants to be an architect when she grows up, so she's always visiting famous monuments and stuff. She's weird that way. She'd e-mailed me the picture after spring break, and every once in a while I'd look at it just to remind myself she was real and Camp Half-Blood hadn't just been my imagination.

I wished Annabeth were here. She'd know what to make of my dream. I'd never admit it to her, but she was smarter than me, even if she was annoying sometimes.

I was about to close my notebook when Matt Sloan reached over and ripped the photo out of the rings.

'Hey!' I protested.

Sloan checked out the picture and his eyes got wide. 'No way, Jackson. Who is that? She is *not* your –'

'Give it back!' My ears felt hot.

Sloan handed the photo to his ugly buddies, who snickered and started ripping it up to make spit wads. They were new kids who must've been visiting, because they were all wearing those stupid HI! MY NAME IS: tags from the admissions office. They must've had a weird sense of humour, too, because they'd all filled in strange names like: MARROW SUCKER, SKULL EATER and JOE BOB. No human beings had names like that.

'These guys are moving here next year,' Sloan bragged, like that was supposed to scare me. 'I bet they can *pay* the tuition, too, unlike your retard friend.'

'He's *not* retarded.' I had to try really, really hard not to punch Sloan in the face.

'You're such a loser, Jackson. Good thing I'm gonna put you out of your misery next period.'

His huge buddies chewed up my photo. I wanted to pulverize them, but I was under strict orders from Chiron never to take my anger out on regular mortals, no matter how obnoxious they were. I had to save my fighting for monsters.

Still, part of me thought, if Sloan only knew who I really was . . .

The bell rang.

As Tyson and I were leaving class, a girl's voice whispered, 'Percy!'

I looked around the locker area, but nobody was paying me any attention. Like any girl at Meriwether would ever be caught dead calling my name.

Before I had time to consider whether or not I'd been imagining things, a crowd of kids rushed for the gym, carrying Tyson and me along with them. It was time for PE. Our coach had promised us a free-for-all dodgeball game, and Matt Sloan had promised to kill me.

* * *

The gym uniform at Meriwether is sky-blue shorts and tie-dyed T-shirts. Fortunately, we did most of our athletic stuff inside, so we didn't have to jog through Tribeca looking like a bunch of boot-camp hippie children.

I changed as quickly as I could in the locker room because I didn't want to deal with Sloan. I was about to leave when Tyson called, 'Percy?'

He hadn't changed yet. He was standing by the weight-room door, clutching his gym clothes. 'Will you . . . uh . . .'

'Oh. Yeah.' I tried not to sound aggravated about it. 'Yeah, sure, man.'

Tyson ducked inside the weight room. I stood guard outside the door while he changed. I felt kind of awkward doing this, but he asked me to most days. I think it's because he's completely hairy and he's got weird scars on his back that I've never had the courage to ask him about.

Anyway, I'd learned the hard way that if people teased Tyson while he was dressing, he'd get upset and start ripping the doors off lockers.

When we got into the gym, Coach Nunley was sitting at his little desk reading *Sports Illustrated*. Nunley was about a million years old, with bifocals and no teeth and a greasy wave of grey hair. He reminded me of the Oracle at Camp Half-Blood – which was a shrivelled-up mummy – except Coach Nunley moved a lot less and he never billowed green smoke. Well, at least not that I'd observed.

Matt Sloan said, 'Coach, can I be captain?'

'Eh?' Coach Nunley looked up from his magazine. 'Yeah,' he mumbled. 'Mm-hmm.'

Sloan grinned and took charge of the picking. He made

me the other team's captain, but it didn't matter who I picked, because all the jocks and the popular kids moved over to Sloan's side. So did the big group of visitors.

On my side I had Tyson, Corey Bailer the computer geek, Raj Mandali the calculus whiz, and a half-dozen other kids who always got harassed by Sloan and his gang. Normally I would've been okay with just Tyson — he was worth half a team all by himself — but the visitors on Sloan's team were almost as tall and strong-looking as Tyson, and there were six of them.

Matt Sloan spilled a cage full of balls in the middle of the gym.

'Scared,' Tyson mumbled. 'Smell funny.'

I looked at him. 'What smells funny?' Because I didn't figure he was talking about himself.

'Them.' Tyson pointed at Sloan's new friends. 'Smell funny.'

The visitors were cracking their knuckles, eyeing us like it was slaughter time. I couldn't help wondering where they were from. Someplace where they fed kids raw meat and beat them with sticks.

Sloan blew the coach's whistle and the game began. Sloan's team ran for the centre line. On my side, Raj Mandali yelled something in Urdu, probably 'I have to go potty!' and ran for the exit. Corey Bailer tried to crawl behind the wall mat and hide. The rest of my team did their best to cower in fear and not look like targets.

'Tyson,' I said. 'Let's g—'

A ball slammed into my gut. I sat down hard in the middle of the gym floor. The other team exploded in laughter.

My eyesight was fuzzy. I felt like I'd just got the Heimlich manoeuvre from a gorilla. I couldn't believe anybody could throw that hard.

Tyson yelled, 'Percy, duck!'

I rolled as another dodgeball whistled past my ear at the speed of sound.

Whooom!

It hit the wall mat, and Corey Bailer yelped.

'Hey!' I yelled at Sloan's team. 'You could kill somebody!'

The visitor named Joe Bob grinned at me evilly. Somehow, he looked a lot bigger now . . . even taller than Tyson. His biceps bulged beneath his T-shirt. 'I hope so, Perseus Jackson! I hope so!'

The way he said my name sent a chill down my back. Nobody called me Perseus except those who knew my true identity. Friends . . . and enemies.

What had Tyson said? *They smell funny.*

Monsters.

All around Matt Sloan, the visitors were growing in size. They were no longer kids. They were two-and-a-half-metre-tall giants with wild eyes, pointy teeth and hairy arms tattooed with snakes and hula women and Valentine hearts.

Matt Sloan dropped his ball. 'Whoa! You're not from Detroit! Who . . .'

The other kids on his team started screaming and backing towards the exit, but the giant named Marrow Sucker threw a ball with deadly accuracy. It streaked past Raj Mandali just as he was about to leave and hit the door, slamming it shut like magic. Raj and some of the other kids banged on it desperately but it wouldn't budge.

'Let them go!' I yelled at the giants.

The one called Joe Bob growled at me. He had a tattoo on his biceps that said: *JB luvs Babycakes*. 'And lose our tasty morsels? No, Son of the Sea God. We Laistrygonians aren't just playing for your death. We want lunch!'

He waved his hand and a new batch of dodgeballs appeared on the centre line – but these balls weren't made of red rubber. They were bronze, the size of cannon balls, perforated like Wiffle balls with fire bubbling out the holes. They must've been searing hot, but the giants picked them up with their bare hands.

'Coach!' I yelled.

Nunley looked up sleepily, but if he saw anything abnormal about the dodgeball game, he didn't let on. That's the problem with mortals. A magical force called the Mist obscures the true appearance of monsters and gods from their vision, so mortals tend to see only what they can understand. Maybe the coach saw a few eighth graders pounding the younger kids like usual. Maybe the other kids saw Matt Sloan's thugs getting ready to toss Molotov cocktails around. (It wouldn't have been the first time.) At any rate, I was pretty sure nobody else realized we were dealing with genuine man-eating bloodthirsty monsters.

'Yeah. Mm-hmm,' Coach muttered. 'Play nice.'

And he went back to his magazine.

The giant named Skull Eater threw his ball. I dived aside as the fiery bronze comet sailed past my shoulder.

'Corey!' I screamed.

Tyson pulled him out from behind the exercise mat just as the ball exploded against it, blasting the mat to smoking shreds.

'Run!' I told my teammates. 'The other exit!'

They ran for the locker room, but with another wave of Joe Bob's hand, that door also slammed shut.

'No one leaves unless you're out!' Joe Bob roared. 'And you're not out until we eat you!'

He launched his own fireball. My teammates scattered as it blasted a crater in the gym floor.

I reached for Riptide, which I always kept in my pocket, but then I realized I was wearing gym shorts. I *had* no pockets. Riptide was tucked in my jeans inside my gym locker. And the locker room door was sealed. I was completely defenceless.

Another fireball came streaking towards me. Tyson pushed me out of the way, but the explosion still blew me head over heels. I found myself sprawled on the gym floor, dazed from smoke, my tie-dyed T-shirt peppered with sizzling holes. Just across the centre line, two hungry giants were glaring down at me.

'Flesh!' they bellowed. 'Hero flesh for lunch!' They both took aim.

'Percy needs help!' Tyson yelled, and he jumped in front of me just as they threw their balls.

'Tyson!' I screamed, but it was too late.

Both balls slammed into him . . . but no . . . he'd caught them. Somehow Tyson, who was so clumsy he knocked over lab equipment and broke playground structures on a regular basis, had caught two fiery metal balls speeding towards him at a zillion miles an hour. He sent them hurtling back towards their surprised owners, who screamed, 'BAAAAAD!' as the bronze spheres exploded against their chests.

The giants disintegrated in twin columns of flame — a sure sign they were monsters, all right. Monsters don't die. They just dissipate into smoke and dust, which saves heroes a lot of trouble cleaning up after a fight.

'My brothers!' Joe Bob the Cannibal wailed. He flexed his muscles and his *Babycakes* tattoo rippled. 'You will pay for their destruction!'

'Tyson!' I said. 'Look out!'

Another comet hurtled towards us. Tyson just had time to swat it aside. It flew straight over Coach Nunley's head and landed in the stands with a huge KA-BOOM!

Kids were running around screaming, trying to avoid the sizzling craters in the floor. Others were banging on the door, calling for help. Sloan himself stood petrified in the middle of the court, watching in disbelief as balls of death flew around him.

Coach Nunley still wasn't seeing anything. He tapped his hearing aid like the explosions were giving him interference, but he kept his eyes on his magazine.

Surely the whole school could hear the noise. The headmaster, the police, somebody would come help us.

'Victory will be ours!' roared Joe Bob the Cannibal. 'We will feast on your bones!'

I wanted to tell him he was taking the dodgeball game way too seriously, but before I could, he hefted another ball. The other three giants followed his lead.

I knew we were dead. Tyson couldn't deflect all those balls at once. His hands *had* to be seriously burned from blocking the first volley. Without my sword . . .

I had a crazy idea.

I ran towards the locker room.

'Move!' I told my teammates. 'Away from the door.'

Explosions behind me. Tyson had batted two of the balls back towards their owners and blasted them to ashes.

That left two giants still standing.

A third ball hurtled straight at me. I forced myself to wait – one Mississippi, two Mississippi – then dived aside as the fiery sphere demolished the locker room door.

Now, I figured that the built-up gas in most boys' locker rooms was enough to cause an explosion, so I wasn't surprised when the flaming dodgeball ignited a huge *WHOOOOOOOM*!

The wall blew apart. Locker doors, socks, athletic supports and other various nasty personal belongings rained all over the gym.

I turned just in time to see Tyson punch Skull Eater in the face. The giant crumpled. But the last giant, Joe Bob, had wisely held on to his own ball, waiting for an opportunity. He threw just as Tyson was turning to face him.

'No!' I yelled.

The ball caught Tyson square in the chest. He slid the length of the court and slammed into the back wall, which cracked and partially crumbled on top of him, making a hole right onto Church Street. I didn't see how Tyson could still be alive, but he only looked dazed. The bronze ball was smoking at his feet. Tyson tried to pick it up, but he fell back, stunned, into a pile of cinder blocks.

'Well!' Joe Bob gloated. 'I'm the last one standing! I'll have enough meat to bring Babycakes a doggy bag!'

He picked up another ball and aimed it at Tyson.

'Stop!' I yelled. 'It's me you want!'

The giant grinned. 'You wish to die first, young hero?'

I had to do something. Riptide had to be around here somewhere.

Then I spotted my jeans in a smoking heap of clothes right by the giant's feet. If I could only get there . . . I knew it was hopeless, but I charged.

The giant laughed. 'My lunch approaches.' He raised his arm to throw. I braced myself to die.

Suddenly the giant's body went rigid. His expression changed from gloating to surprise. Right where his belly button should've been, his T-shirt ripped open and he grew something like a horn — no, not a horn — the glowing tip of a blade.

The ball dropped out of his hand. The monster stared down at the knife that had just run him through from behind.

He muttered, 'Ow,' and burst into a cloud of green flame, which I figured was going to make Babycakes pretty upset.

Standing in the smoke was my friend Annabeth. Her face was grimy and scratched. She had a ragged backpack slung over her shoulder, her baseball cap tucked in her pocket, a bronze knife in her hand, and a wild look in her storm-grey eyes, like she'd just been chased a thousand miles by ghosts.

Matt Sloan, who'd been standing there dumbfounded the whole time, finally came to his senses. He blinked at Annabeth, as if he dimly recognized her from my notebook picture. 'That's the girl . . . That's the girl —'

Annabeth punched him in the nose and knocked him flat. 'And *you*,' she told him, 'lay off my friend.'

The gym was in flames. Kids were still running around screaming. I heard sirens wailing and a garbled voice over the intercom. Through the glass windows of the exit doors, I could see the headmaster, Mr Bonsai, wrestling with the lock, a crowd of teachers piling up behind him.

'Annabeth . . .' I stammered. 'How did you . . . how long have you . . .'

'Pretty much all morning.' She sheathed her bronze knife. 'I've been trying to find a good time to talk to you, but you were never alone.'

'The shadow I saw this morning – that was –' My face felt hot. 'Oh my gods, you were looking in my bedroom window?'

'There's no time to explain!' she snapped, though she looked a little red-faced herself. 'I just didn't want to –'

'There!' a woman screamed. The doors burst open and the adults came pouring in.

'Meet me outside,' Annabeth told me. 'And him.' She pointed to Tyson, who was still sitting dazed against the wall. Annabeth gave him a look of distaste that I didn't quite understand. 'You'd better bring him.'

'*What?*'

'No time!' she said. 'Hurry!'

She put on her Yankees baseball cap, which was a magic gift from her mom, and instantly vanished.

That left me standing alone in the middle of the burning gymnasium when the headmaster came charging in with half the faculty and a couple of police officers.

'Percy Jackson?' Mr Bonsai said. 'What . . . how . . .'

Over by the broken wall, Tyson groaned and stood up from the pile of cinder blocks. 'Head hurts.'

Matt Sloan was coming around, too. He focused on me with a look of terror. 'Percy did it, Mr Bonsai! He set the whole building on fire. Coach Nunley will tell you! He saw it all!'

Coach Nunley had been dutifully reading his magazine, but just my luck — he chose that moment to look up when Sloan said his name. 'Eh? Yeah. Mm-hmm.'

The other adults turned towards me. I knew they would never believe me, even if I could tell them the truth.

I grabbed Riptide out of my ruined jeans, told Tyson, 'Come on!' and jumped through the gaping hole in the side of the building.

WE HAIL THE TAXI OF ETERNAL TORMENT

Annabeth was waiting for us in an alley down Church Street. She pulled Tyson and me off the sidewalk just as a fire truck screamed past, heading for Meriwether Prep.

'Where'd you find *him*?' she demanded, pointing at Tyson.

Now, under different circumstances, I would've been really happy to see her. We'd made our peace last summer, despite the fact that her mom was Athena and didn't get along with my dad. I'd missed Annabeth probably more than I wanted to admit.

But I'd just been attacked by cannibal giants, Tyson had saved my life three or four times, and all Annabeth could do was glare at him like *he* was the problem.

'He's my friend,' I told her.

'Is he homeless?'

'What does that have to do with anything? He can hear you, you know. Why don't you ask him?'

She looked surprised. 'He can talk?'

'I talk,' Tyson admitted. 'You are pretty.'

'Ah! Gross!' Annabeth stepped away from him.

I couldn't believe she was being so rude. I examined Tyson's hands, which I was sure must've been badly scorched by the flaming dodgeballs, but they looked fine – grimy and scarred, with dirty fingernails the size of potato chips

– but they always looked like that. 'Tyson,' I said in disbelief. 'Your hands aren't even burned.'

'Of course not,' Annabeth muttered. 'I'm surprised the Laistrygonians had the guts to attack you with him around.'

Tyson seemed fascinated by Annabeth's blonde hair. He tried to touch it, but she smacked his hand away.

'Annabeth,' I said, 'what are you talking about? Laistry-what?'

'Laistrygonians. The monsters in the gym. They're a race of giant cannibals who live in the far north. Odysseus ran into them once, but I've never seen them as far south as New York before.'

'Laistry – I can't even say that. What would you call them in English?'

She thought about it for a moment. 'Canadians,' she decided. 'Now come on, we have to get out of here.'

'The police'll be after me.'

'That's the least of our problems,' she said. 'Have you been having the dreams?'

'The dreams . . . about Grover?'

Her face turned pale. 'Grover? No, what about Grover?'

I told her my dream. 'Why? What were *you* dreaming about?'

Her eyes looked stormy, like her mind was racing a million miles an hour.

'Camp,' she said at last. 'Big trouble at camp.'

'My mom was saying the same thing! But what *kind* of trouble?'

'I don't know exactly. Something's wrong. We have to get there right away. Monsters have been chasing me all the way from Virginia, trying to stop me. Have you had a lot of attacks?'

I shook my head. 'None all year . . . until today.'

'None? But how . . .' Her eyes drifted to Tyson. 'Oh.'

'What do mean, "oh"?'

Tyson raised his hand like he was still in class. 'Canadians in the gym called Percy something . . . Son of the Sea God?'

Annabeth and I exchanged looks.

I didn't know how I could explain, but I figured Tyson deserved the truth after almost getting killed.

'Big guy,' I said, 'you ever hear those old stories about the Greek gods? Like Zeus, Poseidon, Athena —'

'Yes,' Tyson said.

'Well . . . those gods are still alive. They kind of follow Western Civilization around, living in the strongest countries, so like now they're in the U.S. And sometimes they have kids with mortals. Kids called half-bloods.'

'Yes,' Tyson said, like he was still waiting for me to get to the point.

'Uh, well, Annabeth and I are half-bloods,' I said. 'We're like . . . heroes-in-training. And whenever monsters pick up our scent, they attack us. That's what those giants were in the gym. Monsters.'

'Yes.'

I stared at him. He didn't seem surprised or confused by what I was telling him, which surprised and confused me. 'So . . . you believe me?'

Tyson nodded. 'But you are . . . Son of the Sea God?'

'Yeah,' I admitted. 'My dad is Poseidon.'

Tyson frowned. *Now* he looked confused. 'But then . . .'

A siren wailed. A police car raced past our alley.

'We don't have time for this,' Annabeth said. 'We'll talk in the taxi.'

'A taxi all the way to camp?' I said. 'You know how much money –'

'Trust me.'

I hesitated. 'What about Tyson?'

I imagined escorting my giant friend into Camp Half-Blood. If he freaked out on a regular playground with regular bullies, how would he act at a training camp for demigods? On the other hand, the cops would be looking for us.

'We can't just leave him,' I decided. 'He'll be in trouble, too.'

'Yeah.' Annabeth looked grim. 'We definitely need to take him. Now come on.'

I didn't like the way she said that, as if Tyson were a big disease we needed to get to the hospital, but I followed her down the alley. Together the three of us sneaked through the side streets of downtown while a huge column of smoke billowed up behind us from my school gymnasium.

'Here.' Annabeth stopped us on the corner of Thomas and Trimble. She fished around in her backpack. 'I hope I have one left.'

She looked even worse than I'd realized at first. Her chin was cut. Twigs and grass were tangled in her ponytail, as if she'd slept several nights in the open. The slashes on the hems of her jeans looked suspiciously like claw marks.

'What are you looking for?' I asked.

All around us, sirens wailed. I figured it wouldn't be

long before more cops cruised by, looking for juvenile delinquent gym-bombers. No doubt Matt Sloan had given them a statement by now. He'd probably twisted the story around so that Tyson and I were the bloodthirsty cannibals.

'Found one. Thank the gods.' Annabeth pulled out a gold coin that I recognized as a drachma, the currency of Mount Olympus. It had Zeus's likeness stamped on one side and the Empire State Building on the other.

'Annabeth,' I said, 'New York taxi drivers won't take that.'

'*Anakoche,*' she shouted in Ancient Greek. '*Harma epitribeios!*'

As usual, the moment she spoke in the language of Olympus, I somehow understood it. She'd said, *Stop, Chariot of Damnation!*

That didn't exactly make me feel real excited about whatever her plan was.

She threw her coin into the street, but instead of clattering on the tarmac, the drachma sank right through and disappeared.

For a moment, nothing happened.

Then, just where the coin had fallen, the tarmac darkened. It melted into a rectangular pool about the size of a parking space – bubbling red liquid like blood. Then a car erupted from the ooze.

It was a taxi, all right, but, unlike every other taxi in New York, it wasn't yellow. It was smoky grey. I mean it looked like it was *woven* out of smoke, like you could walk right through it. There were words printed on the door – something like GYAR SSIRES – but my dyslexia made it hard for me to decipher what it said.

The passenger window rolled down, and an old woman stuck her head out. She had a mop of grizzled hair covering her eyes, and she spoke in a weird mumbling way, like she'd just had a shot of Novocain. 'Passage? Passage?'

'Three to Camp Half-Blood,' Annabeth said. She opened the cab's back door and waved at me to get in, like this was all completely normal.

'Ach!' the old woman screeched. 'We don't take *his* kind!'

She pointed a bony finger at Tyson.

What was it? Pick-on-Big-and-Ugly-Kids Day?

'Extra pay,' Annabeth promised. 'Three more drachmas on arrival.'

'Done!' the woman screamed.

Reluctantly I got in the cab. Tyson squeezed in the middle. Annabeth crawled in last.

The interior was also smoky grey, but it felt solid enough. The seat was cracked and lumpy – no different than most taxis. There was no Plexiglas screen separating us from the old lady driving . . . Wait a minute. There wasn't just one old lady. There were three, all crammed in the front seat, each with stringy hair covering her eyes, bony hands and a charcoal-coloured sackcloth dress.

The one driving said, 'Long Island! Out-of-metro fare bonus! Ha!'

She floored the accelerator, and my head slammed against the backrest. A pre-recorded voice came on over the speaker: *Hi, this is Ganymede, cup-bearer to Zeus, and when I'm out buying wine for the Lord of the Skies, I always buckle up!*

I looked down and found a large black chain instead of a seat belt. I decided I wasn't that desperate . . . yet.

The cab sped around the corner of West Broadway, and the grey lady sitting in the middle screeched, 'Look out! Go left!'

'Well, if you'd give me the eye, Tempest, I could *see* that!' the driver complained.

Wait a minute. *Give her the eye?*

I didn't have time to ask questions because the driver swerved to avoid an oncoming delivery truck, ran over the kerb with a jaw-rattling *thump*, and flew into the next block.

'Wasp!' the third lady said to the driver. 'Give me the girl's coin! I want to bite it.'

'You bit it last time, Anger!' said the driver, whose name must've been Wasp. 'It's my turn!'

'Is not!' yelled the one called Anger.

The middle one, Tempest, screamed, 'Red light!'

'Brake!' yelled Anger.

Instead, Wasp floored the accelerator and rode up on the kerb, screeching around another corner, and knocking over a newspaper box. She left my stomach somewhere back on Broome Street.

'Excuse me,' I said. 'But . . . can you see?'

'No!' screamed Wasp from behind the wheel.

'No!' screamed Tempest from the middle.

'Of course!' screamed Anger by the shotgun window.

I looked at Annabeth. 'They're blind?'

'Not completely,' Annabeth said. 'They have an eye.'

'One eye?'

'Yeah.'

'Each?'

'No. One eye total.'

Next to me, Tyson groaned and grabbed the seat. 'Not feeling so good.'

'Oh, man,' I said, because I'd seen Tyson get carsick on school field trips and it was *not* something you wanted to be within fifteen metres of. 'Hang in there, big guy. Anybody got a garbage bag or something?'

The three grey ladies were too busy squabbling to pay me any attention. I looked over at Annabeth, who was hanging on for dear life, and I gave her a *why-did-you-do-this-to-me* look.

'Hey,' she said, 'Grey Sisters Taxi is the fastest way to camp.'

'Then why didn't you take it from Virginia?'

'That's outside their service area,' she said, like that should be obvious. 'They only serve Greater New York and surrounding communities.'

'We've had famous people in this cab!' Anger exclaimed. 'Jason! You remember him?'

'Don't remind me!' Wasp wailed. 'And we didn't have a cab back then, you old bat. That was three thousand years ago!'

'Give me the tooth!' Anger tried to grab at Wasp's mouth, but Wasp swatted her hand away.

'Only if Tempest gives me the eye!'

'No!' Tempest screeched. 'You had it yesterday!'

'But I'm driving, you old hag!'

'Excuses! Turn! That was your turn!'

Wasp swerved hard onto Delancey Street, squishing me between Tyson and the door. She punched the gas and we shot up the Williamsburg Bridge at seventy miles an hour.

The three sisters were fighting for real now, slapping each

other as Anger tried to grab at Wasp's face and Wasp tried to grab at Tempest's. With their hair flying and their mouths open, screaming at each other, I realized that none of the sisters had any teeth except for Wasp, who had one mossy yellow incisor. Instead of eyes, they just had closed, sunken eyelids, except for Anger, who had one bloodshot green eye that stared at everything hungrily, as if it couldn't get enough of anything it saw.

Finally Anger, who had the advantage of sight, managed to yank the tooth out of her sister Wasp's mouth. This made Wasp so mad she swerved towards the edge of the Williamsburg Bridge, yelling, ''Ivit back! 'Ivit back!'

Tyson groaned and clutched his stomach.

'Uh, if anybody's interested,' I said, 'we're going to die!'

'Don't worry,' Annabeth told me, sounding pretty worried. 'The Grey Sisters know what they're doing. They're really very wise.'

This coming from the daughter of Athena, but I wasn't exactly reassured. We were skimming along the edge of a bridge forty metres above the East River.

'Yes, wise!' Anger grinned in the rear-view mirror, showing off her newly acquired tooth. 'We know things!'

'Every street in Manhattan!' Wasp bragged, still hitting her sister. 'The capital of Nepal!'

'The location you seek!' Tempest added.

Immediately her sisters pummelled her from either side, screaming, 'Be quiet! Be quiet! He didn't even ask yet!'

'What?' I said. 'What location? I'm not seeking any –'

'Nothing!' Tempest said. 'You're right, boy. It's nothing!'

'Tell me.'

'No!' they all screamed.

'The last time we told, it was horrible!' Tempest said.

'Eye tossed in a lake!' Anger agreed.

'Years to find it again!' Wasp moaned. 'And speaking of that – give it back!'

'No!' yelled Anger.

'Eye!' Wasp yelled. 'Gimme!'

She whacked her sister Anger on the back. There was a sickening *pop* and something flew out of Anger's face. Anger fumbled for it, trying to catch it, but she only managed to bat it with the back of her hand. The slimy green orb sailed over her shoulder, into the back seat, and straight into my lap.

I jumped so hard, my head hit the ceiling and the eyeball rolled away.

'I can't see!' all three sisters yelled.

'Give me the eye!' Wasp wailed.

'Give her the eye!' Annabeth screamed.

'I don't have it!' I said.

'There, by your foot,' Annabeth said. 'Don't step on it! Get it!'

'I'm not picking that up!'

The taxi slammed against the guardrail and skidded along with a horrible grinding noise. The whole car shuddered, billowing grey smoke as if it were about to dissolve from the strain.

'Going to be sick!' Tyson warned.

'Annabeth,' I yelled, 'let Tyson use your backpack!'

'Are you crazy? Get the eye!'

Wasp yanked the wheel, and the taxi swerved away from the rail. We hurtled down the bridge towards Brooklyn, going faster than any human taxi. The Grey Sisters screeched and pummelled each other and cried out for their eye.

At last I steeled my nerves. I ripped off a chunk of my tie-dyed T-shirt, which was already falling apart from all the burn marks, and used it to pick the eyeball off the floor.

'Nice boy!' Anger cried, as if she somehow knew I had her missing peeper. 'Give it back!'

'Not until you explain,' I told her. 'What were you talking about, the location I seek?'

'No time!' Tempest cried. 'Accelerating!'

I looked out the window. Sure enough, trees and cars and whole neighbourhoods were now zipping by in a grey blur. We were already out of Brooklyn, heading through the middle of Long Island.

'Percy,' Annabeth warned, 'they can't find our destination without the eye. We'll just keep accelerating until we break into a million pieces.'

'First they have to tell me,' I said. 'Or I'll open the window and throw the eye into oncoming traffic.'

'No!' the Grey Sisters wailed. 'Too dangerous!'

'I'm rolling down the window.'

'Wait!' the Grey Sisters screamed. 'Thirty, thirty-one, seventy-five, twelve!'

They belted it out like a quarterback calling a play.

'What do you mean?' I said. 'That makes no sense!'

'Thirty, thirty-one, seventy-five, twelve!' Anger wailed. 'That's all we can tell you. Now give us the eye! Almost to camp!'

We were off the highway now, zipping through the countryside of northern Long Island. I could see Half-

Blood Hill ahead of us, with its giant pine tree at the crest – Thalia's tree, which contained the life force of a fallen hero.

'Percy!' Annabeth said more urgently. 'Give them the eye *now!*'

I decided not to argue. I threw the eye into Wasp's lap.

The old lady snatched it up, pushed it into her eye socket like somebody putting in a contact lens, and blinked. 'Whoa!'

She slammed on the brakes. The taxi spun four or five times in a cloud of smoke and squealed to a halt in the middle of the farm road at the base of Half-Blood Hill.

Tyson let loose a huge belch. 'Better now.'

'All right,' I told the Grey Sisters. 'Now tell me what those numbers mean.'

'No time!' Annabeth opened her door. 'We have to get out *now.*'

I was about to ask why, when I looked up at Half-Blood Hill and understood.

At the crest of the hill was a group of campers. And they were under attack.

4   TYSON PLAYS WITH FIRE

Mythologically speaking, if there's anything I hate worse than trios of old ladies, it's bulls. Last summer, I fought the Minotaur on top of Half-Blood Hill. This time what I saw up there was even worse: two bulls. And not just regular bulls – bronze ones the size of elephants. And even *that* wasn't bad enough. Naturally they had to breathe fire, too.

As soon as we exited the taxi, the Grey Sisters peeled out, heading back to New York, where life was safer. They didn't even wait for their extra three-drachma payment. They just left us on the side of the road, Annabeth with nothing but her backpack and knife, Tyson and me still in our burned-up tie-dyed gym clothes.

'Oh, man,' said Annabeth, looking at the battle raging on the hill.

What worried me most weren't the bulls themselves. Or the ten heroes in full battle armour who were getting their bronze-plated booties whooped. What worried me was that the bulls were ranging all over the hill, even around the back side of the pine tree. That shouldn't have been possible. The camp's magic boundaries didn't allow monsters to cross past Thalia's tree. But the metal bulls were doing it anyway.

One of the heroes shouted, 'Border patrol, to me!' A girl's voice – gruff and familiar.

Border patrol? I thought. The camp didn't *have* a border patrol.

'It's Clarisse,' Annabeth said. 'Come on, we have to help her.'

Normally, rushing to Clarisse's aid would not have been high on my 'to do' list. She was one of the biggest bullies at camp. The first time we'd met she tried to introduce my head to a toilet. She was also a daughter of Ares, and I'd had a very serious disagreement with her father last summer, so now the god of war and all his children basically hated my guts.

Still, she *was* in trouble. Her fellow warriors were scattering, running in panic as the bulls charged. The grass was burning in huge swathes around the pine tree. One hero screamed and waved his arms as he ran in circles, the horsehair plume on his helmet blazing like a fiery Mohawk. Clarisse's own armour was charred. She was fighting with a broken spear shaft, the other end embedded uselessly in the metal joint of one bull's shoulder.

I uncapped my ballpoint pen. It shimmered, growing longer and heavier until I held the bronze sword Anaklusmos in my hands. 'Tyson, stay here. I don't want you taking any more chances.'

'No!' Annabeth said. 'We need him.'

I stared at her. 'He's mortal. He got lucky with the dodgeballs but he can't –'

'Percy, do you know what those are up there? The Colchis bulls, made by Hephaestus himself. We can't fight them without Medea's Sunscreen SPF 50,000. We'll get burned to a crisp.'

'Medea's *what?*'

Annabeth rummaged through her backpack and cursed. 'I had a jar of tropical coconut scent sitting on my nightstand at home. Why didn't I bring it?'

I'd learned a long time ago not to question Annabeth too much. It just made me more confused. 'Look, I don't know what you're talking about, but I'm *not* going to let Tyson get fried.'

'Percy —'

'Tyson, stay back.' I raised my sword. 'I'm going in.'

Tyson tried to protest, but I was already running up the hill towards Clarisse, who was yelling at her patrol, trying to get them into phalanx formation. It was a good idea. The few who were listening lined up shoulder to shoulder, locking their shields to form an ox-hide-and-bronze wall, their spears bristling over the top like porcupine quills.

Unfortunately, Clarisse could only muster six campers. The other four were still running around with their helmets on fire. Annabeth ran towards them, trying to help. She taunted one of the bulls into chasing her, then turned invisible, completely confusing the monster. The other bull charged Clarisse's line.

I was halfway up the hill — not close enough to help. Clarisse hadn't even seen me yet.

The bull moved deadly fast for something so big. Its metal hide gleamed in the sun. It had fist-sized rubies for eyes and horns of polished silver. When it opened its hinged mouth, a column of white-hot flame blasted out.

'Hold the line!' Clarisse ordered her warriors.

Whatever else you could say about Clarisse, she was brave. She was a big girl with cruel eyes like her father's. She looked like she was born to wear Greek battle armour, but I didn't see how even she could stand against that bull's charge.

Unfortunately, at that moment, the other bull lost interest in finding Annabeth. It turned, wheeling around behind Clarisse on her unprotected side.

'Behind you!' I yelled. 'Look out!'

I shouldn't have said anything, because all I did was startle her. Bull Number One crashed into her shield, and the phalanx broke. Clarisse went flying backwards and landed in a smouldering patch of grass. The bull charged past her, but not before blasting the other heroes with its fiery breath. Their shields melted right off their arms. They dropped their weapons and ran as Bull Number Two closed in on Clarisse for the kill.

I lunged forward and grabbed Clarisse by the straps of her armour. I dragged her out of the way just as Bull Number Two freight-trained past. I gave it a good swipe with Riptide and cut a huge gash in its flank, but the monster just creaked and groaned and kept on going.

It hadn't touched me, but I could feel the heat of its metal skin. Its body temperature could've microwaved a frozen burrito.

'Let me go!' Clarisse pummelled my hand. 'Percy, curse you!'

I dropped her in a heap next to the pine tree and turned to face the bulls. We were on the inside slope of the hill now, the valley of Camp Half-Blood directly below us – the cabins, the training facilities, the Big House – all of it at risk if these bulls got past us.

Annabeth shouted orders to the other heroes, telling them to spread out and keep the bulls distracted.

Bull Number One ran a wide arc, making its way back towards me. As it passed the middle of the hill, where the invisible boundary line should've kept it out, it slowed down a little, as if it were struggling against a strong wind; but then it broke through and kept coming. Bull Number Two turned to face me, fire sputtering from the gash I'd cut in its side. I couldn't tell if it felt any pain, but its ruby eyes seemed to glare at me like I'd just made things personal.

I couldn't fight both bulls at the same time. I'd have to take down Bull Number Two first, cut its head off before Bull Number One charged back into range. My arms already felt tired. I realized how long it had been since I'd worked out with Riptide, how out of practice I was.

I lunged but Bull Number Two blew flames at me. I rolled aside as the air turned to pure heat. All the oxygen was sucked out of my lungs. My foot caught on something – a tree root, maybe – and pain shot up my ankle. Still, I managed to slash with my sword and lop off part of the monster's snout. It galloped away, wild and disoriented. But before I could feel too good about that, I tried to stand, and my left leg buckled underneath me. My ankle was sprained, maybe broken.

Bull Number One charged straight towards me. No way could I crawl out of its path.

Annabeth shouted, 'Tyson, help him!'

Somewhere near, towards the crest of the hill, Tyson wailed, 'Can't – get – through!'

'I, Annabeth Chase, give you permission to enter camp!'

Thunder shook the hillside. Suddenly Tyson was there, barrelling towards me, yelling, 'Percy needs help!'

Before I could tell him no, he dived between me and the bull just as it unleashed a nuclear firestorm.

'Tyson!' I yelled.

The blast swirled around him like a red tornado. I could only see the black silhouette of his body. I knew with horrible certainty that my friend had just been turned into a column of ashes.

But when the fire died, Tyson was still standing there, completely unharmed. Not even his grungy clothes were scorched. The bull must've been as surprised as I was, because before it could unleash a second blast, Tyson balled his fists and slammed them into the bull's face. 'BAD COW!'

His fists made a crater where the bronze bull's snout used to be. Two small columns of flame shot out of its ears. Tyson hit it again, and the bronze crumpled under his hands like aluminium foil. The bull's face now looked like a sock puppet pulled inside out.

'Down!' Tyson yelled.

The bull staggered and fell on its back. Its legs moved feebly in the air, steam coming out of its ruined head in odd places.

Annabeth ran over to check on me.

My ankle felt like it was filled with acid, but she gave me some Olympian nectar to drink from her canteen, and I immediately started to feel better. There was a burning smell that I later learned was me. The hair on my arms had been completely singed off.

'The other bull?' I asked.

Annabeth pointed down the hill. Clarisse had taken care of Bad Cow Number Two. She'd impaled it through the back leg with a celestial bronze spear. Now, with its snout half gone and a huge gash in its side, it was trying to run in slow motion, going in circles like some kind of merry-go-round animal.

Clarisse pulled off her helmet and marched towards us. A strand of her stringy brown hair was smouldering, but she didn't seem to notice. 'You – ruin – everything!' she yelled at me. 'I had it under control!'

I was too stunned to answer. Annabeth grumbled, 'Good to see you too, Clarisse.'

'Argh!' Clarisse screamed. 'Don't ever, EVER try saving me again!'

'Clarisse,' Annabeth said, 'you've got wounded campers.'

That sobered her up. Even Clarisse cared about the soldiers under her command.

'I'll be back,' she growled, then trudged off to assess the damage.

I stared at Tyson. 'You didn't die.'

Tyson looked down like he was embarrassed. 'I am sorry. Came to help. Disobeyed you.'

'My fault,' Annabeth said. 'I had no choice. I had to let Tyson cross the boundary line to save you. Otherwise, you would've died.'

'*Let* him cross the boundary line?" I asked. 'But –'

'Percy,' she said, 'have you ever looked at Tyson closely? I mean . . . in the face. Ignore the Mist, and *really* look at him.'

The Mist makes humans see only what their brains can process . . . I knew it could fool demigods, too, but . . .

I looked Tyson in the face. It wasn't easy. I'd always had

trouble looking directly at him, though I'd never quite understood why. I'd thought it was just because he always had peanut butter in his crooked teeth. I forced myself to focus at his big lumpy nose, then a little higher at his eyes.

No, not *eyes*.

One eye. One large, calf-brown eye, right in the middle of his forehead, with thick lashes and big tears trickling down his cheeks on either side.

'Tyson,' I stammered. 'You're a . . .'

'Cyclops,' Annabeth offered. 'A baby, by the looks of him. Probably why he couldn't get past the boundary line as easily as the bulls. Tyson's one of the homeless orphans.'

'One of the what?'

'They're in almost all the big cities,' Annabeth said distastefully. 'They're . . . *mistakes*, Percy. Children of nature spirits and gods . . . Well, one god in particular, usually . . . and they don't always come out right. No one wants them. They get tossed aside. They grow up wild on the streets. I don't know how this one found you, but he obviously likes you. We should take him to Chiron, let him decide what to do.'

'But the fire. How —'

'He's a Cyclops.' Annabeth paused, as if she were remembering something unpleasant. 'They work the forges of the gods. They *have* to be immune to fire. That's what I was trying to tell you.'

I was completely shocked. How had I never realized what Tyson was?

But I didn't have much time to think about it just then. The whole side of the hill was burning. Wounded heroes needed attention. And there were still two banged-up bronze bulls to dispose of, which I didn't figure would fit in our normal recycling bins.

Clarisse came back over and wiped the soot off her forehead. 'Jackson, if you can stand, get up. We need to carry the wounded back to the Big House, let Tantalus know what's happened.'

'Tantalus?' I asked.

'The activities director,' Clarisse said impatiently.

'Chiron is the activities director. And where's Argus? He's head of security. He should be here.'

Clarisse made a sour face. 'Argus got fired. You two have been gone too long. Things are changing.'

'But Chiron . . . He's trained kids to fight monsters for over three thousand years. He can't just be *gone*. What happened?'

'*That* happened,' Clarisse snapped.

She pointed to Thalia's tree.

Every camper knew the story behind the tree. Six years ago, Grover, Annabeth and two other demigods named Thalia and Luke had come to Camp Half-Blood chased by an army of monsters. When they got cornered on top of this hill, Thalia, a daughter of Zeus, had made her last stand here to give her friends time to reach safety. As she was dying, her father Zeus took pity on her and changed her into a pine tree. Her spirit had reinforced the magic borders of the camp, protecting it from monsters. The pine had been here ever since, strong and healthy.

But now, its needles were yellow. A huge pile of dead ones littered the base of the tree. In the centre of the trunk, a metre from the ground, was a puncture mark the size of a bullet hole, oozing green sap.

A sliver of ice ran through my chest. Now I understood why the camp was in danger. The magical borders were failing because Thalia's tree was dying.

Someone had poisoned it.

5 I GET A NEW CABIN MATE

Ever come home and found your room messed up? Like some helpful person (hi, Mom) has tried to 'clean' it, and suddenly you can't find anything? And even if nothing is missing, you get that creepy feeling like somebody's been looking through your private stuff and dusting everything with lemon furniture polish?

That's kind of the way I felt seeing Camp Half-Blood again.

On the surface, things didn't look all that different. The Big House was still there with its blue gabled roof and its wraparound porch. The strawberry fields still baked in the sun. The same white-columned Greek buildings were scattered around the valley – the amphitheatre, the combat arena, the dining pavilion overlooking Long Island Sound. And nestled between the woods and the creek were the same cabins – a crazy assortment of twelve buildings, each representing a different Olympian god.

But there was an air of danger now. You could tell something was wrong. Instead of playing volleyball in the sandpit, counsellors and satyrs were stockpiling weapons in the tool shed. Dryads armed with bows and arrows talked nervously at the edge of the woods. The forest looked sickly, the grass in the meadow was pale yellow, and the fire marks on Half-Blood Hill stood out like ugly scars.

Somebody had messed with my favourite place in the world, and I was not . . . well, a happy camper.

As we made our way to the Big House, I recognized a lot of kids from last summer. Nobody stopped to talk. Nobody said, 'Welcome back.' Some did double takes when they saw Tyson, but most just walked grimly past and carried on with their duties – running messages, toting swords to sharpen on the grinding wheels. The camp felt like a military school. And believe me, I know. I've been kicked out of a couple.

None of that mattered to Tyson. He was absolutely fascinated by everything he saw. 'Whasthat!' he gasped.

'The stables for pegasi,' I said. 'The winged horses.'

'Whasthat!'

'Um . . . those are the toilets.'

'Whasthat!'

'The cabins for the campers. If they don't know who your Olympian parent is, they put you in the Hermes cabin – that brown one over there – until you're determined. Then, once they know, they put you in your dad or mom's group.'

He looked at me in awe. 'You . . . have a *cabin*?'

'Number three.' I pointed to a low grey building made of sea stone.

'You live with friends in the cabin?'

'No. No, just me.' I didn't feel like explaining. The embarrassing truth: I was the only one who stayed in that cabin because I wasn't supposed to be alive. The 'Big Three' gods – Zeus, Poseidon and Hades – had made a pact after World War II not to have any more children with mortals. We were more powerful than regular half-bloods. We were too unpredictable. When we got mad we tended to cause problems . . . like World War II, for instance. The 'Big Three' pact had only been broken twice – once when Zeus sired Thalia, once when Poseidon sired me. Neither of us should've been born.

Thalia had got herself turned into a pine tree when she was twelve. Me . . . well, I was doing my best not to follow her example. I had nightmares about what Poseidon might turn me into if I were ever on the verge of death – plankton, maybe. Or a floating patch of kelp.

When we got to the Big House, we found Chiron in his apartment, listening to his favourite 1960s lounge music while he packed his saddlebags. I guess I should mention – Chiron is a centaur. From the waist up he looks like a regular middle-aged guy with curly brown hair and a scraggly beard. From the waist down, he's a white stallion. He can pass for human by compacting his lower half into a magic wheelchair. In fact, he'd passed himself off as my Latin teacher during my sixth-grade year. But most of the time, if the ceilings are high enough, he prefers hanging out in full centaur form.

As soon as we saw him, Tyson froze. 'Pony!' he cried in total rapture.

Chiron turned, looking offended. 'I beg your pardon?'

Annabeth ran up and hugged him. 'Chiron, what's happening? You're not . . . leaving?' Her voice was shaky. Chiron was like a second father to her.

Chiron ruffled her hair and gave her a kindly smile. 'Hello, child. And Percy, my goodness. You've grown over the year!'

I swallowed. 'Clarisse said you were . . . you were . . .'

'Fired.' Chiron's eyes glinted with dark humour. 'Ah, well, someone had to take the blame. Lord Zeus was most upset. The tree he'd created from the spirit of his daughter, poisoned! Mr D had to punish someone.'

'Besides himself, you mean,' I growled. Just the thought of the camp director, Mr D, made me angry.

'But this is crazy!' Annabeth cried. 'Chiron, you couldn't have had anything to do with poisoning Thalia's tree!'

'Nevertheless,' Chiron sighed, 'some in Olympus do not trust me now, under the circumstances.'

'What circumstances?' I asked.

Chiron's face darkened. He stuffed a Latin–English dictionary into his saddlebag while the Frank Sinatra music oozed from his boom box.

Tyson was still staring at Chiron in amazement. He whimpered like he wanted to pat Chiron's flank but was afraid to come closer. 'Pony?'

Chiron sniffed. 'My dear young Cyclops! I am a *centaur*.'

'Chiron,' I said. 'What about the tree? What happened?'

He shook his head sadly. 'The poison used on Thalia's pine is something from the Underworld, Percy. Some venom even I have never seen. It must have come from a monster quite deep in the pits of Tartarus.'

'Then we know who's responsible. Kro–'

'Do not invoke the titan lord's name, Percy. Especially not here, not now.'

'But last summer he tried to cause a civil war in Olympus! This *has* to be his idea. He'd get Luke to do it, that traitor.'

'Perhaps,' Chiron said. 'But I fear I am being held responsible because I did not prevent it and I cannot cure it. The tree has only a few weeks of life left unless . . .'

'Unless what?' Annabeth asked.

'No,' Chiron said. 'A foolish thought. The whole valley is feeling the shock of the poison. The magical borders are deteriorating. The camp itself is dying. Only one source of magic would be strong enough to reverse the poison, and it was lost centuries ago.'

'What *is* it?' I asked. 'We'll go find it!'

Chiron closed his saddlebag. He pressed the STOP button on his boom box. Then he turned and rested his hand on my shoulder, looking me straight in the eyes. 'Percy, you must promise me that you will *not* act rashly. I told your mother I did not want you to come here at all this summer. It's much too dangerous. But now that you are here, *stay* here. Train hard. Learn to fight. But do not leave.'

'Why?' I asked. 'I want to do something! I can't just let the borders fail. The whole camp will be —'

'Overrun by monsters,' Chiron said. 'Yes, I fear so. But you must not let yourself be baited into hasty action! This could be a trap of the titan lord. Remember last summer! He almost took your life.'

It was true, but still, I wanted to help so badly. I also wanted to make Kronos pay. I mean, you'd think the titan lord would've learned his lesson aeons ago when he was overthrown by the gods. You'd think getting chopped into a million pieces and cast into the darkest part of the Underworld would give him a subtle clue that nobody wanted him around. But no. Because he was immortal, he was still alive down there in Tartarus — suffering in eternal pain, hungering to return and take revenge on Olympus. He couldn't act on his own, but he was great at twisting the minds of mortals and even gods to do his dirty work.

The poisoning *had* to be his doing. Who else would be so low as to attack Thalia's tree, the only thing left of a hero who'd given her life to save her friends?

Annabeth was trying hard not to cry. Chiron brushed a tear from her cheek. 'Stay with Percy, child,' he told her. 'Keep him safe. The prophecy – remember it!'

'I-I will.'

'Um . . .' I said. 'Would this be the super-dangerous prophecy that has me in it, but the gods have forbidden you to tell me about?'

Nobody answered.

'Right,' I muttered. 'Just checking.'

'Chiron . . .' Annabeth said. 'You told me the gods made you immortal only so long as you were needed to train heroes. If they dismiss you from camp –'

'Swear you will do your best to keep Percy from danger,' he insisted. 'Swear upon the River Styx.'

'I-I swear it upon the River Styx,' Annabeth said.

Thunder rumbled outside.

'Very well,' Chiron said. He seemed to relax just a little. 'Perhaps my name will be cleared and I shall return. Until then, I go to visit my wild kinsmen in the Everglades. It's possible they know of some cure for the poisoned tree that I have forgotten. In any event, I will stay in exile until this matter is resolved . . . one way or another.'

Annabeth stifled a sob. Chiron patted her shoulder awkwardly. 'There, now, child. I must entrust your safety to Mr D and the new activities director. We must hope

. . . well, perhaps they won't destroy the camp quite as quickly as I fear.'

'Who is this Tantalus guy, anyway?' I demanded. 'Where does he get off taking your job?'

A conch horn blew across the valley. I hadn't realized how late it was. It was time for the campers to assemble for dinner.

'Go,' Chiron said. 'You will meet him at the pavilion. I will contact your mother, Percy, and let her know you're safe. No doubt she'll be worried by now. Just remember my warning! You are in grave danger. Do not think for a moment that the titan lord has forgotten you!'

With that, he clopped out of the apartment and down the hall, Tyson calling after him, 'Pony! Don't go!'

I realized I'd forgotten to tell Chiron about my dream of Grover. Now it was too late. The best teacher I'd ever had was gone, maybe for good.

Tyson started bawling almost as bad as Annabeth.

I tried to tell them that things would be okay, but I didn't believe it.

The sun was setting behind the dining pavilion as the campers came up from their cabins. We stood in the shadow of a marble column and watched them file in. Annabeth was still pretty shaken up, but she promised she'd talk to us later. Then she went off to join her siblings from the Athena cabin – a dozen boys and girls with blonde hair and grey eyes like hers. Annabeth wasn't the oldest, but she'd been at camp more summers than just about anybody. You could tell that by looking at her camp necklace – one bead for every summer, and

Annabeth had six. No one questioned her right to lead the line.

Next came Clarisse, leading the Ares cabin. She had one arm in a sling and a nasty-looking gash on her cheek, but otherwise her encounter with the bronze bulls didn't seem to have fazed her. Someone had taped a piece of paper to her back that said, YOU MOO, GIRL! But nobody in her cabin was bothering to tell her about it.

After the Ares kids came the Hephaestus cabin – six guys led by Charles Beckendorf, a big fifteen-year-old African American kid. He had hands the size of catchers' mitts and a face that was hard and squinty from looking into a blacksmith's forge all day. He was nice enough once you got to know him, but no one ever called him Charlie or Chuck or Charles. Most just called him Beckendorf. Rumour was he could make anything. Give him a chunk of metal and he could create a razor-sharp sword or a robotic warrior or a singing birdbath for your grandmother's garden. Whatever you wanted.

The other cabins filed in: Demeter, Apollo, Aphrodite, Dionysus. Naiads came up from the canoe lake. Dryads melted out of the trees. From the meadow came a dozen satyrs, who reminded me painfully of Grover.

I'd always had a soft spot for the satyrs. When they were at camp, they had to do all kinds of odd jobs for Mr D, the director, but their most important work was out in the real world. They were the camp's seekers. They went undercover into schools all over the world, looking for potential half-bloods and escorting them back to camp. That's how I'd met Grover. He had been the first one to recognize I was a demigod.

After the satyrs filed in to dinner, the Hermes cabin brought up the rear. They were always the biggest cabin. Last summer, it had been led by Luke, the guy who'd fought with Thalia and Annabeth on top of Half-Blood Hill. For a while, before Poseidon had claimed me, I'd lodged in the Hermes cabin. Luke had befriended me . . . and then he'd tried to kill me.

Now the Hermes cabin was led by Travis and Connor Stoll. They weren't twins, but they looked so much alike it didn't matter. I could never remember which one was older. They were both tall and skinny, with mops of brown hair that hung in their eyes. They wore orange CAMP HALF-BLOOD T-shirts untucked over baggy shorts, and they had those elfish features all Hermes's kids had: upturned eyebrows, sarcastic smiles, a gleam in their eyes whenever they looked at you – like they were about to drop a firecracker down your shirt. I'd always thought it was funny that the god of thieves would have kids with the last name 'Stoll', but the only time I mentioned it to Travis and Connor, they both stared at me blankly like they didn't get the joke.

As soon as the last campers had filed in, I led Tyson into the middle of the pavilion. Conversations faltered. Heads turned. 'Who invited *that*?' somebody at the Apollo table murmured.

I glared in their direction, but I couldn't figure out who'd spoken.

From the head table a familiar voice drawled, 'Well, well, if it isn't Peter Johnson. My millennium is complete.'

I gritted my teeth. '*Percy Jackson* . . . sir.'

Mr D sipped his Diet Coke. 'Yes. Well, as you young people say these days, *whatever*.'

He was wearing his usual leopard-pattern Hawaiian shirt, walking shorts and tennis shoes with black socks. With his pudgy belly and his blotchy red face, he looked like a Las Vegas tourist who'd stayed up too late in the casinos. Behind him, a nervous-looking satyr was peeling the skins off grapes and handing them to Mr D one at a time.

Mr D's real name is Dionysus. The god of wine. Zeus appointed him director of Camp Half-Blood to dry out for a hundred years – a punishment for chasing some off-limits wood nymph.

Next to him, where Chiron usually sat (or stood, in centaur form), was someone I'd never seen before – a pale, horribly thin man in a threadbare orange prisoner's jumpsuit. The number over his pocket read 0001. He had blue shadows under his eyes, dirty fingernails and badly cut grey hair, like his last haircut had been done with a weed whacker. He stared at me; his eyes made me nervous. He looked . . . fractured. Angry and frustrated and hungry all at the same time.

'This boy,' Dionysus told him, 'you need to watch. Poseidon's child, you know.'

'Ah!' the prisoner said. 'That one.'

His tone made it obvious that he and Dionysus had already discussed me at length.

'I am Tantalus,' the prisoner said, smiling coldly. 'On special assignment here until, well, until my Lord Dionysus decides otherwise. And you, Perseus Jackson, I *do* expect you to refrain from causing any more trouble.'

'Trouble?' I demanded.

Dionysus snapped his fingers. A newspaper appeared

on the table – the front page of today's *New York Post*. There was my yearbook picture from Meriwether Prep. It was hard for me to make out the headline, but I had a pretty good guess what it said. Something like: *Thirteen-Year-Old Lunatic Torches Gymnasium.*

'Yes, trouble,' Tantalus said with satisfaction. 'You caused plenty of it last summer, I understand.'

I was too mad to speak. Like it was *my* fault the gods had almost got into a civil war?

A satyr inched forward nervously and set a plate of barbecued meat in front of Tantalus. The new activities director licked his lips. He looked at his empty goblet and said, 'Root beer. Barq's special stock. 1967.'

The glass filled itself with foamy soda. Tantalus stretched out his hand hesitantly, as if he were afraid the goblet was hot.

'Go on, then, old fellow,' Dionysus said, a strange sparkle in his eyes. 'Perhaps now it will work.'

Tantalus grabbed for the glass, but it scooted away before he could touch it. A few drops of root beer spilled, and Tantalus tried to dab them up with his fingers, but the drops rolled away like quicksilver before he could touch them. He growled and turned towards the plate of meat. He picked up a fork and tried to stab a piece of brisket, but the plate skittered down the table and flew off the end, straight into the coals of the brazier.

'Blast!' Tantalus muttered.

'Ah, well,' Dionysus said, his voice dripping with false sympathy. 'Perhaps a few more days. Believe me, old chap, working at this camp will be torture enough. I'm sure your old curse will fade eventually.'

'Eventually,' muttered Tantalus, staring at Dionysus's Diet Coke. 'Do you have any idea how dry one's throat gets after three thousand years?'

'You're that spirit from the Fields of Punishment,' I said. 'The one who stands in the lake with the fruit tree hanging over you, but you can't eat or drink.'

Tantalus sneered at me. 'A real scholar, aren't you, boy?'

'You must've done something really horrible when you were alive,' I said, mildly impressed. 'What was it?'

Tantalus's eyes narrowed. Behind him, the satyrs were shaking their heads vigorously, trying to warn me.

'I'll be watching you, Percy Jackson,' Tantalus said. 'I don't want any problems at my camp.'

'*Your* camp has problems already . . . sir.'

'Oh, go sit down, Johnson,' Dionysus sighed. 'I believe that table over there is yours — the one where no one else ever wants to sit.'

My face was burning, but I knew better than to talk back. Dionysus was an overgrown brat, but he was an immortal, superpowerful overgrown brat. I said, 'Come on, Tyson.'

'Oh, no,' Tantalus said. 'The monster stays here. We must decide what to do with it.'

'*Him*,' I snapped. 'His name is Tyson.'

The new activities director raised an eyebrow.

'Tyson saved the camp,' I insisted. 'He pounded those bronze bulls. Otherwise they would've burned down this whole place.'

'Yes,' Tantalus sighed, 'and *what* a pity that would've been.'

Dionysus snickered.

'Leave us,' Tantalus ordered, 'while we decide this creature's fate.'

Tyson looked at me with fear in his one big eye, but I knew I couldn't disobey a direct order from the camp directors. Not openly, anyway.

'I'll be right over here, big guy,' I promised. 'Don't worry. We'll find you a good place to sleep tonight.'

Tyson nodded. 'I believe you. You are my friend.'

Which made me feel a whole lot guiltier.

I trudged over to the Poseidon table and slumped onto the bench. A wood nymph brought me a plate of Olympian olive-and-pepperoni pizza, but I wasn't hungry. I'd been almost killed twice today. I'd managed to end my school year with a complete disaster. Camp Half-Blood was in serious trouble and Chiron had told me not to do anything about it.

I didn't feel very thankful, but I took my dinner, as was customary, up to the bronze brazier and scraped part of it into the flames.

'Poseidon,' I murmured, 'accept my offering.'

And send me some help while you're at it, I prayed silently. *Please.*

The smoke from the burning pizza changed into something fragrant – the smell of a clean sea breeze with wildflowers mixed in – but I had no idea if that meant my father was really listening.

I went back to my seat. I didn't think things could get much worse. But then Tantalus had one of the satyrs blow the conch horn to get our attention for announcements.

* * *

'Yes, well,' Tantalus said, once the talking had died down. 'Another fine meal! Or so I am told.' As he spoke, he inched his hand towards his refilled dinner plate, as if maybe the food wouldn't notice what he was doing, but it did. It shot away down the table as soon as he got within twenty centimetres.

'And here on my first day of authority,' he continued, 'I'd like to say what a pleasant form of punishment it is to be here. Over the course of the summer, I hope to torture, er, interact with each and every one of you children. You all look good enough to eat.'

Dionysus clapped politely, leading to some half-hearted applause from the satyrs. Tyson was still standing at the head table, looking uncomfortable, but every time he tried to scoot out of the limelight, Tantalus pulled him back.

'And now some changes!' Tantalus gave the campers a crooked smile. 'We are reinstituting the chariot races!'

Murmuring broke out at all the tables – excitement, fear, disbelief.

'Now I know,' Tantalus continued, raising his voice, 'that these races were discontinued some years ago due to, ah, technical problems.'

'Three deaths and twenty-six mutilations,' someone at the Apollo table called.

'Yes, yes!' Tantalus said. 'But I know that you will all join me in welcoming the return of this camp tradition. Golden laurels will go to the winning charioteers each month. Teams may register in the morning! The first race will be held in three days' time. We will release you from most of your regular activities to prepare your chariots and choose your horses. Oh, and did I mention, the victorious team's cabin will have no chores for the month in which they win?'

An explosion of excited conversation – no KP for a whole month? No stable cleaning? Was he serious?

Then the last person I expected to object did so.

'But, sir!' Clarisse said. She looked nervous, but she stood up to speak from the Ares table. Some of the campers snickered when they saw the YOU MOO, GIRL! sign on her back. 'What about patrol duty? I mean, if we drop everything to ready our chariots –'

'Ah, the hero of the day,' Tantalus exclaimed. 'Brave Clarisse, who single-handedly bested the bronze bulls!'

Clarisse blinked, then blushed. 'Um, I didn't –'

'And modest, too.' Tantalus grinned. 'Not to worry, my dear! This is a summer camp. We are here to enjoy ourselves, yes?'

'But the tree –'

'And now,' Tantalus said, as several of Clarisse's cabin mates pulled her back into her seat, 'before we proceed to the campfire and sing-along, one slight housekeeping issue. Percy Jackson and Annabeth Chase have seen fit, for some reason, to bring *this* here.' Tantalus waved a hand towards Tyson.

Uneasy murmuring spread among the campers. A lot of sideways looks at me. I wanted to kill Tantalus.

'Now, of course,' he said, 'Cyclopes have a reputation for being bloodthirsty monsters with a very small brain capacity. Under normal circumstances, I would release this beast into the woods and have you hunt it down with torches and pointed sticks. But who knows? Perhaps this Cyclops is not as horrible as most of its brethren. Until it proves worthy of destruction, we need a place to keep it! I've thought about the stables, but that will make the horses nervous. Hermes's cabin, possibly?'

Silence at the Hermes table. Travis and Connor Stoll developed a sudden interest in the tablecloth. I couldn't blame them. The Hermes cabin was always full to bursting. There was no way they could take in a two-metre Cyclops.

'Come now,' Tantalus chided. 'The monster may be able to do some menial chores. Any suggestions as to where such a beast should be kennelled?'

Suddenly everybody gasped.

Tantalus scooted away from Tyson in surprise. All I could do was stare in disbelief at the brilliant green light that was about to change my life – a dazzling holographic image that had appeared above Tyson's head.

With a sickening twist in my stomach, I remembered what Annabeth had said about Cyclopes, *They're the children of nature spirits and gods . . . Well, one god in particular, usually . . .*

Swirling over Tyson was a glowing green trident – the same symbol that had appeared above me the day Poseidon had claimed me as his son.

There was a moment of awed silence.

Being claimed was a rare event. Some campers waited in vain for it their whole lives. When I'd been claimed by Poseidon last summer, everyone had reverently knelt. But now, they followed Tantalus's lead, and Tantalus roared with laughter. 'Well! I think we know where to put the beast now. By the gods, I can see the family resemblance!'

Everybody laughed except Annabeth and a few of my other friends.

Tyson didn't seem to notice. He was too mystified, trying to swat the glowing trident that was now fading over his head. He was too innocent to understand how much they were making fun of him, how cruel people were.

But I got it.

I had a new cabin mate. I had a monster for a half-brother.

6 DEMON PIGEONS ATTACK

The next few days were torture, just like Tantalus wanted.

First there was Tyson moving into the Poseidon cabin, giggling to himself every fifteen seconds and saying, 'Percy is my brother?' like he'd just won the lottery.

'Aw, Tyson,' I'd say. 'It's not that simple.'

But there was no explaining it to him. He was in heaven. And me . . . as much as I liked the big guy, I couldn't help feeling embarrassed. Ashamed. There, I said it.

My father, the all-powerful Poseidon, had got moony-eyed for some nature spirit, and Tyson had been the result. I mean, I'd read the myths about Cyclopes. I even remembered that they were often Poseidon's children. But I'd never really processed that this made them my . . . family. Until I had Tyson living with me in the next bunk.

And then there were the comments from the other campers. Suddenly, I wasn't Percy Jackson, the cool guy who'd retrieved Zeus's lightning bolt last summer. Now I was Percy Jackson, the poor schmuck with the ugly monster for a brother.

'He's not my *real* brother!' I protested whenever Tyson wasn't around. 'He's more like a half-brother on the monstrous side of the family. Like . . . a half-brother twice removed, or something.'

Nobody bought it.

I admit — I was angry at my dad. I felt like being his son was now a joke.

Annabeth tried to make me feel better. She suggested we team up for the chariot race to take our minds off our problems. Don't get me wrong — we both hated Tantalus and we were worried sick about camp — but we didn't know what to do about it. Until we could come up with some brilliant plan to save Thalia's tree, we figured we might as well go along with the races. After all, Annabeth's mom, Athena, had invented the chariot, and my dad had created horses. Together we would *own* that track.

One morning Annabeth and I were sitting by the canoe lake sketching chariot designs when some jokers from Aphrodite's cabin walked by and asked me if I needed to borrow some eyeliner for my eye . . . 'Oh, sorry, *eyes*.'

As they walked away laughing, Annabeth grumbled, 'Just ignore them, Percy. It isn't your fault you have a monster for a brother.'

'He's *not* my brother!' I snapped. 'And he's not a monster, either!'

Annabeth raised her eyebrows. 'Hey, don't get mad at me! And technically, he *is* a monster.'

'Well, *you* gave him permission to enter the camp.'

'Because it was the only way to save your life! I mean . . . I'm sorry, Percy, I didn't expect Poseidon to *claim* him. Cyclopes are the most deceitful, treacherous —'

'He is not! What have you got against Cyclopes, anyway?'

Annabeth's ears turned pink. I got the feeling there was something she wasn't telling me — something bad.

'Just forget it,' she said. 'Now, the axle for this chariot —'

'You're treating him like he's this horrible thing,' I said. 'He saved my life.'

Annabeth threw down her pencil and stood. 'Then maybe you should design a chariot with *him*.'

'Maybe I should.'

'Fine!'

'Fine!'

She stormed off and left me feeling even worse than before.

The next couple of days, I tried to keep my mind off my problems.

Silena Beauregard, one of the nicer girls from Aphrodite's cabin, gave me my first riding lesson on a pegasus. She explained that there was only one immortal winged horse named Pegasus, who still wandered free somewhere in the skies, but over the aeons he'd sired a lot of children, none quite so fast or heroic, but all named after the first and greatest.

Being the son of the sea god, I never liked going into the air. My dad had this rivalry with Zeus, so I tried to stay out of the lord of the sky's domain as much as possible. But riding a winged horse felt different. It didn't make me nearly as nervous as being in an aeroplane. Maybe that was because my dad had created horses out of sea foam, so the pegasi were sort of . . . neutral territory. I could understand their thoughts. I wasn't surprised when my pegasus went galloping over the treetops or chased a flock of seagulls into a cloud.

The problem was that Tyson wanted to ride the 'chicken ponies', too, but the pegasi got skittish whenever he approached. I told them telepathically that Tyson wouldn't hurt them, but they didn't seem to believe me. That made Tyson cry.

The only person at camp who had *no* problem with Tyson was Beckendorf from the Hephaestus cabin. The blacksmith god had always worked with Cyclopes in his forges, so Beckendorf took Tyson down to the armoury to teach him metalworking. He said he'd have Tyson crafting magic items like a master in no time.

After lunch, I worked out in the arena with Apollo's cabin. Swordplay had always been my strength. People said I was better at it than any camper in the last hundred years, except maybe Luke. People always compared me to Luke.

I thrashed the Apollo guys easily. I should've been testing myself against the Ares and Athena cabins, since they had the best sword fighters, but I didn't get along with Clarisse and her siblings, and after my argument with Annabeth, I just didn't want to see her.

I went to archery class, even though I was terrible at it, and it wasn't the same without Chiron teaching. In arts and crafts, I started a marble bust of Poseidon, but it started looking like Sylvester Stallone, so I ditched it. I scaled the climbing wall in full lava-and-earthquake mode. And in the evenings, I did border patrol. Even though Tantalus had insisted we forget trying to protect the camp, some of the campers had quietly kept it up, working out a schedule during our free times.

I sat at the top of Half-Blood Hill and watched the dryads come and go, singing to the dying pine tree. Satyrs brought their reed pipes and played nature magic songs, and for a while the pine needles seemed to get fuller. The flowers on the hill smelled a little sweeter and the grass looked greener. But as soon as the music stopped, the sickness crept back into the air. The whole hill seemed to be infected, dying from the poison that had sunk into the tree's roots. The longer I sat there, the angrier I got.

Luke had done this. I remembered his sly smile, the dragon-claw scar across his face. He'd pretended to be my friend, and the whole time he'd been Kronos's number-one servant.

I opened the palm of my hand. The scar Luke had given me last summer was fading, but I could still see it – a white asterisk-shaped wound where his pit scorpion had stung me.

I thought about what Luke had told me right before he'd tried to kill me: *Goodbye, Percy. There is a new Golden Age coming. You won't be part of it.*

At night, I had more dreams of Grover. Sometimes, I just heard snatches of his voice. Once, I heard him say, *It's here.* Another time, *He likes sheep.*

I thought about telling Annabeth about my dreams, but I would've felt stupid. I mean, *He likes sheep*? She would've thought I was crazy.

The night before the race, Tyson and I finished our chariot. It was wicked cool. Tyson had made the metal parts in the armoury's forges. I'd sanded the wood and put the carriage together. It was blue and white, with wave designs on the sides and a trident painted on the front. After all that work, it seemed only fair that Tyson would ride shotgun with me, though I knew the horses wouldn't like it, and Tyson's extra weight would slow us down.

As we were turning in for bed, Tyson said, 'You are mad?'

I realized I'd been scowling. 'Nah. I'm not mad.'

He lay down in his bunk and was quiet in the dark. His body was way too long for his bed. When he pulled up the covers, his feet stuck out the bottom. 'I am a monster.'

'Don't say that.'

'It is okay. I will be a *good* monster. Then you will not have to be mad.'

I didn't know what to say. I stared at the ceiling and felt like I was dying slowly, right along with Thalia's tree.

'It's just . . . I never had a half-brother before.' I tried to keep my voice from cracking. 'It's really different for me. And I'm worried about the camp. And another friend of mine, Grover . . . he might be in trouble. I keep feeling like I should be doing something to help, but I don't know what.'

Tyson said nothing.

'I'm sorry,' I told him. 'It's not your fault. I'm mad at Poseidon. I feel like he's trying to embarrass me, like he's trying to compare us or something, and I don't understand why.'

I heard a deep rumbling sound. Tyson was snoring.

I sighed. 'Goodnight, big guy.'

And I closed my eyes, too.

* * *

In my dream, Grover was wearing a wedding dress.

It didn't fit him very well. The gown was too long and the hem was caked with dried mud. The neckline kept falling off his shoulders. A tattered veil covered his face.

He was standing in a dank cave, lit only by torches. There was a cot in one corner and an old-fashioned loom in the other, a length of white cloth half woven on the frame. And he was staring right at me, like I was a TV programme he'd been waiting for. 'Thank the gods!' he yelped. 'Can you hear me?'

My dream-self was slow to respond. I was still looking around, taking in the stalactite ceiling, the stench of sheep and goats, the growling and grumbling and bleating sounds that seemed to echo from behind a refrigerator-sized boulder, which was blocking the room's only exit, as if there were a much larger cavern beyond it.

'Percy?' Grover said. 'Please, I don't have the strength to project any better. You *have* to hear me!'

'I hear you,' I said. 'Grover, what's going on?'

From behind the boulder, a monstrous voice yelled, 'Honeypie! Are you done yet?'

Grover flinched. He called out in falsetto, 'Not quite, dearest! A few more days!'

'Bah! Hasn't it been two weeks yet?'

'N-no, dearest. Just five days. That leaves twelve more to go.'

The monster was silent, maybe trying to do the maths. He must've been worse at arithmetic than I was, because he said, 'All right, but hurry! I want to SEEEEE under that veil, heh-heh-heh.'

Grover turned back to me. 'You have to help me! No time! I'm stuck in this cave. On an island in the sea.'

'*Where?*'

'I don't know exactly! I went to Florida and turned left.'

'What? How did you –'

'It's a trap!' Grover said. 'It's the reason no satyr has ever returned from this quest. He's a shepherd, Percy! And he *has* it. Its nature magic is *so* powerful it smells just like the great god Pan! The satyrs come here thinking they've found Pan, and they get trapped and eaten by Polyphemus!'

'Poly-who?'

'The Cyclops!' Grover said, exasperated. 'I almost got away. I made it all the way to St Augustine.'

'But he followed you,' I said, remembering my first dream. 'And trapped you in a bridal boutique.'

'That's right,' Grover said. 'My first empathy link must've worked then. Look, this bridal dress is the only thing keeping me alive. He thinks I smell good, but I told him it was just goat-scented perfume. Thank goodness he can't see very well. His eye is still half blind from the last time somebody poked it out. But soon he'll realize what I am. He's only giving me two weeks to finish the bridal train, and he's getting impatient!'

'Wait a minute. This Cyclops thinks you're –'

'Yes!' Grover wailed. 'He thinks I'm a lady Cyclops and he wants to marry me!'

Under different circumstances, I might've busted out laughing, but Grover's voice was deadly serious. He was shaking with fear.

'I'll come rescue you,' I promised. 'Where are you?'

'The Sea of Monsters, of course!'

'The sea of *what?*'

'I told you! I don't know exactly where! And look, Percy . . . um, I'm really sorry about this, but this empathy link . . . well, I had no choice. Our emotions are connected now. If I die . . .'

'Don't tell me, I'll die, too.'

'Oh, well, perhaps not. You might live for years in a vegetative state. But, uh, it would be a lot better if you got me out of here.'

'Honeypie!' the monster bellowed. 'Dinnertime! Yummy yummy sheep meat!'

Grover whimpered. 'I have to go. Hurry!'

'Wait! You said "it" was here. What?'

But Grover's voice was already growing fainter. 'Sweet dreams. Don't let me die!'

The dream faded and I woke with a start. It was early morning. Tyson was staring down at me, his one big brown eye full of concern.

'Are you okay?' he asked.

His voice sent a chill down my back, because he sounded almost exactly like the monster I'd heard in my dream.

The morning of the race was hot and humid. Fog lay low on the ground like sauna steam. Millions of birds were roosting in the trees – fat grey-and-white pigeons, except they didn't coo like regular pigeons. They made this annoying metallic screeching sound that reminded me of submarine radar.

The racetrack had been built in a grassy field between

the archery range and the woods. Hephaestus's cabin had used the bronze bulls, which were completely tame since they'd had their heads smashed in, to plough an oval track in a matter of minutes.

There were rows of stone steps for the spectators – Tantalus, the satyrs, a few dryads and all of the campers who weren't participating. Mr D didn't show. He never got up before ten o'clock.

'Right!' Tantalus announced as the teams began to assemble. A naiad had brought him a big platter of pastries, and as Tantalus spoke his right hand chased a chocolate eclair across the judge's table. 'You all know the rules. A quarter-mile track. Twice around to win. Two horses per chariot. Each team will consist of a driver and a fighter. Weapons are allowed. Dirty tricks are expected. But try not to kill anybody!' Tantalus smiled at us like we were all naughty children. 'Any killing will result in harsh punishment. No s'mores at the campfire for a week! Now ready your chariots!'

Beckendorf led the Hephaestus team onto the track. They had a sweet ride made of bronze and iron – even the horses, which were magical automatons like the Colchis bulls. I had no doubt that their chariot had all kinds of mechanical traps and more fancy options than a fully loaded Maserati.

The Ares chariot was blood-red, and pulled by two grisly horse skeletons. Clarisse climbed aboard with a batch of javelins, spiked balls, caltrops and a bunch of other nasty toys.

Apollo's chariot was trim and graceful and completely gold, pulled by two beautiful palominos. Their fighter was armed with a bow, though he had promised not to shoot regular pointed arrows at the opposing drivers.

Hermes's chariot was green and kind of old-looking, as if it hadn't been out of the garage in years. It didn't look like anything special, but it was manned by the Stoll brothers, and I shuddered to think what dirty tricks they'd schemed up.

That left two chariots: one driven by Annabeth, and the other by me.

Before the race began, I tried to approach Annabeth and tell her about my dream.

She perked up when I mentioned Grover, but when I told her what he'd said, she seemed to get distant again, suspicious.

'You're trying to distract me,' she decided.

'What? No, I'm not!'

'Oh, right! Like Grover would just happen to stumble across the *one* thing that could save the camp.'

'What do you mean?'

She rolled her eyes. 'Go back to your chariot, Percy.'

'I'm not making this up. He's in trouble, Annabeth.'

She hesitated. I could tell she was trying to decide whether or not to trust me. Despite our occasional fights, we'd been through a lot together. And I knew she would never want anything bad to happen to Grover.

'Percy, an empathy link is so hard to do. I mean, it's more likely you really were dreaming.'

'The Oracle,' I said. 'We could consult the Oracle.'

Annabeth frowned.

Last summer, before my quest, I'd visited the strange spirit that lived in the Big House attic and it had given me a prophecy that came true in ways I'd never expected. The experience had freaked me out for months. Annabeth knew I'd never suggest going back there if I wasn't completely serious.

Before she could answer, the conch horn sounded.

'Charioteers!' Tantalus called. 'To your mark!'

'We'll talk later,' Annabeth told me, '*after* I win.'

As I was walking back to my own chariot, I noticed how many more pigeons were in the trees now – screeching like crazy, making the whole forest rustle. Nobody else seemed to be paying them much attention, but they made me nervous. Their beaks glinted strangely. Their eyes seemed shinier than regular birds.

Tyson was having trouble getting our horses under control. I had to talk to them a long time before they would settle down.

He's a monster, lord! they complained to me.

He's a son of Poseidon, I told them. *Just like . . . well, just like me.*

No! they insisted. *Monster! Horse-eater! Not trusted!*

I'll give you sugar cubes at the end of the race, I said.

Sugar cubes?

Very big sugar cubes. And apples. Did I mention the apples?

Finally they agreed to let me harness them.

Now, if you've never seen a Greek chariot, it's built for speed, not safety or comfort. It's basically a wooden basket, open at the back, mounted on an axle between two wheels. The driver stands up the whole time, and you can feel every bump in the road. The carriage is made of such light wood that if you wipe out making the hairpin turns at either end of the track, you'll probably tip over and crush both the chariot and yourself. It's an even better rush than skateboarding.

I took the reins and manoeuvred the chariot to the starting line. I gave Tyson a three-metre pole and told him that his job was to push the other chariots away if they got too close, and to deflect anything they might try to throw at us.

'No hitting ponies with the stick,' he insisted.

'No,' I agreed. 'Or people, either, if you can help it. We're going to run a clean race. Just keep the distractions away and let me concentrate on driving.'

'We will win!' He beamed.

We are *so* going to lose, I thought to myself, but I *had* to try. I wanted to show the others . . . well, I wasn't sure what, exactly. That Tyson wasn't such a bad guy? That I wasn't ashamed of being seen with him in public? Maybe that they hadn't hurt me with all their jokes and name-calling?

As the chariots lined up, more shiny-eyed pigeons gathered in the woods. They were screeching so loudly the campers in the stands were starting to take notice, glancing nervously at the trees, which shivered under the weight of the birds. Tantalus didn't look concerned, but he did have to speak up to be heard over the noise.

'Charioteers!' he shouted. 'Attend your mark!'

He waved his hand and the starting signal dropped. The chariots roared to life. Hooves thundered against the dirt. The crowd cheered.

Almost immediately there was a loud nasty *crack!* I looked back in time to see the Apollo chariot flip over. The Hermes chariot had rammed into it – maybe by mistake, maybe not. The riders were thrown free, but their panicked horses dragged the golden chariot diagonally across the track. The Hermes team, Travis and Connor Stoll, were laughing at their good luck, but not for long. The Apollo horses crashed into theirs, and the Hermes chariot flipped too, leaving a pile of broken wood and four rearing horses in the dust.

Two chariots down in the first six metres. I loved this sport.

I turned my attention back to the front. We were making good time, pulling ahead of Ares, but Annabeth's chariot was way ahead of us. She was already making her turn around the first post, her javelin man grinning and waving at us, shouting, 'See ya!'

The Hephaestus chariot was starting to gain on us, too.

Beckendorf pressed a button, and a panel slid open on the side of his chariot.

'Sorry, Percy!' he yelled. Three sets of balls and chains shot straight towards our wheels. They would've wrecked us completely if Tyson hadn't whacked them aside with a quick swipe of his pole. He gave the Hephaestus chariot a good shove and sent them skittering sideways while we pulled ahead.

'Nice work, Tyson!' I yelled.

'Birds!' he cried.

'What?'

We were whipping along so fast it was hard to hear or see anything, but Tyson pointed towards the woods and I saw what he was worried about. The pigeons had risen from the trees. They were spiralling like a huge tornado, heading towards the track.

No big deal, I told myself. *They're just pigeons.*

I tried to concentrate on the race.

We made our first turn, the wheels creaking under us, the chariot threatening to tip, but we were now only three metres behind Annabeth. If I could just get a little closer, Tyson could use his pole . . .

Annabeth's fighter wasn't smiling now. He pulled a javelin from his collection and took aim at me. He was about to throw when we heard the screaming.

The pigeons were swarming – thousands of them dive-bombing the spectators in the stands, attacking the other chariots. Beckendorf was mobbed. His fighter tried to bat the birds away but he couldn't see anything. The chariot veered off course and ploughed through the strawberry fields, the mechanical horses steaming.

In the Ares chariot, Clarisse barked an order to her fighter, who quickly threw a screen of camouflage netting over their basket. The birds swarmed around it, pecking and clawing at the fighter's hands as he tried to hold up the net, but Clarisse just gritted her teeth and kept driving. Her skeletal horses seemed immune to the distraction. The pigeons pecked uselessly at their empty eye sockets and flew through their rib cages, but the stallions kept right on running.

The spectators weren't so lucky. The birds were slashing at any bit of exposed flesh, driving everyone into a panic. Now that the birds were closer, it was clear they weren't normal pigeons. Their eyes were beady and evil-looking. Their beaks were made of bronze, and, judging from the yelps of the campers, they must've been razor sharp.

'Stymphalian birds!' Annabeth yelled. She slowed down and pulled her chariot alongside mine. 'They'll strip everyone to bones if we don't drive them away!'

'Tyson,' I said, 'we're turning around!'

'Going the wrong way?' he asked.

'Always,' I grumbled, but I steered the chariot towards the stands.

Annabeth rode right next to me. She shouted, 'Heroes, to arms!' But I wasn't sure anyone could hear her over the screeching of the birds and the general chaos.

I held my reins in one hand and managed to draw Riptide as a wave of birds dived at my face, their metal beaks snapping. I slashed them out of the air and they exploded into dust and feathers, but there were still millions of them left. One nailed me in the back end and I almost jumped straight out of the chariot.

Annabeth wasn't having much better luck. The closer we got to the stands, the thicker the cloud of birds became.

Some of the spectators were trying to fight back. The Athena campers were calling for shields. The archers from Apollo's cabin brought out their bows and arrows, ready to slay the menace, but with so many campers mixed in with the birds, it wasn't safe to shoot.

'Too many!' I yelled to Annabeth. 'How do you get rid of them?'

She stabbed at a pigeon with her knife. 'Heracles used noise! Brass bells! He scared them away with the most horrible sound he could –'

Her eyes got wide. 'Percy . . . Chiron's collection!'

I understood instantly. 'You think it'll work?'

She handed her fighter the reins and leaped from her

chariot into mine like it was the easiest thing in the world. 'To the Big House! It's our only chance!'

Clarisse had just pulled across the finish line, completely unopposed, and seemed to notice for the first time how serious the bird problem was.

When she saw us driving away, she yelled, 'You're *running?* The fight is here, cowards!' She drew her sword and charged for the stands.

I urged our horses into a gallop. The chariot rumbled through the strawberry fields, across the volleyball pit, and lurched to a halt in front of the Big House. Annabeth and I ran inside, tearing down the hallway to Chiron's apartment.

His boom box was still on his nightstand. So were his favourite CDs. I grabbed the most repulsive one I could find, Annabeth snatched the boom box, and together we ran back outside.

Down at the track, the chariots were in flames. Wounded campers ran in every direction, with birds shredding their clothes and pulling out their hair, while Tantalus chased breakfast pastries around the stands, every once in a while yelling, 'Everything's under control! Not to worry!'

We pulled up to the finish line. Annabeth got the boom box ready. I prayed the batteries weren't dead.

I pressed PLAY and started up Chiron's favourite – the *All-Time Greatest Hits of Dean Martin.* Suddenly the air was filled with violins and a bunch of guys moaning in Italian.

The demon pigeons went nuts. They started flying in circles, running into each other like they wanted to bash their own brains out. Then they abandoned the track altogether and flew skywards in a huge dark wave.

'Now!' shouted Annabeth. 'Archers!'

With clear targets, Apollo's archers had flawless aim. Most of them could nock five or six arrows at once. Within minutes, the ground was littered with dead bronze-beaked pigeons, and the survivors were a distant trail of smoke on the horizon.

The camp was saved, but the wreckage wasn't pretty. Most of the chariots had been completely destroyed. Almost everyone was wounded, bleeding from multiple bird pecks. The kids from Aphrodite's cabin were screaming because their hairdos had been ruined and their clothes pooped on.

'Bravo!' Tantalus said, but he wasn't looking at me or Annabeth. 'We have our first winner!' He walked to the finish line and awarded the golden laurels for the race to a stunned-looking Clarisse.

Then he turned and smiled at me. 'And now to punish the troublemakers who disrupted this race.'

7   I ACCEPT GIFTS FROM A STRANGER

The way Tantalus saw it, the Stymphalian birds had simply been minding their own business in the woods and would not have attacked if Annabeth, Tyson and I hadn't disturbed them with our bad chariot driving.

This was so completely unfair, I told Tantalus to go chase a doughnut, which didn't help his mood. He sentenced us to kitchen patrol — scrubbing pots and platters all afternoon in the underground kitchen with the cleaning harpies. The harpies washed with lava instead of water, to get that extra-clean sparkle and kill ninety-nine point nine percent of all germs, so Annabeth and I had to wear asbestos gloves and aprons.

Tyson didn't mind. He plunged his bare hands right in and started scrubbing, but Annabeth and I had to suffer through hours of hot, dangerous work, especially since there were tons of extra plates. Tantalus had ordered a special luncheon banquet to celebrate Clarisse's chariot victory — a full-course meal featuring country-fried Stymphalian death-bird.

The only good thing about our punishment was that it gave Annabeth and me a common enemy and lots of time to talk. After listening to my dream about Grover again, she looked like she might be starting to believe me.

'If he's really found it,' she murmured, 'and if we could retrieve it —'

'Hold on,' I said. 'You act like this . . . whatever-it-is Grover found is the only thing in the world that could save the camp. What *is* it?'

'I'll give you a hint. What do you get when you skin a ram?'

'Messy?'

She sighed. 'A *fleece*. The coat of a ram is called a fleece. And if that ram happens to have golden wool —'

'The Golden Fleece. Are you serious?'

Annabeth scraped a plateful of death-bird bones into the lava. 'Percy, remember the Grey Sisters? They said they knew the location of the thing you seek. And they mentioned Jason. Three thousand years ago, they told *him* how to find the Golden Fleece. You *do* know the story of Jason and the Argonauts?'

'Yeah,' I said. 'That old movie with the clay skeletons.'

Annabeth rolled her eyes. 'Oh my gods, Percy! You are so hopeless.'

'*What?*' I demanded.

'Just listen. The real story of the Fleece: there were these two children of Zeus, Cadmus and Europa, okay? They were about to get offered up as human sacrifices, when they prayed to Zeus to save them. So Zeus sent this magical flying ram with golden wool, which picked them up in Greece and carried them all the way to Colchis in Asia Minor. Well, actually it carried Cadmus. Europa fell off and died along the way, but that's not important.'

'It was probably important to her.'

'The *point* is, when Cadmus got to Colchis, he sacrificed the golden ram to the gods and hung the Fleece in a tree in the middle of the kingdom. The Fleece brought prosperity to the land. Animals stopped getting sick. Plants grew better. Farmers had bumper crops. Plagues never visited. That's why Jason wanted the Fleece. It can revitalize any land where it's placed. It cures sickness, strengthens nature, cleans up pollution –'

'It could cure Thalia's tree.'

Annabeth nodded. 'And it would totally strengthen the borders of Camp Half-Blood. But Percy, the Fleece has been missing for centuries. Tons of heroes have searched for it with no luck.'

'But Grover found it,' I said. 'He went looking for Pan and he found the Fleece instead because they both radiate nature magic. It makes sense, Annabeth. We can rescue him and save the camp at the same time. It's perfect!'

Annabeth hesitated. 'A little *too* perfect, don't you think? What if it's a trap?'

I remembered last summer, how Kronos had manipulated our quest. He'd almost fooled us into helping him start a war that would've destroyed Western Civilization.

'What choice do we have?' I asked. 'Are you going to help me rescue Grover or not?'

She glanced at Tyson, who'd lost interest in our conversation and was happily making toy boats out of cups and spoons in the lava.

'Percy,' she said under her breath, 'we'll have to fight a Cyclops. Polyphemus, the *worst* of the Cyclopes. And there's only one place his island could be. The Sea of Monsters.'

'Where's that?'

She stared at me like she thought I was playing dumb.

'The Sea of Monsters. The same sea Odysseus sailed through, and Jason, and Aeneas and all the others.'

'You mean the Mediterranean?'

'No. Well, yes . . . but no.'

'Another straight answer. Thanks.'

'Look, Percy, the Sea of Monsters is the sea all heroes sail through on their adventures. It used to be in the Mediterranean, yes. But like everything else, it shifts locations as the West's centre of power shifts.'

'Like Mount Olympus being above the Empire State Building,' I said. 'And Hades being under Los Angeles.'

'Right.'

'But a whole sea full of monsters — how could you hide something like that? Wouldn't the mortals notice weird things happening . . . like, ships getting eaten and stuff?'

'Of course they notice. They don't understand, but they know something is strange about that part of the ocean. The Sea of Monsters is off the east coast of the U.S. now, just north-east of Florida. The mortals even have a name for it.'

'The Bermuda Triangle?'

'Exactly.'

I let that sink in. I guess it wasn't stranger than anything else I'd learned since coming to Camp Half-Blood. 'Okay . . . so at least we know where to look.'

'It's still a huge area, Percy. Searching for one tiny island in monster-infested waters —'

'Hey, I'm the son of the sea god. This is my home turf. How hard can it be?'

Annabeth knitted her eyebrows. 'We'll have to talk to Tantalus, get approval for a quest. He'll say no.'

'Not if we tell him tonight at the campfire in front of everybody. The whole camp will hear. They'll pressure him. He won't be able to refuse.'

'Maybe.' A little bit of hope crept into Annabeth's voice. 'We'd better get these dishes done. Hand me the lava spray gun, will you?'

That night at the campfire, Apollo's cabin led the sing-along. They tried to get everybody's spirits up, but it wasn't easy after that afternoon's bird attack. We all sat around a semicircle of stone steps, singing half-heartedly and watching the bonfire blaze while the Apollo guys strummed their guitars and picked their lyres.

We did all the standard camp numbers: 'Down by the Aegean', 'I Am My Own Great-Great-Great-Great-Grandpa', 'This Land is Minos's Land'. The bonfire was enchanted, so the louder you sang, the higher it rose, changing colour and heat with the mood of the crowd. On a good night, I'd seen it six metres high, bright purple, and so hot the whole front row's marshmallows burst into flames. Tonight, the fire was only a metre high, barely warm, and the flames were the colour of lint.

Dionysus left early. After suffering through a few songs, he muttered something about how even pinochle with Chiron had been more exciting than this. Then he gave Tantalus a distasteful look and headed back towards the Big House.

When the last song was over, Tantalus said, 'Well, that was lovely!'

He came forward with a toasted marshmallow on a stick and tried to pluck it off, real casual-like. But before he could touch it, the marshmallow flew off the stick. Tantalus made a wild grab, but the marshmallow committed suicide, diving into the flames.

Tantalus turned back towards us, smiling coldly. 'Now then! Some announcements about tomorrow's schedule.'

'Sir,' I said.

Tantalus's eye twitched. 'Our kitchen boy has something to say?'

Some of the Ares campers snickered, but I wasn't going to let anybody embarrass me into silence. I stood and looked at Annabeth. Thank the gods, she stood up with me.

I said, 'We have an idea to save the camp.'

Dead silence, but I could tell I'd got everybody's interest, because the campfire flared bright yellow.

'Indeed,' Tantalus said blandly. 'Well, if it has anything to do with chariots –'

'The Golden Fleece,' I said. 'We know where it is.'

The flames burned orange. Before Tantalus could stop me, I blurted out my dream about Grover and Polyphemus's island. Annabeth stepped in and reminded everybody what the Fleece could do. It sounded more convincing coming from her.

'The Fleece can save the camp,' she concluded. 'I'm certain of it.'

'Nonsense,' said Tantalus. 'We don't need saving.'

Everybody stared at him until Tantalus started looking uncomfortable.

'Besides,' he added quickly, 'the Sea of Monsters? That's hardly an exact location. You wouldn't even know where to look.'

'Yes, I would,' I said.

Annabeth leaned towards me and whispered, 'You would?'

I nodded, because Annabeth had jogged something in my memory when she reminded me about our taxi drive with the Grey Sisters. At the time, the information they'd given me made no sense. But now . . .

'Thirty, thirty-one, seventy-five, twelve,' I said.

'Ooo-kay,' Tantalus said. 'Thank you for sharing those meaningless numbers.'

'They're sailing coordinates,' I said. 'Latitude and longitude. I, uh, learned about it in social studies.'

Even Annabeth looked impressed. 'Thirty degrees, thirty-one minutes north, seventy-five degrees, twelve minutes west. He's right! The Grey Sisters gave us those coordinates. That'd be somewhere in the Atlantic, off the coast of Florida. The Sea of Monsters. We need a quest!'

'Wait just a minute,' Tantalus said.

But the campers took up the chant. 'We need a quest! We need a quest!'

The flames rose higher.

'It isn't necessary!' Tantalus insisted.

'WE NEED A QUEST! WE NEED A QUEST!'

'Fine!' Tantalus shouted, his eyes blazing with anger. 'You brats want me to assign a quest?'

'YES!'

'Very well,' he agreed. 'I shall authorize a champion to undertake this perilous journey, to retrieve the Golden Fleece and bring it back to camp. Or die trying.'

My heart filled with excitement. I wasn't going to let Tantalus scare me. This was what I needed to do. I was going to save Grover and the camp. Nothing would stop me.

'I will allow our champion to consult the Oracle!' Tantalus announced. 'And choose two companions for the journey. And I think the choice of champions is obvious.'

Tantalus looked at Annabeth and me as if he wanted to flay us alive. 'The champion should be one who has earned the camp's respect, who has proven resourceful in the chariot races and courageous in the defence of the camp. *You* shall lead this quest . . . Clarisse!'

The fire flickered a thousand different colours. The Ares cabin started stomping and cheering, 'CLARISSE! CLARISSE!'

Clarisse stood up, looking stunned. Then she swallowed, and her chest swelled with pride. 'I accept the quest!'

'Wait!' I shouted. 'Grover is my friend. The dream came to *me*.'

'Sit down!' yelled one of the Ares campers. 'You had your chance last summer!'

'Yeah, he just wants to be in the spotlight again!' another said.

Clarisse glared at me. 'I accept the quest!' she repeated. 'I, Clarisse, daughter of Ares, will save the camp!'

The Ares campers cheered even louder. Annabeth protested, and the other Athena campers joined in. Everybody else started taking sides – shouting and arguing and throwing marshmallows. I thought it was going to turn into a fully fledged s'more war until Tantalus shouted, 'Silence, you brats!'

His tone stunned even me.

'Sit down!' he ordered. 'And I will tell you a ghost story.'

I didn't know what he was up to, but we all moved

reluctantly back to our seats. The evil aura radiating from Tantalus was as strong as any monster I'd ever faced.

'Once upon a time there was a mortal king who was beloved of the gods!' Tantalus put his hand on his chest, and I got the feeling he was talking about himself.

'This king,' he said, 'was even allowed to feast on Mount Olympus. But when he tried to take some ambrosia and nectar back to earth to figure out the recipe – just one little doggy bag, mind you – the gods punished him. They banned him from their halls forever! His own people mocked him! His children scolded him! And, oh yes, campers, he had horrible children. Children – just – like – you!'

He pointed a crooked finger at several people in the audience, including me.

'Do you know what he did to his ungrateful children?' Tantalus asked softly. 'Do you know how he paid back the gods for their cruel punishment? He invited the Olympians to a feast at his palace, just to show there were no hard feelings. No one noticed that his children were missing. And when he served the gods dinner, my dear campers, can you guess what was in the stew?'

No one dared answer. The firelight glowed dark blue, reflecting evilly on Tantalus's crooked face.

'Oh, the gods punished him in the afterlife,' Tantalus croaked. 'They did indeed. But he'd had his moment of satisfaction, hadn't he? His children never again spoke back to him or questioned his authority. And do you know what? Rumour has it that the king's spirit now dwells at this very camp, waiting for a chance to take revenge on ungrateful, rebellious children. And so . . . are there any more complaints, before we send Clarisse off on her quest?'

Silence.

Tantalus nodded at Clarisse. 'The Oracle, my dear. Go on.'

She shifted uncomfortably, like even *she* didn't want glory at the price of being Tantalus's pet. 'Sir —'

'Go!' he snarled.

She bowed awkwardly and hurried off towards the Big House.

'What about you, Percy Jackson?' Tantalus asked. 'No comments from our dishwasher?'

I didn't say anything. I wasn't going to give him the satisfaction of punishing me again.

'Good,' Tantalus said. 'And let me remind everyone — no one leaves this camp without my permission. Anyone who tries . . . well, if they survive the attempt, they will be expelled forever, but it won't come to that. The harpies will be enforcing curfew from now on, and they are always hungry! Good night, my dear campers. Sleep well.'

With a wave of Tantalus's hand, the fire was extinguished, and the campers trailed off towards their cabins in the dark.

I couldn't explain things to Tyson. He knew I was sad. He knew I wanted to go on a trip and Tantalus wouldn't let me.

'You will go anyway?' he asked.

'I don't know,' I admitted. 'It would be hard. Very hard.'

'I will help.'

'No. I — uh, I couldn't ask you to do that, big guy. Too dangerous.'

Tyson looked down at the pieces of metal he was assembling in his lap – springs and gears and tiny wires. Beckendorf had given him some tools and spare parts, and now Tyson spent every night tinkering, though I wasn't sure how his huge hands could handle such delicate little pieces.

'What are you building?' I asked.

Tyson didn't answer. Instead he made a whimpering sound in the back of his throat. 'Annabeth doesn't like Cyclopes. You . . . don't want me along?'

'Oh, that's not it,' I said half-heartedly. 'Annabeth likes you. Really.'

He had tears in the corners of his eye.

I remembered that Grover, like all satyrs, could read human emotions. I wondered if Cyclopes had the same ability.

Tyson folded up his tinkering project in an oilcloth. He lay down on his bunk bed and hugged his bundle like a teddy bear. When he turned towards the wall, I could see the weird scars on his back, like somebody had ploughed over him with a tractor. I wondered for the millionth time how he'd got hurt.

'Daddy always cared for m-me,' he sniffled. 'Now . . . I think he was mean to have a Cyclops boy. I should not have been born.'

'Don't talk that way! Poseidon claimed you, didn't he? So . . . he must care about you . . . a lot . . .'

My voice trailed off as I thought about all those years Tyson had lived on the streets of New York in a cardboard refrigerator box. How could Tyson think that Poseidon had cared for him? What kind of dad let that happen to his kid, even if his kid was a monster?

'Tyson . . . camp will be a good home for you. The others will get used to you. I promise.'

Tyson sighed. I waited for him to say something. Then I realized he was already asleep.

I lay back on my bed and tried to close my eyes, but I just couldn't. I was afraid I might have another dream about Grover. If the empathy link was real . . . if something happened to Grover . . . would I ever wake up?

The full moon shone through my window. The sound of the surf rumbled in the distance. I could smell the warm scent of the strawberry fields, and hear the laughter of the dryads as they chased owls through the forest. But something felt wrong about the night – the sickness of Thalia's tree, spreading across the valley.

Could Clarisse save Half-Blood Hill? I thought the odds were better of me getting a 'Best Camper' award from Tantalus.

I got out of bed and pulled on some clothes. I grabbed a beach blanket and a six-pack of Coke from under my bunk. The Cokes were against the rules. No outside snacks or drinks were allowed, but if you talked to the right guy in Hermes's cabin and paid him a few golden drachmas, he could smuggle in almost anything from the nearest convenience store.

Sneaking out after curfew was against the rules, too. If I got caught I'd either get in big trouble or be eaten by the harpies. But I wanted to see the ocean. I always felt better there. My thoughts were clearer. I left the cabin and headed for the beach.

* * *

I spread my blanket near the surf and popped open a Coke. For some reason sugar and caffeine always calmed down my hyperactive brain. I tried to decide what to do to save the camp, but nothing came to me. I wished Poseidon would talk to me, give me some advice or something.

The sky was clear and starry. I was checking out the constellations Annabeth had taught me – Sagittarius, Heracles, Corona Borealis – when somebody said, 'Beautiful, aren't they?'

I almost spewed soda.

Standing right next to me was a guy in nylon running shorts and a New York City Marathon T-shirt. He was slim and fit, with salt-and-pepper hair and a sly smile. He looked kind of familiar, but I couldn't figure out why.

My first thought was that he must've been taking a midnight jog down the beach and strayed inside the camp borders. That wasn't supposed to happen. Regular mortals couldn't enter the valley. But maybe with the tree's magic weakening he'd managed to slip in. But in the middle of the night? And there was nothing around except farmland and state preserves. Where would this guy have jogged from?

'May I join you?' he asked. 'I haven't sat down in ages.'

Now, I know – a strange guy in the middle of the night. Common sense: I was supposed to run away, yell for help, etc. But the guy acted so calm about the whole thing that I found it hard to be afraid.

I said, 'Uh, sure.'

He smiled. 'Your hospitality does you credit. Oh, and Coca-Cola! May I?'

He sat at the other end of the blanket, popped a soda

and took a drink. 'Ah . . . that hits the spot. Peace and quiet at –'

A cell phone went off in his pocket.

The jogger sighed. He pulled out his phone and my eyes got big, because it glowed with a bluish light. When he extended the antenna, two creatures began writhing around it – green snakes, no bigger than earthworms.

The jogger didn't seem to notice. He checked his LCD screen and cursed. 'I've got to take this. Just a sec . . .' Then into the phone, 'Hello?'

He listened. The mini-snakes writhed up and down the antenna right next to his ear.

'Yeah,' the jogger said. 'Listen – I know, but . . . I don't care if he *is* chained to a rock with vultures pecking at his liver, if he doesn't have a tracking number, we can't locate his package . . . A gift to humankind, great . . . You know how many of those we deliver – Oh, never mind. Listen, just refer him to Eris in customer service. I gotta go.'

He hung up. 'Sorry. The overnight express business is just booming. Now, as I was saying –'

'You have snakes on your phone.'

'What? Oh, they don't bite. Say hello, George and Martha.'

Hello, George and Martha, a raspy male voice said inside my head.

Don't be sarcastic, said a female voice.

Why not? George demanded. *I do all the* real *work.*

'Oh, let's not go into that again!' The jogger slipped his phone back into his pocket. 'Now, where were we . . . Ah, yes. Peace and quiet.'

He crossed his ankles and stared up at the stars. 'Been a long time since I've got to relax. Ever since the telegraph – rush, rush, rush. Do you have a favourite constellation, Percy?'

I was still kind of wondering about the little green snakes he'd shoved into his jogging shorts, but I said, 'Uh, I like Heracles.'

'Why?'

'Well . . . because he had rotten luck. Even worse than mine. It makes me feel better.'

The jogger chuckled. 'Not because he was strong and famous and all that?'

'No.'

'You're an interesting young man. And so, what now?'

I knew immediately what he was asking. What did I intend to do about the Fleece?

Before I could answer, Martha the snake's muffled voice came from his pocket, *I have Demeter on line two.*

'Not now,' the jogger said. 'Tell her to leave a message.'

She's not going to like that. The last time you put her off, all the flowers in the floral delivery division wilted.

'Just tell her I'm in a meeting!' The jogger rolled his eyes. 'Sorry again, Percy. You were saying . . .'

'Um . . . who are you, exactly?'

'Haven't you guessed by now, a smart boy like you?'

Show him! Martha pleaded. *I haven't been full-size for months.*

Don't listen to her! George said. *She just wants to show off!*

The man took out his phone again. 'Original form, please.'

The phone glowed a brilliant blue. It stretched into a

metre-long wooden staff with dove wings sprouting out the top. George and Martha, now full-sized green snakes, coiled together around the middle. It was a caduceus, the symbol of Cabin Eleven.

My throat tightened. I realized who the jogger reminded me of with his elfish features, the mischievous twinkle in his eyes. . . .

'You're Luke's father,' I said. 'Hermes.'

The god pursed his lips. He stuck his caduceus in the sand like an umbrella pole. '"Luke's father." Normally, that's not the first way people introduce me. God of thieves, yes. God of messengers and travellers, if they wish to be kind.'

God of thieves works, George said.

Oh, don't mind George. Martha flicked her tongue at me. *He's just bitter because Hermes likes me best.*

He does not!

Does too!

'Behave, you two,' Hermes warned, 'or I'll turn you back into a cell phone and set you on vibrate! Now, Percy, you still haven't answered my question. What do you intend to do about the quest?'

'I — I don't have permission to go.'

'No, indeed. Will that stop you?'

'I want to go. I have to save Grover.'

Hermes smiled. 'I knew a boy once . . . oh, younger than you by far. A mere baby, really.'

Here we go again, George said. *Always talking about himself.*

Quiet! Martha snapped. *Do you want to get set on vibrate?*

Hermes ignored them. 'One night, when this boy's mother wasn't watching, he sneaked out of their cave and stole some cattle that belonged to Apollo.'

'Did he get blasted to tiny pieces?' I asked.

'Hmm . . . no. Actually, everything turned out quite well. To make up for his theft, the boy gave Apollo an instrument he'd invented – a lyre. Apollo was so enchanted with the music that he forgot all about being angry.'

'So what's the moral?'

'The moral?' Hermes asked. 'Goodness, you act like it's a fable. It's a true story. Does truth have a moral?'

'Um . . .'

'How about this: stealing is not always bad?'

'I don't think my mom would like that moral.'

Rats are delicious, suggested George.

What does that have to do with the story? Martha demanded.

Nothing, George said. *But I'm hungry.*

'I've got it,' Hermes said. 'Young people don't always do what they're told, but if they can pull it off and do something wonderful, sometimes they escape punishment. How's that?'

'You're saying I should go anyway,' I said, 'even without permission.'

Hermes's eyes twinkled. 'Martha, may I have the first package, please?'

Martha opened her mouth . . . and kept opening it until it was as wide as my arm. She belched out a stainless steel canister – an old-fashioned lunch box flask with a black plastic top. The sides of the flask were enamelled with red and yellow Ancient Greek scenes – a hero killing a lion; a hero lifting up Cerberus, the three-headed dog.

'That's Heracles,' I said. 'But how –'

'Never question a gift,' Hermes chided. 'This is a collector's item from *Heracles Busts Heads*. The first season.'

'*Heracles Busts Heads?*'

'Great show.' Hermes sighed. 'Back before Hephaestus-TV was all reality programming. Of course, the Flask would be worth much more if I had the whole lunch box –'

Or if it hadn't been in Martha's mouth, George added.

I'll get you for that. Martha began chasing him around the caduceus.

'Wait a minute,' I said. 'This is a gift?'

'One of two,' Hermes said. 'Go on, pick it up.'

I almost dropped it because it was freezing cold on one side and burning hot on the other. The weird thing was, when I turned the Flask, the side facing the ocean – north – was always the cold side . . .

'It's a compass!' I said.

Hermes looked surprised. 'Very clever. I never thought of that. But its intended use is a bit more dramatic. Uncap it, and you will release the winds from the four corners of the earth to speed you on your way. Not now! And please, when the time comes, only unscrew the lid a tiny bit. The winds are a bit like me – always restless. Should all four escape at once . . . ah, but I'm sure you'll be careful. And now my second gift. George?'

She's touching me, George complained as he and Martha slithered around the pole.

'She's *always* touching you,' Hermes said. 'You're intertwined. And if you don't stop that, you'll get knotted again!'

The snakes stopped wrestling.

George unhinged his jaw and coughed up a little plastic bottle filled with chewable vitamins.

'You're kidding,' I said. 'Are those Minotaur-shaped?'

Hermes picked up the bottle and rattled it. 'The lemon ones, yes. The grape ones are Furies, I think. Or are they hydras? At any rate, these are potent. Don't take one unless you really, really need it.'

'How will I know if I really, really need it?'

'You'll know, believe me. Nine essential vitamins, minerals, amino acids . . . oh, everything you need to feel yourself again.'

He tossed me the bottle.

'Um, thanks,' I said. 'But Lord Hermes, why are you helping me?'

He gave me a melancholy smile. 'Perhaps because I hope that you can save many people on this quest, Percy. Not just your friend Grover.'

I stared at him. 'You don't mean . . . *Luke?*'

Hermes didn't answer.

'Look,' I said. 'Lord Hermes, I mean, thanks and everything, but you might as well take back your gifts. Luke can't be saved. Even if I could find him . . . he told me he wanted to tear down Olympus stone by stone. He betrayed everybody he knew. He – he hates you especially.'

Hermes gazed up at the stars. 'My dear young cousin, if there's one thing I've learned over the aeons, it's that you *can't* give up on your family, no matter how tempting they make it. It doesn't matter if they hate you, or embarrass you, or simply don't appreciate your genius for inventing the internet –'

'You invented the internet?'

It was my idea, Martha said.

Rats are delicious, George said.

'It was *my* idea!' Hermes said. 'I mean the internet, not the rats. But that's not the point. Percy, do you understand what I'm saying about family?'

'I — I'm not sure.'

'You will some day.' Hermes got up and brushed the sand off his legs. 'In the meantime, I must be going.'

You have sixty calls to return, Martha said.

And one thousand and thirty-eight emails, George added. *Not counting the offers for online discount ambrosia.*

'And you, Percy,' Hermes said, 'have a shorter deadline than you realize to complete your quest. Your friends should be coming right about . . . now.'

I heard Annabeth's voice calling my name from the sand dunes. Tyson, too, was shouting from a little bit further away.

'I hope I packed well for you,' Hermes said. 'I do have some experience with travel.'

He snapped his fingers and three yellow duffel bags appeared at my feet. 'Waterproof, of course. If you ask nicely, your father should be able to help you reach the ship.'

'Ship?'

Hermes pointed. Sure enough, a big cruise ship was cutting across Long Island Sound, its white-and-gold lights glowing against the dark water.

'Wait,' I said. 'I don't understand any of this. I haven't even agreed to go!'

'I'd make up your mind in the next five minutes, if I were you,' Hermes advised. 'That's when the harpies will come to eat you. Now, goodnight, cousin, and dare I say it? May the gods go with you.'

He opened his hand and the caduceus flew into it.

Good luck, Martha told me.

Bring me back a rat, George said.

The caduceus changed into a cell phone and Hermes slipped it into his pocket.

He jogged off down the beach. Twenty paces away, he shimmered and vanished, leaving me alone with a flask, a bottle of chewable vitamins and five minutes to make an impossible decision.

8 WE BOARD THE *PRINCESS ANDROMEDA*

I was staring at the waves when Annabeth and Tyson found me.

'What's going on?' Annabeth asked. 'I heard you calling for help!'

'Me, too!' Tyson said. 'Heard you yell, "Bad things are attacking!"'

'I didn't call you guys,' I said. 'I'm fine.'

'But then who . . .' Annabeth noticed the three yellow duffel bags, then the Flask and the bottle of vitamins I was holding. 'What –'

'Just listen,' I said. 'We don't have much time.'

I told them about my conversation with Hermes. By the time I was finished, I could hear screeching in the distance – patrol harpies picking up our scent.

'Percy,' Annabeth said, 'we have to do the quest.'

'We'll get expelled, you know. Trust me, I'm an expert at getting expelled.'

'So? If we fail, there won't be any camp to come back to.'

'Yeah, but you promised Chiron –'

'I promised I'd keep you from danger. I can only do that by coming with you! Tyson can stay behind and tell them –'

'I want to go,' Tyson said.

'No!' Annabeth's voice sounded close to panic. 'I mean . . . Percy, come on. You know that's impossible.'

I wondered again why she had such a grudge against Cyclopes. There was something she wasn't telling me.

She and Tyson both looked at me, waiting for an answer. Meanwhile, the cruise ship was getting further and further away.

The thing was, part of me didn't want Tyson along. I'd spent the last three days in close quarters with the guy, getting teased by the other campers and embarrassed a million times a day, constantly reminded that I was related to him. I needed some space.

Plus, I didn't know how much help he'd be, or how I'd keep him safe. Sure, he was strong, but Tyson was a little kid in Cyclops terms, maybe seven or eight years old, mentally. I could see him freaking out and starting to cry while we were trying to sneak past a monster or something. He'd get us all killed.

On the other hand, the sound of the harpies was getting closer . . .

'We can't leave him,' I decided. 'Tantalus will punish him for us being gone.'

'Percy,' Annabeth said, trying to keep her cool, 'we're going to Polyphemus's island! Polyphemus is an S-i-k . . . a C-y-k . . .' She stamped her foot in frustration. As smart as she was, Annabeth was dyslexic, too. We could've been there all night while she tried to spell Cyclops. 'You know what I mean!'

'Tyson can go,' I insisted, 'if he wants to.'

Tyson clapped his hands. 'Want to!'

Annabeth gave me the evil eye, but I guess she could

tell I wasn't going to change my mind. Or maybe she just knew we didn't have time to argue.

'All right,' she said. 'How do we get to that ship?'

'Hermes said my father would help.'

'Well then, Seaweed Brain? What are you waiting for?'

I'd always had a hard time calling on my father, or praying, or whatever you want to call it, but I stepped into the waves.

'Um, Dad?' I called. 'How's it going?'

'Percy!' Annabeth whispered. 'We're in a hurry!'

'We need your help,' I called a little louder. 'We need to get to that ship, like, before we get eaten and stuff, so . . .'

At first, nothing happened. Waves crashed against the shore like normal. The harpies sounded like they were right behind the sand dunes. Then, about a hundred metres out to sea, three white lines appeared on the surface. They moved fast towards the shore, like claws ripping through the ocean.

As they neared the beach, the surf burst apart and the heads of three white stallions reared out of the waves.

Tyson caught his breath. 'Fish ponies!'

He was right. As the creatures pulled themselves onto the sand, I saw that they were only horses in the front; their back halves were silvery fish bodies, with glistening scales and rainbow-tail fins.

'Hippocampi!' Annabeth said. 'They're beautiful.'

The nearest one whinnied in appreciation and nuzzled Annabeth.

'We'll admire them later,' I said. 'Come on!'

'There!' a voice screeched behind us. 'Bad children out of cabins! Snack time for lucky harpies!'

Five of them were fluttering over the top of the dunes – plump little hags with pinched faces and talons and feathery wings too small for their bodies. They reminded me of miniature cafeteria ladies who'd been crossbred with dodo birds. They weren't very fast, thank the gods, but they were vicious if they caught you.

'Tyson!' I said. 'Grab a duffel bag!'

He was still staring at the hippocampi with his mouth hanging open.

'Tyson!'

'Uh?'

'Come on!'

With Annabeth's help I got him moving. We gathered the bags and mounted our steeds. Poseidon must've known Tyson was one of the passengers, because one hippocampus was much larger than the other two – just right for carrying a Cyclops.

'Giddy-up!' I said. My hippocampus turned and plunged into the waves. Annabeth's and Tyson's followed right behind.

The harpies cursed at us, wailing for their snacks to come back, but the hippocampi raced over the water at the speed of jet skis. The harpies fell behind, and soon the shore of Camp Half-Blood was nothing but a dark smudge. I wondered if I'd ever see the place again. But right then I had other problems.

The cruise ship was now looming in front of us – our ride towards Florida and the Sea of Monsters.

* * *

Riding the hippocampus was even easier than riding a pegasus. We zipped along with the wind in our faces, speeding through the waves so smoothly and steadily I hardly needed to hold on at all.

As we got closer to the cruise ship, I realized just how huge it was. I felt as though I were looking up at a building in Manhattan. The white hull was at least ten storeys tall, topped with another dozen levels of decks with brightly lit balconies and portholes. The ship's name was painted just above the bow line in black letters, lit with a spotlight. It took me a few seconds to decipher it:

PRINCESS ANDROMEDA

Attached to the bow was a huge masthead – a three-storey-tall woman wearing a white Greek chiton, sculpted to look as if she were chained to the front of the ship. She was young and beautiful, with flowing black hair, but her expression was one of absolute terror. Why anybody would want a screaming princess' on the front of their vacation ship, I had no idea.

I remembered the myth about Andromeda and how she had been chained to a rock by her own parents as a sacrifice to a sea monster. Maybe she'd got too many Fs on her report card or something. Anyway, my namesake, Perseus, had saved her just in time and turned the sea monster to stone using the head of Medusa.

That Perseus always won. That's why my mom had named me after him, even though he was a son of Zeus and I was a son of Poseidon. The original Perseus was one of the only heroes in the Greek myths who got a happy ending.

The others died – betrayed, mauled, mutilated, poisoned, or cursed by the gods. My mom hoped I would inherit Perseus's luck. Judging by how my life was going so far, I wasn't really optimistic.

'How do we get aboard?' Annabeth shouted over the noise of the waves, but the hippocampi seemed to know what we needed. They skimmed along the starboard side of the ship, riding easily through its huge wake, and pulled up next to a service ladder riveted to the side of the hull.

'You first,' I told Annabeth.

She slung her duffel bag over her shoulder and grabbed the bottom rung. Once she'd hoisted herself onto the ladder, her hippocampus whinnied a farewell and dived underwater. Annabeth began to climb. I let her get a few rungs up, then followed her.

Finally it was just Tyson in the water. His hippocampus was treating him to 360° aerials and backwards ollies, and Tyson was laughing so hysterically, the sound echoed up the side of the ship.

'Tyson, shhh!' I said. 'Come on, big guy!'

'Can't we take Rainbow?' he asked, his smile fading.

I stared at him. *Rainbow?*

The hippocampus whinnied as if he liked his new name.

'Um, we have to go,' I said. 'Rainbow . . . well, he can't climb ladders.'

Tyson sniffled. He buried his face in the hippocampus's mane. 'I will miss you, Rainbow!'

The hippocampus made a neighing sound I could've sworn was crying.

'Maybe we'll see him again sometime,' I suggested.

'Oh, please!' Tyson said, perking up immediately. 'Tomorrow!'

I didn't make any promises, but I finally convinced Tyson to say his farewells and grab hold of the ladder. With a final sad whinny, Rainbow the hippocampus did a backflip and dived into the sea.

The ladder led to a maintenance deck stacked with yellow lifeboats. There was a set of locked double doors, which Annabeth managed to prise open with her knife and a fair amount of cursing in Ancient Greek.

I figured we'd have to sneak around, being stowaways and all, but after checking a few corridors and peering over a balcony into a huge central promenade lined with closed shops, I began to realize there was nobody to hide from. I mean, sure it was the middle of the night, but we walked half the length of the boat and met no one. We passed forty or fifty cabin doors and heard no sound behind any of them.

'It's a ghost ship,' I murmured.

'No,' Tyson said, fiddling with the strap of his duffel bag. 'Bad smell.'

Annabeth frowned. 'I don't smell anything.'

'Cyclopes are like satyrs,' I said. 'They can smell monsters. Isn't that right, Tyson?'

He nodded nervously. Now that we were away from Camp Half-Blood, the Mist had distorted his face again. Unless I concentrated very hard, it seemed that he had two eyes instead of one.

'Okay,' Annabeth said. 'So what exactly do you smell?'

'Something bad,' Tyson answered.

'Great,' Annabeth grumbled. 'That clears it up.'

We came outside on the swimming pool level. There were rows of empty deckchairs and a bar closed off with a chain curtain. The water in the pool glowed eerily, sloshing back and forth from the motion of the ship.

Above us fore and aft were more levels – a climbing wall, a pitch-and-putt golf course, a revolving restaurant, but no sign of life.

And yet . . . I sensed something familiar. Something dangerous. I had the feeling that if I weren't so tired and burned out on adrenalin from our long night, I might be able to put a name to what was wrong.

'We need a hiding place,' I said. 'Somewhere safe to sleep.'

'Sleep,' Annabeth agreed wearily.

We explored a few more corridors until we found an empty suite on the ninth level. The door was open, which struck me as weird. There was a basket of chocolate goodies on the table, an iced-down bottle of sparkling cider on the nightstand and a mint on the pillow with a handwritten note that said: *Enjoy your cruise!*

We opened our duffel bags for the first time and found that Hermes really had thought of everything – extra clothes, toiletries, camp rations, an airtight bag full of cash, a leather pouch full of golden drachmas. He'd even managed to pack Tyson's oilcloth with his tools and metal bits, and Annabeth's cap of invisibility, which made them both feel a lot better.

'I'll be next door,' Annabeth said. 'You guys *don't* drink or eat anything.'

'You think this place is enchanted?'

She frowned. 'I don't know. Something isn't right. Just . . . be careful.'

We locked our doors.

Tyson crashed on the couch. He tinkered for a few minutes on his metalworking project – which he still wouldn't show me – but soon enough he was yawning. He wrapped up his oilcloth and passed out.

I lay on the bed and stared out of the porthole. I thought I heard voices out in the hallway, like whispering. I knew that couldn't be. We'd walked all over the ship and had seen nobody. But the voices kept me awake. They reminded me of my trip to the Underworld – the way the spirits of the dead sounded as they drifted past.

Finally my weariness got the best of me. I fell asleep . . . and had my worst dream yet.

I was standing in a cavern at the edge of an enormous pit. I knew the place too well. The entrance to Tartarus. And I recognized the cold laugh that echoed from the darkness below.

If it isn't the young hero. The voice was like a knife blade scraping across stone. *On his way to another great victory.*

I wanted to shout at Kronos to leave me alone. I wanted to draw Riptide and strike him down. But I couldn't move. And even if I could, how could I kill something that had already been destroyed – chopped to pieces and cast into eternal darkness?

Don't let me stop you, the titan said. *Perhaps this time, when you fail, you'll wonder if it's worthwhile slaving for the gods. How exactly has your father shown his appreciation lately?*

His laughter filled the cavern, and suddenly the scene changed.

It was a different cave – Grover's bedroom prison in the Cyclops's lair.

Grover was sitting at the loom in his soiled wedding dress, madly unravelling the threads of the unfinished bridal train.

'Honeypie!' the monster shouted from behind the boulder.

Grover yelped and began weaving the threads back together.

The room shook as the boulder was pushed aside. Looming in the doorway was a Cyclops so huge he made Tyson look vertically challenged. He had jagged yellow teeth and gnarled hands as big as my whole body. He wore a faded purple T-shirt that said WORLD SHEEP EXPO 2001. He must've been at least five metres tall, but the most startling thing was his enormous milky eye, scarred and webbed with cataracts. If he wasn't completely blind, he had to be pretty darn close.

'What are you doing?' the monster demanded.

'Nothing!' Grover said in his falsetto voice. 'Just weaving my bridal train, as you can see.'

The Cyclops stuck one hand into the room and groped around until he found the loom. He pawed at the cloth. 'It hasn't got any longer!'

'Oh, um, yes it has, dearest. See? I've added at least three centimetres.'

'Too many delays!' the monster bellowed. Then he sniffed the air. 'You smell good! Like goats!'

'Oh.' Grover forced a weak giggle. 'Do you like it? It's *Eau de Chévre*. I wore it just for you.'

'Mmmm!' The Cyclops bared his pointed teeth. 'Good enough to eat!'

'Oh, you're such a flirt!'

'No more delays!'

'But dear, I'm not done!'

'Tomorrow!'

'No, no. Ten more days.'

'Five!'

'Oh, well, seven then. If you insist.'

'Seven! That is less than five, right?'

'Certainly. Oh yes.'

The monster grumbled, still not happy with his deal, but he left Grover to his weaving and rolled the boulder back into place.

Grover closed his eyes and took a shaky breath, trying to calm his nerves.

'Hurry, Percy,' he muttered. 'Please, please, please!'

I woke to a ship's whistle and a voice on the intercom — some guy with an Australian accent who sounded way too happy.

'Good morning, passengers! We'll be at sea all day today. Excellent weather for the poolside mambo party! Don't forget million-dollar bingo in the Kraken Lounge at one o'clock, and for our *special guests*, disembowelling practice on the Promenade!'

I sat up in bed. 'What did he say?'

Tyson groaned, still half asleep. He was lying face down on the couch, his feet so far over the edge they were in the bathroom. 'The happy man said . . . bowling practice?'

I hoped he was right, but then there was an urgent knock on the suite's interior door. Annabeth stuck her head in – her blonde hair in a rat's nest. '*Disembowelling* practice?'

Once we were all dressed, we ventured out into the ship and were surprised to see other people. A dozen senior citizens were heading to breakfast. A dad was taking his kids to the pool for a morning swim. Crew members in crisp white uniforms strolled the deck, tipping their hats to the passengers.

Nobody asked who we were. Nobody paid us much attention. But there was something wrong.

As the family of swimmers passed us, the dad told his kids, 'We are on a cruise. We are having fun.'

'Yes,' his three kids said in unison, their expressions blank. 'We are having a blast. We will swim in the pool.'

They wandered off.

'Good morning,' a crew member told us, his eyes glazed. 'We are all enjoying ourselves aboard the *Princess Andromeda*. Have a nice day.' He drifted away.

'Percy, this is weird,' Annabeth whispered. 'They're all in some kind of trance.'

Then we passed a cafeteria and saw our first monster. It was a hellhound – a black mastiff with its front paws up on the buffet counter and its muzzle buried in the scrambled eggs. It must've been young, because it was small compared to most – no bigger than a grizzly bear. Still, my blood turned cold. I'd almost got killed by one of those before.

The weird thing was, a middle-aged couple was standing in the buffet queue right behind the devil dog, patiently waiting their turn for the eggs. They didn't seem to notice anything out of the ordinary.

'Not hungry any more,' Tyson murmured.

Before Annabeth or I could reply, a reptilian voice came from down the corridor, 'Ssssix more joined yesssterday.'

Annabeth gestured frantically towards the nearest hiding place – the women's room – and all three of us ducked inside. I was so freaked out it didn't even occur to me to be embarrassed.

Something – or more like *two* somethings – slithered past the restroom door, making sounds like sandpaper against the carpet.

'Yesss,' a second reptilian voice said. 'He drawssss them. Ssssoon we will be sssstrong.'

The things slithered into the cafeteria with a cold hissing that might have been snake laughter.

Annabeth looked at me. 'We have to get out of here.'

'You think I *want* to be in the girls' restroom?'

'I mean the ship, Percy! We have to get off the ship.'

'Smells bad,' Tyson agreed. 'And dogs eat all the eggs. Annabeth is right. We must leave the restroom and ship.'

I shuddered. If Annabeth and Tyson were actually *agreeing* about something, I figured I'd better listen.

Then I heard another voice outside – one that chilled me worse than any monster's.

'– only a matter of time. Don't push me, Agrius!'

It was Luke, beyond a doubt. I could never forget his voice.

'I'm not pushing you!' another guy growled. His voice was deeper and even angrier than Luke's. 'I'm just saying, if this gamble doesn't pay off –'

'It'll pay off,' Luke snapped. 'They'll take the bait. Now, come, we've got to get to the admiralty suite and check on the casket.'

Their voices receded down the corridor.

Tyson whimpered. 'Leave now?'

Annabeth and I exchanged looks and came to a silent agreement.

'We can't,' I told Tyson.

'We have to find out what Luke is up to,' Annabeth agreed. 'And if possible, we're going to beat him up, bind him in chains and drag him to Mount Olympus.'

I HAVE THE WORST FAMILY REUNION EVER

Annabeth volunteered to go alone since she had the cap of invisibility, but I convinced her it was too dangerous. Either we all went together, or nobody went.

'Nobody!' Tyson voted. 'Please?'

But in the end he came along, nervously chewing on his huge fingernails. We stopped at our cabin long enough to gather our stuff. We figured whatever happened, we would *not* be staying another night aboard the zombie cruise ship, even if they did have million-dollar bingo. I made sure Riptide was in my pocket and the vitamins and flask from Hermes were at the top of my bag. I didn't want Tyson to carry everything, but he insisted, and Annabeth told me not to worry about it. Tyson could carry three full duffel bags over his shoulder as easily as I could carry a backpack.

We sneaked through the corridors, following the ship's YOU ARE HERE signs towards the admiralty suite. Annabeth scouted ahead invisibly. We hid whenever someone passed by, but most of the people we saw were just glassy-eyed zombie passengers.

As we came up the stairs to deck thirteen, where the admiralty suite was supposed to be, Annabeth hissed, 'Hide!' and shoved us into a supply closet.

I heard a couple of guys coming down the hall.

'You see that Aethiopian drakon in the cargo hold?' one of them said.

The other laughed. 'Yeah, it's awesome.'

Annabeth was still invisible, but she squeezed my arm hard. I got a feeling I should know that second guy's voice.

'I hear they got two more coming,' the familiar voice said. 'They keep arriving at this rate, oh, man — no contest!'

The voices faded down the corridor.

'That was Chris Rodriguez!' Annabeth took off her cap and turned visible. 'You remember — from Cabin Eleven.'

I sort of recalled Chris from the summer before. He was one of those undetermined campers who got stuck in the Hermes cabin because his Olympian dad or mom never claimed him. Now that I thought about it, I realized I hadn't seen Chris at camp this summer. 'What's another half-blood doing here?'

Annabeth shook her head, clearly troubled.

We kept going down the corridor. I didn't need maps any more to know I was getting close to Luke. I sensed something cold and unpleasant — the presence of evil.

'Percy.' Annabeth stopped suddenly. 'Look.'

She stood in front of a glass wall looking down into the multistorey canyon that ran through the middle of the ship. At the bottom was the Promenade — a mall full of shops — but that's not what had caught Annabeth's attention.

A group of monsters had assembled in front of the candy store: a dozen Laistrygonian giants like the ones who'd attacked me with dodgeballs, two hellhounds and a few even stranger creatures — humanoid females with twin serpent tails instead of legs.

'Scythian Dracaenae,' Annabeth whispered. 'Dragon women.'

The monsters made a semicircle around a young guy in Greek armour who was hacking on a straw dummy. A lump formed in my throat when I realized the dummy was wearing an orange Camp Half-Blood T-shirt. As we watched, the guy in armour stabbed the dummy through its belly and ripped upwards. Straw flew everywhere. The monsters cheered and howled.

Annabeth stepped away from the window. Her face was ashen.

'Come on,' I told her, trying to sound braver than I felt. 'The sooner we find Luke the better.'

At the end of the hallway were double oak doors that looked like they must lead somewhere important. When we were ten metres away, Tyson stopped. 'Voices inside.'

'You can hear that far?' I asked.

Tyson closed his eye like he was concentrating hard. Then his voice changed, becoming a husky approximation of Luke's. '– the prophecy ourselves. The fools won't know which way to turn.'

Before I could react, Tyson's voice changed again, becoming deeper and gruffer, like the other guy we'd heard talking to Luke outside the cafeteria. 'You really think the old horseman is gone for good?'

Tyson laughed Luke's laugh. 'They can't trust him. Not with the skeletons in *his* closet. The poisoning of the tree was the final straw.'

Annabeth shivered. 'Stop that, Tyson! How do you do that? It's creepy.'

Tyson opened his eye and looked puzzled. 'Just listening.'

'Keep going,' I said. 'What else are they saying?'

Tyson closed his eye again.

He hissed in the gruff man's voice, 'Quiet!' Then Luke's voice, whispering, 'Are you sure?'

'Yes,' Tyson said in the gruff voice. 'Right outside.'

Too late, I realized what was happening.

I just had time to say, 'Run!' when the doors of the stateroom burst open and there was Luke, flanked by two hairy giants armed with javelins, their bronze tips aimed right at our chests.

'Well,' Luke said with a crooked smile. 'If it isn't my two favourite cousins. Come right in.'

The stateroom was beautiful, and it was horrible.

The beautiful part: huge windows curved along the back wall, looking out over the stern of the ship. Green sea and blue sky stretched all the way to the horizon. A Persian rug covered the floor. Two plush sofas occupied the middle of the room, with a canopied bed in one corner and a mahogany dining table in the other. The table was loaded with food: pizza boxes, bottles of soda and a stack of roast beef sandwiches on a silver platter.

The horrible part: on a velvet dais at the back of the room lay a three-metre-long golden casket. A sarcophagus, engraved with Ancient Greek scenes of cities in flames and heroes dying grisly deaths. Despite the sunlight streaming through the windows, the casket made the whole room feel cold.

'Well,' Luke said, spreading his arms proudly. 'A little nicer than Cabin Eleven, huh?'

He'd changed since last summer. Instead of Bermuda shorts and a T-shirt, he wore a button-down shirt, khaki trousers and leather loafers. His sandy hair, which used to be so unruly, was now clipped short. He looked like an evil male model, showing off what the fashionable college-age villain was wearing to Harvard this year.

He still had the scar under his eye – a jagged white line from his battle with a dragon. And propped against the sofa was his magical sword, Backbiter, glinting strangely with its half steel, half Celestial bronze blade that could kill both mortals and monsters.

'Sit,' he told us. He waved his hand and three dining chairs scooted themselves into the centre of the room.

None of us sat.

Luke's large friends were still pointing their javelins at us. They looked like twins, but they weren't human. They stood about two and a half metres tall, for one thing, and wore only blue jeans, probably because their enormous chests were already shag-carpeted with thick brown fur. They had claws for fingernails, feet like paws. Their noses were snoutlike, and their teeth were all pointed canines.

'Where are my manners?' Luke said smoothly. 'These are my assistants, Agrius and Oreius. Perhaps you've heard of them.'

I said nothing. Despite the javelins pointed at me, it wasn't the bear twins who scared me.

I'd imagined meeting Luke again many times since he'd tried to kill me last summer. I'd pictured myself boldly standing up to him, challenging him to a duel. But now that we were face to face, I could barely stop my hands from shaking.

'You don't know Agrius and Oreius's story?' Luke asked. 'Their mother . . . well, it's sad, really. Aphrodite ordered the young woman to fall in love. She refused and ran to Artemis for help. Artemis let her become one of her maiden huntresses, but Aphrodite got her revenge. She bewitched the young woman into falling in love with a bear. When Artemis found out, she abandoned the girl in disgust. Typical of the gods, wouldn't you say? They fight with one another and the poor humans get caught in the middle. The girl's twin sons here, Agrius and Oreius, have no love for Olympus. They like half-bloods well enough, though . . .'

'For lunch,' Agrius growled. His gruff voice was the one I'd heard talking with Luke earlier.

'Hehe! Hehe!' His brother Oreius laughed, licking his fur-lined lips. He kept laughing like he was having an asthmatic fit until Luke and Agrius both stared at him.

'Shut up, you idiot!' Agrius growled. 'Go punish yourself!'

Oreius whimpered. He trudged over to the corner of the room, slumped onto a stool, and banged his forehead against the dining table, making the silver plates rattle.

Luke acted like this was perfectly normal behaviour. He made himself comfortable on the sofa and propped his feet up on the coffee table. 'Well, Percy, we let you survive another year. I hope you appreciated it. How's your mom? How's school?'

'You poisoned Thalia's tree.'

Luke sighed. 'Right to the point, eh? Okay, sure I poisoned the tree. So what?'

'How could you?' Annabeth sounded so angry I thought she'd explode. 'Thalia saved your life! *Our* lives! How could you dishonour her –'

'I didn't dishonour her!' Luke snapped. 'The gods dishonoured her, Annabeth! If Thalia were alive, she'd be on my side.'

'Liar!'

'If you knew what was coming, you'd understand –'

'I understand you want to destroy the camp!' she yelled. 'You're a monster!'

Luke shook his head. 'The gods have blinded you. Can't you imagine a world without them, Annabeth? What good is that ancient history you study? Three thousand years of baggage! The West is rotten to the core. It has to be destroyed. Join me! We can start the world anew. We could use your intelligence, Annabeth.'

'Because you have none of your own!'

His eyes narrowed. 'I know you, Annabeth. You deserve better than tagging along on some hopeless quest to save the camp. Half-Blood Hill will be overrun by monsters within the month. The heroes who survive will have no choice but to join us or be hunted to extinction. You really want to be on a losing team . . . with company like this?' Luke pointed at Tyson.

'Hey!' I said.

'Travelling with a *Cyclops*,' Luke chided. 'Talk about dishonouring Thalia's memory! I'm surprised at you, Annabeth. You of all people –'

'Stop it!' she shouted.

I didn't know what Luke was talking about, but Annabeth buried her head in her hands like she was about to cry.

'Leave her alone,' I said. 'And leave Tyson out of this.'

Luke laughed. 'Oh, yeah, I heard. Your father claimed him.'

I must have looked surprised, because Luke smiled. 'Yes, Percy, I know all about that. And about your plan to find the Fleece. What were those coordinates, again . . . thirty, thirty-one, seventy-five, twelve? You see, I still have friends at camp who keep me posted.'

'Spies, you mean.'

He shrugged. 'How many insults from your father can you stand, Percy? You think he's grateful to you? You think Poseidon cares for you any more than he cares for this monster?'

Tyson clenched his fists and made a rumbling sound down in his throat.

Luke just chuckled. 'The gods are *so* using you, Percy. Do you have any idea what's in store for you if you reach your sixteenth birthday? Has Chiron even *told* you the prophecy?'

I wanted to get in Luke's face and tell him off, but as usual, he knew just how to throw me off balance.

Sixteenth birthday?

I mean, I knew Chiron had received a prophecy from the Oracle many years ago. I knew part of it was about me. But, *if* I reached my sixteenth birthday? I didn't like the sound of that.

'I know what I need to know,' I managed. 'Like, who my enemies are.'

'Then you're a fool.'

Tyson smashed the nearest dining chair to splinters. 'Percy is not a fool!'

Before I could stop him, he charged Luke. His fists came down towards Luke's head — a double overhead blow that would've knocked a hole in titanium — but the bear twins intercepted. They each caught one of Tyson's arms and stopped him cold. They pushed him back and Tyson stumbled. He fell to the carpet so hard the deck shook.

'Too bad, Cyclops,' Luke said. 'Looks like my grizzly friends together are more than a match for your strength. Maybe I should let them —'

'Luke,' I cut in. 'Listen to me. Your father sent us.'

His face turned the colour of pepperoni. 'Don't — *even* — mention him.'

'He told us to take this boat. I thought it was just for a ride, but he sent us here to find you. He told me he won't give up on you, no matter how angry you are.'

'*Angry?*' Luke roared. '*Give up on me?* He abandoned me, Percy! I want Olympus destroyed! Every throne crushed to rubble! You tell Hermes it's going to happen, too. Each time a half-blood joins us, the Olympians grow weaker and we grow stronger. *He* grows stronger.' Luke pointed to the gold sarcophagus.

The box creeped me out, but I was determined not to show it. 'So?' I demanded. 'What's so special . . .'

Then it hit me, what might be inside the sarcophagus. The temperature in the room seemed to drop twenty degrees. 'Whoa, you don't mean —'

'He is re-forming,' Luke said. 'Little by little, we're calling his life force out of the pit. With every recruit who pledges our cause, another small piece appears —'

'That's disgusting!' Annabeth said.

Luke sneered at her. 'Your mother was born from Zeus's

split skull, Annabeth. I wouldn't talk. Soon there will be enough of the titan lord so that we can make him whole again. We will piece together a new body for him, a work worthy of the forges of Hephaestus.'

'You're insane,' Annabeth said.

'Join us and you'll be rewarded. We have powerful friends, sponsors rich enough to buy this cruise ship and much more. Percy, your mother will never have to work again. You can buy her a mansion. You can have power, fame – whatever you want. Annabeth, you can realize your dream of being an architect. You can build a monument to last a thousand years. A temple to the lords of the next age!'

'Go to Tartarus,' she said.

Luke sighed. 'A shame.'

He picked up something that looked like a TV remote and pressed a red button. Within seconds the door of the stateroom opened and two uniformed crew members came in, armed with nightsticks. They had the same glassy-eyed look as the other mortals I'd seen, but I had a feeling this wouldn't make them any less dangerous in a fight.

'Ah, good, security,' Luke said. 'I'm afraid we have some stowaways.'

'Yes, sir,' they said dreamily.

Luke turned to Oreius. 'It's time to feed the Aethiopian drakon. Take these fools below and show them how it's done.'

Oreius grinned stupidly. 'Hehe! Hehe!'

'Let me go, too,' Agrius grumbled. 'My brother is worthless. That Cyclops –'

'Is no threat,' Luke said. He glanced back at the golden

casket, as if something were troubling him. 'Agrius, stay here. We have important matters to discuss.'

'But —'

'Oreius, don't fail me. Stay in the hold to make sure the drakon is properly fed.'

Oreius prodded us with his javelin and herded us out of the stateroom, followed by the two human security guards.

As I walked down the corridor with Orieus's javelin poking me in the back, I thought about what Luke had said — that the bear twins *together* were a match for Tyson's strength. But maybe separately . . .

We exited the corridor amidships and walked across an open deck lined with lifeboats. I knew the ship well enough to realize this would be our last look at sunlight. Once we got to the other side, we'd take the elevator down into the hold, and that would be it.

I looked at Tyson and said, 'Now.'

Thank the gods, he understood. He turned and smacked Oreius ten metres backwards into the swimming pool, right into the middle of the zombie tourist family.

'Ah!' the kids yelled in unison. 'We are *not* having a blast in the pool!'

One of the security guards drew his nightstick, but Annabeth knocked the wind out of him with a well-placed kick. The other guard ran for the nearest alarm box.

'Stop him!' Annabeth yelled, but it was too late.

Just before I banged him on the head with a deckchair, he hit the alarm.

Red lights flashed. Sirens wailed.

'Lifeboat!' I yelled.

We ran for the nearest one.

By the time we got the cover off, monsters and more security men were swarming the deck, pushing aside tourists and waiters with trays of tropical drinks. A guy in Greek armour drew his sword and charged, but slipped in a puddle of piña colada. Laistrygonian archers assembled on the deck above us, notching arrows in their enormous bows.

'How do you launch this thing?' screamed Annabeth.

A hellhound leaped at me, but Tyson slammed it aside with a fire extinguisher.

'Get in!' I yelled. I uncapped Riptide and slashed the first volley of arrows out of the air. Any second we would be overwhelmed.

The lifeboat was hanging over the side of the ship, high above the water. Annabeth and Tyson were having no luck with the release pulley.

I jumped in beside them.

'Hold on!' I yelled, and I cut the ropes.

A shower of arrows whistled over our heads as we free-fell towards the ocean.

10 WE HITCH A RIDE WITH DEAD CONFEDERATES

'Flask!' I screamed as we hurtled towards the water.

'*What?*' Annabeth must've thought I'd lost my mind. She was holding on to the boat straps for dear life, her hair flying straight up like a torch.

But Tyson understood. He managed to open my duffel bag and take out Hermes's magical flask without losing his grip on it or the boat.

Arrows and javelins whistled past us.

I grabbed the Flask and hoped I was doing the right thing. 'Hang on!'

'I *am* hanging on!' Annabeth yelled.

'Tighter!'

I hooked my feet under the boat's inflatable bench, and, as Tyson grabbed Annabeth and me by the backs of our shirts, I gave the Flask cap a quarter turn.

Instantly, a white sheet of wind jetted out of the flask and propelled us sideways, turning our downward plummet into a forty-five-degree crash landing.

The wind seemed to laugh as it shot from the flask, like it was glad to be free. As we hit the ocean, we bumped once, twice, skipping like a stone, then we were whizzing along like a speed boat, salt spray in our faces and nothing but sea ahead.

I heard a wail of outrage from the ship behind us, but

we were already out of weapon range. The *Princess Andromeda* faded to the size of a white toy boat in the distance, and then it was gone.

As we raced over the sea, Annabeth and I tried to send an Iris-message to Chiron. We figured it was important we let somebody know what Luke was doing, and we didn't know who else to trust.

The wind from the Flask stirred up a nice sea spray that made a rainbow in the sunlight – perfect for an Iris-message – but our connection was still poor. When Annabeth threw a gold drachma into the mist and prayed for the rainbow goddess to show us Chiron, his face appeared all right, but there was some kind of weird strobe light flashing in the background and rock music blaring, like he was at a dance club.

We told him about sneaking away from camp, and Luke and the *Princess Andromeda* and the golden box for Kronos's remains, but between the noise on his end and the rushing wind and water on our end, I'm not sure how much he heard.

'Percy,' Chiron yelled, 'you have to watch out for –'

His voice was drowned out by loud shouting behind him – a bunch of voices whooping it up like Comanche warriors.

'What?' I yelled.

'Curse my relatives!' Chiron ducked as a plate flew over his head and shattered somewhere out of sight. 'Annabeth, you shouldn't have let Percy leave camp! But if you *do* get the Fleece –'

'Yeah, baby!' somebody behind Chiron yelled. 'Woo-hoooooo!'

The music got cranked up, subwoofers so loud it made our boat vibrate.

'– Miami,' Chiron was yelling. 'I'll try to keep watch –'

Our misty screen smashed apart like someone on the other side had thrown a bottle at it, and Chiron was gone.

An hour later we spotted land – a long stretch of beach lined with high-rise hotels. The water became crowded with fishing boats and tankers. A coastguard cruiser passed on our starboard side, then turned like it wanted a second look. I guess it isn't every day they see a yellow lifeboat with no engine going a hundred knots an hour, manned by three kids.

'That's Virginia Beach!' Annabeth said as we approached the shoreline. 'Oh my gods, how did the *Princess Andromeda* travel so far overnight? That's like –'

'Five hundred and thirty nautical miles,' I said.

She stared at me. 'How did you know that?'

'I – I'm not sure.'

Annabeth thought for a moment. 'Percy, what's our position?'

'Thirty-six degrees, forty-four minutes north, seventy-six degrees, two minutes west,' I said immediately. Then I shook my head. 'Whoa. How did I know that?'

'Because of your dad,' Annabeth guessed. 'When you're at sea, you have perfect bearings. That is *so* cool.'

I wasn't sure about that. I didn't want to be a human GPS unit. But before I could say anything, Tyson tapped my shoulder. 'Other boat is coming.'

I looked back. The coastguard vessel was definitely on

our tail now. Its lights were flashing and it was gaining speed.

'We can't let them catch us,' I said. 'They'll ask too many questions.'

'Keep going into Chesapeake Bay,' Annabeth said. 'I know a place we can hide.'

I didn't ask what she meant, or how she knew the area so well. I risked loosening the Flask cap a little more, and a fresh burst of wind sent us rocketing around the northern tip of Virginia Beach into Chesapeake Bay. The coastguard boat fell further and further behind. We didn't slow down until the shores of the bay narrowed on either side, and I realized we'd entered the mouth of a river.

I could feel the change from salt water to fresh water. Suddenly I was tired and frazzled, like I was coming down off a sugar high. I didn't know where I was any more, or which way to steer the boat. It was a good thing Annabeth was directing me.

'There,' she said. 'Past that sandbar.'

We veered into a swampy area choked with marsh grass. I beached the lifeboat at the foot of a giant cypress.

Vine-covered trees loomed above us. Insects chirred in the woods. The air was muggy and hot, and steam curled off the river. Basically, it wasn't Manhattan, and I didn't like it.

'Come on,' Annabeth said. 'It's just down the bank.'

'What is?' I asked.

'Just follow.' She grabbed a duffel bag. 'And we'd better cover the boat. We don't want to draw attention.'

After burying the lifeboat with branches, Tyson and I

followed Annabeth along the shore, our feet sinking in red mud. A snake slithered past my shoe and disappeared into the grass.

'Not a good place,' Tyson said. He swatted the mosquitoes that were forming a buffet queue on his arm.

After another few minutes, Annabeth said, 'Here.'

All I saw was a patch of brambles. Then Annabeth moved aside a woven circle of branches, like a door, and I realized I was looking into a camouflaged shelter.

The inside was big enough for three, even with Tyson being the third. The walls were woven from plant material, like a Native American hut, but they looked pretty waterproof. Stacked in the corner was everything you could want for a campout – sleeping bags, blankets, an ice chest and a kerosene lamp. There were demigod provisions, too – bronze javelin tips, a quiver full of arrows, an extra sword and a box of ambrosia. The place smelled musty, like it had been vacant for a long time.

'A half-blood hideout.' I looked at Annabeth in awe. 'You *made* this place?'

'Thalia and I,' she said quietly. 'And Luke.'

That shouldn't have bothered me. I mean, I knew Thalia and Luke had taken care of Annabeth when she was little. I knew the three of them had been runaways together, hiding from monsters, surviving on their own before Grover found them and tried to get them to Half-Blood Hill. But whenever Annabeth talked about the time she'd spent with them, I kind of felt . . . I don't know. Uncomfortable?

No. That's not the word.

The word was *jealous*.

'So . . .' I said. 'You don't think Luke will look for us here?'

She shook her head. 'We made a dozen safe houses like this. I doubt Luke even remembers where they are. Or cares.'

She threw herself down on the blankets and started going through her duffel bag. Her body language made it pretty clear she didn't want to talk.

'Um, Tyson?' I said. 'Would you mind scouting around outside? Like, look for a wilderness convenience store or something?'

'Convenience store?'

'Yeah, for snacks. Powdered doughnuts or something. Just don't go too far.'

'Powdered doughnuts,' Tyson said earnestly. 'I will look for powdered doughnuts in the wilderness.' He headed outside and started calling, 'Here, doughnuts!'

Once he was gone, I sat down across from Annabeth. 'Hey, I'm sorry about, you know, seeing Luke.'

'It's not your fault.' She unsheathed her knife and started cleaning the blade with a rag.

'He let us go too easily,' I said.

I hoped I'd been imagining it, but Annabeth nodded. 'I was thinking the same thing. What we overheard him say about a gamble, and "they'll take the bait" . . . I think he was talking about us.'

'The Fleece is the bait? Or Grover?'

She studied the edge of her knife. 'I don't know, Percy. Maybe he wants the Fleece for himself. Maybe he's hoping we'll do the hard work and then he can steal it from us. I just can't believe he would poison the tree.'

'What did he mean,' I asked, 'that Thalia would've been on his side?'

'He's wrong.'

'You don't sound sure.'

Annabeth glared at me, and I started to wish I hadn't asked her about this while she was holding a knife.

'Percy, you know who you remind me of most? *Thalia.* You guys are so much alike it's scary. I mean, either you would've been best friends or you would've strangled each other.'

'Let's go with "best friends."'

'Thalia got angry with her dad sometimes. So do you. Would *you* turn against Olympus because of that?'

I stared at the quiver of arrows in the corner. 'No.'

'Okay, then. Neither would she. Luke's wrong.' Annabeth stuck her knife blade into the dirt.

I wanted to ask her about the prophecy Luke had mentioned and what it had to do with my sixteenth birthday. But I figured she wouldn't tell me. Chiron had made it pretty clear that I wasn't allowed to hear it until the gods decided otherwise.

'So what did Luke mean about Cyclopes?' I asked. 'He said you of all people –'

'I know what he said. He . . . he was talking about the *real* reason Thalia died.'

I waited, not sure what to say.

Annabeth drew a shaky breath. 'You can never trust a Cyclops, Percy. Six years ago, on the night Grover was leading us to Half-Blood Hill –'

She was interrupted when the door of the hut creaked open. Tyson crawled in.

'Powdered doughnuts!' he said proudly, holding up a pastry box.

Annabeth stared at him. 'Where did you get that? We're in the middle of the wilderness. There's nothing around for —'

'Fifteen metres,' Tyson said. 'Monster Doughnut shop — just over the hill!'

'This is bad,' Annabeth muttered.

We were crouching behind a tree, staring at the doughnut shop in the middle of the woods. It looked brand new, with brightly lit windows, a parking area and a little road leading off into the forest, but there was nothing else around, and no cars parked in the lot. We could see one employee reading a magazine behind the cash register. That was it. On the store's awning, in huge black letters that even I could read, it said:

MONSTER DOUGHNUT

A cartoon ogre was taking a bite out of the *O* in *MONSTER*. The place smelled good, like fresh-baked chocolate doughnuts.

'This shouldn't be here,' Annabeth whispered. 'It's wrong.'

'What?' I asked. 'It's a doughnut shop.'

'Shhh!'

'Why are we whispering? Tyson went in and bought a dozen. Nothing happened to him.'

'*He's* a monster.'

'Aw, c'mon, Annabeth. Monster Doughnut doesn't mean

monsters! It's a chain. We've got them in New York.'

'A chain,' she agreed. 'And don't you think it's strange that one appeared immediately after you told Tyson to get doughnuts? Right here in the middle of the woods?'

I thought about it. It did seem a little weird, but, I mean, doughnut shops weren't real high on my list of sinister forces.

'It could be a nest,' Annabeth explained.

Tyson whimpered. I doubt he understood what Annabeth was saying any better than I did, but her tone was making him nervous. He'd ploughed through half a dozen doughnuts from his box and was getting powdered sugar all over his face.

'A nest for what?' I asked.

'Haven't you ever wondered how franchise stores pop up so fast?' she asked. 'One day there's nothing and then the next day – *boom*, there's a new burger place or a coffee shop or whatever? First a single store, then two, then four – exact replicas spreading across the country?'

'Um, no. Never thought about it.'

'Percy, some of the chains multiply so fast because all their locations are magically linked to the life force of a monster. Some children of Hermes figured out how to do it back in the 1950s. They breed –'

She froze.

'What?' I demanded. 'They breed what?'

'No – sudden – moves,' Annabeth said, like her life depended on it. 'Very slowly, turn around.'

Then I heard it: a scraping noise, like something large dragging its belly through the leaves.

I turned and saw a rhino-size *thing* moving through the

shadows of the trees. It was hissing, its front half writhing in all different directions. I couldn't understand what I was seeing at first. Then I realized the thing had multiple necks — at least seven, each topped with a hissing reptilian head. Its skin was leathery, and under each neck it wore a plastic bib that read: I'M A MONSTER DOUGHNUT KID!

I took out my ballpoint pen, but Annabeth locked eyes with me — a silent warning. *Not yet.*

I understood. A lot of monsters have terrible eyesight. It was possible the Hydra might pass us by. But if I uncapped my sword now, the bronze glow would certainly get its attention.

We waited.

The Hydra was only a metre or so away. It seemed to be sniffing the ground and the trees like it was hunting for something. Then I noticed that two of the heads were ripping apart a piece of yellow canvas — one of our duffel bags. The thing had already been to our campsite. It was following our scent.

My heart pounded. I'd seen a stuffed Hydra-head trophy at camp before, but that did nothing to prepare me for the real thing. Each head was diamond-shaped, like a rattlesnake's, but the mouths were lined with jagged rows of sharklike teeth.

Tyson was trembling. He stepped back and accidentally snapped a twig. Immediately, all seven heads turned towards us and hissed.

'Scatter!' Annabeth yelled. She dived to the right.

I rolled to the left. One of the Hydra heads spat an arc of green liquid that shot past my shoulder and splashed against an elm. The trunk smoked and began to disintegrate. The whole tree toppled straight towards Tyson, who still hadn't moved, petrified by the monster that was now right in front of him.

'Tyson!' I tackled him with all my might, knocking him aside just as the Hydra lunged and the tree crashed on top of two of its heads.

The Hydra stumbled backwards, yanking its heads free and wailing in outrage at the fallen tree. All seven heads shot acid, and the elm melted into a steaming pool of muck.

'Move!' I told Tyson. I ran to one side and uncapped Riptide, hoping to draw the monster's attention.

It worked.

The sight of celestial bronze is hateful to most monsters. As soon as my glowing blade appeared, the Hydra whipped towards it with all its heads, hissing and baring its teeth.

The good news: Tyson was momentarily out of danger. The bad news: I was about to be melted into a puddle of goo.

One of the heads snapped at me experimentally. Without thinking, I swung my sword.

'No!' Annabeth yelled.

Too late. I sliced the Hydra's head clean off. It rolled away into the grass, leaving a flailing stump, which immediately stopped bleeding and began to swell like a balloon.

In a matter of seconds the wounded neck split into two necks, each of which grew a full-size head. Now I was looking at an eight-headed Hydra.

'Percy!' Annabeth scolded. 'You just opened another Monster Doughnut shop somewhere!'

I dodged a spray of acid. 'I'm about to die and you're worried about *that*? How do we kill it?'

'Fire!' Annabeth said. 'We have to have fire!'

As soon as she said that, I remembered the story. The Hydra's heads would only stop multiplying if we burned the stumps before they regrew. That's what Heracles had done, anyway. But we had no fire.

I backed up towards the river. The Hydra followed.

Annabeth moved in on my left and tried to distract one of the heads, parrying its teeth with her knife, but another head swung sideways like a club and knocked her into the muck.

'No hitting my friends!' Tyson charged in, putting himself between the Hydra and Annabeth. As Annabeth got to her feet, Tyson started smashing at the monster heads with his fists so fast it reminded me of the whack-a-mole game at the arcade. But even Tyson couldn't fend off the Hydra forever.

We kept inching backwards, dodging acid splashes and deflecting snapping heads without cutting them off, but I knew we were only postponing our deaths. Eventually, we would make a mistake and the thing would kill us.

Then I heard a strange sound — a chug-chug-chug that at first I thought was my heartbeat. It was so powerful it made the riverbank shake.

'What's that noise?' Annabeth shouted, keeping her eyes on the Hydra.

'Steam engine,' Tyson said.

'*What?*' I ducked as the Hydra spat acid over my head.

Then from the river behind us, a familiar female voice shouted, 'There! Prepare the thirty-two-pounder!'

I didn't dare look away from the Hydra, but if that was who I thought it was behind us, I figured we now had enemies on two fronts.

A gravelly male voice said, 'They're too close, m'lady!'

'Damn the heroes!' the girl said. 'Full steam ahead!'

'Aye, m'lady.'

'Fire at will, Captain!'

Annabeth understood what was happening a split second before I did. She yelled, 'Hit the dirt!' and we dived for the ground as an earth-shattering *BOOM* echoed from the river. There was a flash of light, a column of smoke and the Hydra exploded right in front of us, showering us with nasty green slime that vaporized as soon as it hit, the way monster guts tend to do.

'Gross!' screamed Annabeth.

'Steamship!' yelled Tyson.

I stood, coughing from the cloud of gunpowder smoke that was rolling across the banks.

Chugging towards us down the river was the strangest ship I'd ever seen. It rode low in the water like a submarine, its deck plated with iron. In the middle was a trapezoid-shaped casemate with slats on each side for cannons. A flag waved from the top – a wild boar and spear on a blood-red field. Lining the deck were zombies in grey uniforms – dead soldiers with shimmering faces that only partially covered their skulls, like the ghouls I'd seen in the Underworld guarding Hades's palace.

The ship was an ironclad. A Civil War battle cruiser. I could just make out the name along the prow in moss-covered letters: CSS *Birmingham*.

And standing next to the smoking cannon that had

almost killed us, wearing full Greek battle armour, was Clarisse.

'Losers,' she sneered. 'But I suppose I have to rescue you. Come aboard.'

11   CLARISSE BLOWS UP EVERYTHING

'You are in *so* much trouble,' Clarisse said.

We'd just finished a ship tour we didn't want, through dark rooms overcrowded with dead sailors. We'd seen the coal bunker, the boilers and engine, which huffed and groaned like it would explode any minute. We'd seen the pilot house and the powder magazine and gunnery deck (Clarisse's favourite) with two Dahlgren smoothbore cannons on the port and starboard sides and a Brooke nine-inch rifled gun fore and aft – all specially refitted to fire celestial bronze cannonballs.

Everywhere we went, dead Confederate sailors stared at us, their ghostly bearded faces shimmering over their skulls. They approved of Annabeth because she told them she was from Virginia. They were interested in me, too, because my name was Jackson – like the Southern general – but then I ruined it by telling them I was from New York. They all hissed and muttered curses about Yankees.

Tyson was terrified of them. All through the tour, he insisted Annabeth hold his hand, which she didn't look too thrilled about.

Finally, we were escorted to dinner. The CSS *Birmingham* captain's quarters were about the size of a walk-in closet, but still much bigger than any other room on board. The table was set with white linen and china. Peanut butter and jelly sandwiches, potato chips and Dr Peppers were served by skeletal crewmen. I didn't want to eat anything served by ghosts, but my hunger overruled my fear.

'Tantalus expelled you for eternity,' Clarisse told us smugly. 'Mr D said if any of you show your face at camp again, he'll turn you into squirrels and run you over with his SUV.'

'Did *they* give you this ship?' I asked.

'Course not. My father did.'

'*Ares?*'

Clarisse sneered. 'You think your daddy is the only one with sea power? The spirits on the losing side of every war owe a tribute to Ares. That's their curse for being defeated. I prayed to my father for a naval transport and here it is. These guys will do anything I tell them. Won't you, Captain?'

The captain stood behind her looking stiff and angry. His glowing green eyes fixed me with a hungry stare. 'If it means an end to this infernal war, ma'am, peace at last, we'll do anything. Destroy anyone.'

Clarisse smiled. 'Destroy anyone. I like that.'

Tyson gulped.

'Clarisse,' Annabeth said, 'Luke might be after the Fleece, too. We saw him. He's got the coordinates and he's heading south. He has a cruise ship full of monsters —'

'Good! I'll blow him out of the water.'

'You don't understand,' Annabeth said. 'We have to combine forces. Let us help you —'

'No!' Clarisse pounded the table. 'This is *my* quest, smart girl! Finally *I* get to be the hero, and you two will *not* steal my chance.'

'Where are your cabin mates?' I asked. 'You were allowed to take two friends with you, weren't you?'

'They didn't . . . I let them stay behind. To protect the camp.'

'You mean even the people in your own cabin wouldn't help you?'

'Shut up, Prissy! I don't need them! Or you!'

'Clarisse,' I said, 'Tantalus is using you. He doesn't care about the camp. He'd love to see it destroyed. He's setting you up to fail.'

'No! I don't care what the Oracle —' She stopped herself.

'What?' I said. 'What did the Oracle tell you?'

'Nothing.' Clarisse's ears turned pink. 'All you need to know is that I'm finishing this quest and you're *not* helping. On the other hand, I can't let you go . . .'

'So we're prisoners?' Annabeth asked.

'Guests. For now.' Clarisse propped her feet up on the white linen tablecloth and opened another Dr Pepper. 'Captain, take them below. Assign them hammocks on the berth deck. If they don't mind their manners, show them how we deal with enemy spies.'

The dream came as soon as I fell asleep.

Grover was sitting at his loom, desperately unravelling his wedding train, when the boulder door rolled aside and the Cyclops bellowed, 'Aha!'

Grover yelped. 'Dear! I didn't — you were so quiet!'

'Unravelling!' Polyphemus roared. 'So that's the problem!'

'Oh, no. I-I wasn't —'

'Come!' Polyphemus grabbed Grover around the waist and half carried, half dragged him through the tunnels of the cave. Grover struggled to keep his high heels on his hooves. His veil kept tilting on his head, threatening to come off.

The Cyclops pulled him into a warehouse-size cavern decorated with sheep junk. There was a wool-covered Lay-Z-Boy recliner and a wool-covered television set, crude bookshelves loaded with sheep collectibles – coffee mugs shaped like sheep faces, plaster figurines of sheep, sheep board games and picture books and action figures. The floor was littered with piles of sheep bones, and other bones that didn't look exactly like sheep – the bones of satyrs who'd come to the island looking for Pan.

Polyphemus set Grover down only long enough to move another huge boulder. Daylight streamed into the cave, and Grover whimpered with longing. Fresh air!

The Cyclops dragged him outside to a hilltop overlooking the most beautiful island I'd ever seen.

It was shaped kind of like a saddle cut in half by an axe. There were lush green hills on either side and a wide valley in the middle, split by a deep chasm that was spanned by a rope bridge. Beautiful streams rolled to the edge of the canyon and dropped off in rainbow-coloured waterfalls. Parrots fluttered in the trees. Pink and purple flowers bloomed on the bushes. Hundreds of sheep grazed in the meadows, their wool glinting strangely like copper and silver coins.

And at the centre of the island, right next to the rope bridge, was an enormous twisted oak tree with something glittering in its lowest bough.

The Golden Fleece.

Even in a dream, I could feel its power radiating across the island, making the grass greener, the flowers more beautiful. I could almost smell the nature magic at work. I could only imagine how powerful the scent would be for a satyr.

Grover whimpered.

'Yes,' Polyphemus said proudly. 'See over there? Fleece is the prize of my collection! Stole it from heroes long ago, and ever since – free food! Satyrs come from all over the world, like moths to flame. Satyrs good eating! And now –'

Polyphemus scooped up a wicked set of bronze shears.

Grover yelped, but Polyphemus just picked up the nearest sheep like it was a stuffed animal and shaved off its wool. He handed a fluffy mass of it to Grover.

'Put that on the spinning wheel!' he said proudly. 'Magic. Cannot be unravelled.'

'Oh . . . well . . .'

'Poor Honeypie!' Polyphemus grinned. 'Bad weaver. Ha-ha! Not to worry. That thread will solve problem. Finish wedding train by tomorrow!'

'Isn't that . . . thoughtful of you!'

'Hehe.'

'But-but, dear,' Grover gulped, 'what if someone were to rescue – I mean attack this island?' Grover looked straight at me, and I knew he was asking for my benefit. 'What would keep them from marching right up here to your cave?'

'Wifey scared! So cute! Not to worry. Polyphemus has state-of-the-art security system. Have to get through my pets.'

'Pets?'

Grover looked across the island, but there was nothing to see except sheep grazing peacefully in the meadows.

'And then,' Polyphemus growled, 'they would have to get through me!'

He pounded his fist against the nearest rock, which cracked and split in half. 'Now, come!' he shouted. 'Back to the cave.'

Grover looked about ready to cry – so close to freedom, but so hopelessly far. Tears welled in his eyes as the boulder door rolled shut, sealing him once again in the stinky torch-lit dankness of the Cyclops's cave.

I woke to alarm bells ringing throughout the ship.

The captain's gravelly voice: 'All hands on deck! Find Lady Clarisse! Where is that girl?'

Then his ghostly face appeared above me. 'Get up, Yankee. Your friends are already above. We are approaching the entrance.'

'The entrance to what?'

He gave me a skeletal smile. 'The Sea of Monsters, of course.'

I stuffed my few belongings that had survived the Hydra into a sailor's canvas knapsack and slung it over my shoulder. I had a sneaking suspicion that one way or another I would not be spending another night aboard the CSS *Birmingham*.

I was on my way upstairs when something made me freeze. A presence nearby – something familiar and unpleasant. For no particular reason, I felt like picking a fight. I wanted to punch a dead Confederate. The last time I'd felt like that kind of anger . . .

Instead of going up, I crept to the edge of the ventilation grate and peered down into the boiler deck.

Clarisse was standing right below me, talking to an image that shimmered in the steam from the boilers — a muscular man in black leather biker clothes, with a military haircut, red-tinted sunglasses and a knife strapped to his side.

My fists clenched. It was my least favourite Olympian: Ares, the god of war.

'I don't want excuses, little girl!' he growled.

'Y-yes, Father,' Clarisse mumbled.

'You don't want to see me mad, do you?'

'No, Father.'

'*No, Father,*' Ares mimicked. 'You're pathetic. I should've let one of my *sons* take this quest.'

'I'll succeed!' Clarisse promised, her voice trembling. 'I'll make you proud.'

'You'd better,' he warned. 'You asked me for this quest, girl. If you let that slimeball Jackson kid steal it from you —'

'But the Oracle said —'

'I DON'T CARE WHAT IT SAID!' Ares bellowed with such force that his image shimmered. 'You *will* succeed. And if you don't . . .'

He raised his fist. Even though he was only a figure in the steam, Clarisse flinched.

'Do we understand each other?' Ares growled.

The alarm bells rang again. I heard voices coming towards me, officers yelling orders to ready the cannons.

I crept back from the ventilation grate and made my way upstairs to join Annabeth and Tyson on the spar deck.

'What's wrong?' Annabeth asked me. 'Another dream?'

I nodded, but I didn't say anything. I didn't know what to think about what I'd seen downstairs. It bothered me almost as much as the dream about Grover.

Clarisse came up the stairs right after me. I tried not to look at her.

She grabbed a pair of binoculars from a zombie officer and peered towards the horizon. 'At last. Captain, full steam ahead!'

I looked in the same direction as she was, but I couldn't see much. The sky was overcast. The air was hazy and humid, like steam from an iron. If I squinted real hard, I could just make out a couple of dark fuzzy splotches in the distance.

My nautical senses told me we were somewhere off the coast of northern Florida, so we'd come a long way overnight, further than any mortal ship should've been able to travel.

The engine groaned as we increased speed.

Tyson muttered nervously, 'Too much strain on the pistons. Not meant for deep water.'

I wasn't sure how he knew that, but it made me nervous.

After a few more minutes, the dark splotches ahead of us came into focus. To the north, a huge mass of rock rose out of the sea – an island with cliffs at least thirty metres tall. About half a mile south of that, the other patch of darkness was a storm brewing. The sky and sea boiled together in a roaring mass.

'Hurricane?' Annabeth asked.

'No,' Clarisse said. 'Charybdis.'

Annabeth paled. 'Are you crazy?'

'Only way into the Sea of Monsters. Straight between Charybdis and her sister Scylla.' Clarisse pointed to the top of the cliffs, and I got the feeling something lived up there that I did not want to meet.

'What do you mean the only way?' I asked. 'The sea is wide open! Just sail around them.'

Clarisse rolled her eyes. 'Don't you know anything? If I tried to sail around them, they would just appear in my path again. If you want to get into the Sea of Monsters, you *have* to sail through them.'

'What about the Clashing Rocks?' Annabeth said. 'That's another gateway. Jason used it.'

'I can't blow apart rocks with my cannons,' Clarisse said. 'Monsters, on the other hand . . .'

'You *are* crazy,' Annabeth decided.

'Watch and learn, Wise Girl.' Clarisse turned to the captain. 'Set course for Charybdis!'

'Aye, m'lady.'

The engine groaned, the iron plating rattled, and the ship began to pick up speed.

'Clarisse,' I said, 'Charybdis sucks up the sea. Isn't that the story?'

'And spits it back out again, yeah.'

'What about Scylla?'

'She lives in a cave, up on those cliffs. If we get too close, her snaky heads will come down and start plucking sailors off the ship.'

'Choose Scylla then,' I said. 'Everybody goes below deck and we chug right past.'

'No!' Clarisse insisted. 'If Scylla doesn't get her easy meat, she might pick up the whole ship. Besides, she's too high to make a good target. My cannon can't shoot straight up. Charybdis just sits there at the centre of her whirlpool. We're going to steam straight towards her, train our guns on her, and blow her to Tartarus!'

She said it with such relish I almost wanted to believe her.

The engine hummed. The boilers were heating up so much I could feel the deck getting warm beneath my feet. The smokestacks billowed. The red Ares flag whipped in the wind.

As we got closer to the monsters, the sound of Charybdis got louder and louder – a horrible wet roar like the galaxy's biggest toilet being flushed. Every time Charybdis inhaled, the ship shuddered and lurched forward. Every time she exhaled, we rose in the water and were buffeted by three-metre waves.

I tried to time the whirlpool. As near as I could figure, it took Charybdis about three minutes to suck up and destroy everything within a half-mile radius. To avoid her, we would have to skirt right next to Scylla's cliffs. And as bad as Scylla might be, those cliffs were looking awfully good to me.

Undead sailors calmly went about their business on the spar deck. I guess they'd fought a losing cause before, so this didn't bother them. Or maybe they didn't care about getting destroyed because they were already deceased. Neither thought made me feel any better.

Annabeth stood next to me, gripping the rail. 'You still have your Flask full of wind?'

I nodded. 'But it's too dangerous to use with a whirl-pool like that. More wind might just make things worse.'

'What about controlling the water?' she asked. 'You're Poseidon's son. You've done it before.'

She was right. I closed my eyes and tried to calm the sea, but I couldn't concentrate. Charybdis was too loud and powerful. The waves wouldn't respond.

'I-I can't,' I said miserably.

'We need a backup plan,' Annabeth said. 'This isn't going to work.'

'Annabeth is right,' Tyson said. 'Engine's no good.'

'What do you mean?' she asked.

'Pressure. Pistons need fixing.'

Before he could explain, the cosmic toilet flushed with a mighty *roaaar*! The ship lurched forward and I was thrown to the deck. We were in the whirlpool.

'Full reverse!' Clarisse screamed above the noise. The sea churned around us, waves crashing over the deck. The iron plating was now so hot it steamed. 'Get us within firing range! Make ready starboard cannons!'

Dead Confederates rushed back and forth. The propeller grinded into reverse, trying to slow the ship, but we kept sliding towards the centre of the vortex.

A zombie sailor burst out of the hold and ran to Clarisse. His grey uniform was smoking. His beard was on fire. 'Boiler room overheating, ma'am! She's going to blow!'

'Well, get down there and fix it!'

'Can't!' the sailor yelled. 'We're vaporizing in the heat.'

Clarisse pounded the side of the casemate. 'All I need is a few more minutes! Just enough to get in range!'

'We're going in too fast,' the captain said grimly. 'Prepare yourself for death.'

'No!' Tyson bellowed. 'I can fix it.'

Clarisse looked at him incredulously. 'You?'

'He's a Cyclops,' Annabeth said. 'He's immune to fire. And he knows mechanics.'

'Go!' yelled Clarisse.

'Tyson, no!' I grabbed his arm. 'It's too dangerous!'

He patted my hand. 'Only way, brother.' His expression was determined – confident, even. I'd never seen him look like this before. 'I will fix it. Be right back.'

As I watched him follow the smouldering sailor down the hatch, I had a terrible feeling. I wanted to run after him, but the ship lurched again – and then I saw Charybdis.

She appeared only a few hundred metres away, through a swirl of mist and smoke and water. The first thing I noticed was the reef – a black crag of coral with a fig tree clinging to the top, an oddly peaceful thing in the middle of a maelstrom. All around it, water curved into a funnel, like light around a black hole. Then I saw the horrible thing anchored to the reef just below the waterline – an enormous mouth with slimy lips and mossy teeth the size of rowboats. And worse, the teeth had braces, bands of corroded scummy metal with pieces of fish and driftwood and floating garbage stuck between them.

Charybdis was an orthodontist's nightmare. She was nothing but a huge black maw with bad teeth alignment and a serious overbite, and she'd done nothing for centuries but eat without brushing after meals. As I watched, the entire sea around her was sucked into the void — sharks, schools of fish, a giant squid. And I realized that in a few seconds, the CSS *Birmingham* would be next.

'Lady Clarisse,' the captain shouted. 'Starboard and forward guns are in range!'

'Fire!' Clarisse ordered.

Three rounds were blasted into the monster's maw. One blew off the edge of an incisor. Another disappeared into her gullet. The third hit one of Charybdis's retaining bands and shot back at us, snapping the Ares flag off its pole.

'Again!' Clarisse ordered. The gunners reloaded, but I knew it was hopeless. We would have to pound the monster a hundred more times to do any real damage, and we didn't have that long. We were being sucked in too fast.

Then the vibrations in the deck changed. The hum of the engine got stronger and steadier. The ship shuddered and we started pulling away from the mouth.

'Tyson did it!' Annabeth said.

'Wait!' Clarisse said. 'We need to stay close!'

'We'll die!' I said. 'We *have* to move away.'

I gripped the rail as the ship fought against the suction. The broken Ares flag raced past us and lodged in Charybdis's braces. We weren't making much progress, but at least we were holding our own. Tyson had somehow given us just enough juice to keep the ship from being sucked in.

Suddenly, the mouth snapped shut. The sea died to absolute calm. Water washed over Charybdis.

Then, just as quickly as it had closed, the mouth

exploded open, spitting out a wall of water, ejecting everything inedible, including our cannonballs, one of which slammed into the side of the CSS *Birmingham* with a *ding* like the bell on a carnival game.

We were thrown backwards on a wave that must've been fifteen metres high. I used all of my willpower to keep the ship from capsizing, but we were still spinning out of control, hurtling towards the cliffs on the opposite side of the strait.

Another smouldering sailor burst out of the hold. He stumbled into Clarisse, almost knocking them both overboard. 'The engine is about to blow!'

'Where's Tyson?' I demanded.

'Still down there,' the sailor said. 'Holding it together somehow, though I don't know for how much longer.'

The captain said, 'We have to abandon ship.'

'No!' Clarisse yelled.

'We have no choice, m'lady. The hull is already cracking apart! She can't –'

He never finished his sentence. Quick as lightning, something brown and green shot from the sky, snatched up the captain, and lifted him away. All that was left were his leather boots.

'Scylla!' a sailor yelled, as another column of reptilian flesh shot from the cliffs and snapped him up. It happened so fast it was like watching a laser beam rather than a monster. I couldn't even make out the thing's face, just a flash of teeth and scales.

I uncapped Riptide and tried to swipe at the monster as it carried off another deckhand, but I was way too slow.

'Everyone get below!' I yelled.

'We can't!' Clarisse drew her own sword. 'Below deck is in flames.'

'Lifeboats!' Annabeth said. 'Quick!'

'They'll never get clear of the cliffs,' Clarisse said. 'We'll all be eaten.'

'We have to try. Percy, the Flask.'

'I can't leave Tyson!'

'We have to get the boats ready!'

Clarisse took Annabeth's command. She and a few of her undead sailors uncovered one of the two emergency rowboats while Scylla's heads rained from the sky like a meteor shower with teeth, picking off Confederate sailors one after another.

'Get the other boat.' I threw Annabeth the Flask. 'I'll get Tyson.'

'You can't!' she said. 'The heat will kill you!'

I didn't listen. I ran for the boiler room hatch, when suddenly my feet weren't touching the deck any more. I was flying straight up, the wind whistling in my ears, the side of the cliff only inches from my face.

Scylla had somehow caught me by the knapsack, and was lifting me up towards her lair. Without thinking, I swung my sword behind me and managed to jab the thing in her beady yellow eye. She grunted and dropped me.

The fall would've been bad enough, considering I was thirty metres in the air. But, as I fell, the CSS *Birmingham* exploded below me.

KAROOM!

The engine room blew, sending chunks of ironclad flying in either direction like a fiery set of wings.

'Tyson!' I yelled.

The lifeboats had managed to get away from the ship, but not very far. Flaming wreckage was raining down. Clarisse and Annabeth would either be smashed or burned or pulled to the bottom by the force of the sinking hull, and that was thinking optimistically, assuming they got away from Scylla.

Then I heard a different kind of explosion – the sound of Hermes's magic Flask being opened a little too far. White sheets of wind blasted in every direction, scattering the lifeboats, lifting me out of my free fall and propelling me across the ocean.

I couldn't see anything. I spun in the air, got clonked on the head by something hard, and hit the water with a crash that would've broken every bone in my body if I hadn't been the son of the Sea God.

The last thing I remembered was sinking in a burning sea, knowing that Tyson was gone forever, and wishing I were able to drown.

I woke up in a rowboat with a makeshift sail stitched of grey uniform fabric. Annabeth sat next to me, tacking into the wind.

I tried to sit up and immediately felt woozy.

'Rest,' she said. 'You're going to need it.'

'Tyson. . .?'

She shook her head. 'Percy, I'm really sorry.'

We were silent while the waves tossed us up and down.

'He may have survived,' she said half-heartedly. 'I mean, fire can't kill him.'

I nodded, but I had no reason to feel hopeful. I'd seen that explosion rip through solid iron. If Tyson had been down in the boiler room, there was no way he could've lived.

He'd given his life for us, and all I could think about were the times I'd felt embarrassed by him and had denied that the two of us were related.

Waves lapped at the boat. Annabeth showed me some things she'd salvaged from the wreckage – Hermes's Flask (now empty), an airtight bag full of ambrosia, a couple of sailors' shirts and a bottle of Dr Pepper. She'd fished me out of the water and found my knapsack, bitten in half by Scylla's teeth. Most of my stuff had floated away, but I still had Hermes's bottle of multivitamins, and of course

I had Riptide. The ballpoint pen always appeared back in my pocket no matter where I lost it.

We sailed for hours. Now that we were in the Sea of Monsters, the water glittered a more brilliant green, like Hydra acid. The wind smelled fresh and salty, but it carried a strange metallic scent, too – as if a thunderstorm were coming. Or something even more dangerous. I knew what direction we needed to go. I knew we were exactly one hundred and thirteen nautical miles west by northwest of our destination. But that didn't make me feel any less lost.

No matter which way we turned, the sun seemed to shine straight into my eyes. We took turns sipping from the Dr Pepper, shading ourselves with the sail as best we could. And we talked about my latest dream of Grover.

By Annabeth's estimate, we had less than twenty-four hours to find Grover, assuming my dream was accurate, and assuming the Cyclops Polyphemus didn't change his mind and try to marry Grover earlier.

'Yeah,' I said bitterly. 'You can never trust a Cyclops.'

Annabeth stared across the water. 'I'm sorry, Percy. I was wrong about Tyson, okay? I wish I could tell him that.'

I tried to stay mad at her, but it wasn't easy. We'd been through a lot together. She'd saved my life plenty of times. It was stupid of me to resent her.

I looked down at our measly possessions – the empty wind Flask, the bottle of multivitamins. I thought about Luke's look of rage when I'd tried to talk to him about his dad.

'Annabeth, what's Chiron's prophecy?'

She pursed her lips. 'Percy, I shouldn't –'

'I know Chiron promised the gods he wouldn't tell me. But *you* didn't promise, did you?'

'Knowledge isn't always good for you.'

'Your mom is the wisdom goddess!'

'I know! But every time heroes learn the future, they try to change it, and it never works.'

'The gods are worried about something I'll do when I get older,' I guessed. 'Something when I turn sixteen.'

Annabeth twisted her Yankees cap in her hands. 'Percy, I don't know the full prophecy, but it warns about a half-blood child of the Big Three – the next one who lives to the age of sixteen. That's the real reason Zeus, Poseidon and Hades swore a pact after World War II not to have any more kids. The next child of the Big Three who reaches sixteen will be a dangerous weapon.'

'Why?'

'Because that hero will decide the fate of Olympus. He or she will make a decision that either saves the Age of the Gods, or destroys it.'

I let that sink in. I don't get seasick, but suddenly I felt ill. 'That's why Kronos didn't kill me last summer.'

She nodded. 'You could be very useful to him. If he can get you on his side, the gods will be in serious trouble.'

'But if it's *me* in the prophecy –'

'We'll only know that if you survive three more years. That can be a long time for a half-blood. When Chiron first learned about Thalia, he assumed *she* was the one in the prophecy. That's why he was so desperate to get her safely to camp. Then she went down fighting and got turned into a pine tree and none of us knew what to think. Until you came along.'

On our port side, a spiky green dorsal fin about five metres long curled out of the water and disappeared.

'This kid in the prophecy . . . he or she couldn't be like, a Cyclops?' I asked. 'The Big Three have lots of monster children.'

Annabeth shook her head. 'The Oracle said "half-blood". That always means half human, half god. There's really nobody alive who it could be, except you.'

'Then why do the gods even let me live? It would be safer to kill me.'

'You're right.'

'Thanks a lot.'

'Percy, I don't know. I guess some of the gods *would* like to kill you, but they're probably afraid of offending Poseidon. Other gods . . . maybe they're still watching you, trying to decide what kind of hero you're going to be. You could be a weapon for their survival, after all. The real question is . . . what will you do in three years? What decision will you make?'

'Did the prophecy give any hints?'

Annabeth hesitated.

Maybe she would've told me more, but just then a sea-gull swooped down out of nowhere and landed on our makeshift mast. Annabeth looked startled as the bird dropped a small cluster of leaves into her lap.

'Land,' she said. 'There's land nearby!'

I sat up. Sure enough, there was a line of blue and brown in the distance. Another minute and I could make out an island with a small mountain in the centre, a dazzling white collection of buildings, a beach dotted with palm trees and a harbour filled with a strange assortment of boats.

The current was pulling our rowboat towards what looked like a tropical paradise.

'Welcome!' said the lady with the clipboard.

She looked like a flight attendant – blue business suit, perfect makeup, hair pulled back in a ponytail. She shook our hands as we stepped onto the dock. With the dazzling smile she gave us, you would've thought we'd just got off the *Princess Andromeda* rather than a bashed-up rowboat.

Then again, our rowboat wasn't the weirdest ship in port. Along with a bunch of pleasure yachts, there was a U.S. Navy submarine, several dugout canoes and an old-fashioned three-masted sailing ship. There was a helipad with a 'Channel Five Fort Lauderdale' helicopter on it, and a short runway with a Learjet and a propeller plane that looked like a World War II fighter. Maybe they were replicas for tourists to look at or something.

'Is this your first time with us?' the clipboard lady enquired.

Annabeth and I exchanged looks. Annabeth said, 'Umm . . .'

'First – time – at – spa,' the lady said as she wrote on her clipboard. 'Let's see . . .'

She looked us up and down critically. 'Mmm. An herbal wrap to start for the young lady. And of course, a complete makeover for the young gentleman.'

'A what?' I asked.

She was too busy jotting down notes to answer.

'Right!' she said with a breezy smile. 'Well, I'm sure C.C. will want to speak with you personally before the luau. Come, please.'

Now here's the thing. Annabeth and I were used to traps, and usually those traps looked good at first. So I expected the clipboard lady to turn into a snake or a demon, or something, any minute. But, on the other hand, we'd been floating in a rowboat for most of the day. I was hot, tired and hungry, and when this lady mentioned a luau, my stomach sat up on its hind legs and begged like a dog.

'I guess it couldn't hurt,' Annabeth muttered.

Of course it could, but we followed the lady anyway. I kept my hands in my pockets where I'd stashed my only magic defences — Hermes's multivitamins and Riptide — but the further we wandered into the resort, the more I forgot about them.

The place was amazing. There was white marble and blue water everywhere I looked. Terraces climbed up the side of the mountain, with swimming pools on every level, connected by waterslides and waterfalls and underwater tubes you could swim through. Fountains sprayed water into the air, forming impossible shapes, like flying eagles and galloping horses.

Tyson loved horses, and I knew he'd love those fountains. I almost turned around to see the expression on his face before I remembered: Tyson was gone.

'You okay?' Annabeth asked me. 'You look pale.'

'I'm okay,' I lied. 'Just . . . let's keep walking.'

We passed all kinds of tame animals. A sea turtle napped in a stack of beach towels. A leopard stretched out asleep on the diving board. The resort guests — only young women, as far as I could see — lounged in deckchairs, drinking fruit smoothies or reading magazines while herbal gunk dried on their faces and manicurists in white uniforms did their nails.

As we headed up a staircase towards what looked like the main building, I heard a woman singing. Her voice drifted through the air like a lullaby. Her words were in some language other than Ancient Greek, but just as old – Minoan, maybe, or something like that. I could understand what she sang about – moonlight in the olive groves, the colours of the sunrise. And magic. Something about magic. Her voice seemed to lift me off the steps and carry me towards her.

We came into a big room where the whole front wall was windows. The back wall was covered in mirrors, so the room seemed to go on forever. There was a bunch of expensive-looking white furniture, and on a table in one corner was a large wire pet cage. The cage seemed out of place, but I didn't think about it too much, because just then I saw the lady who'd been singing . . . and whoa.

She sat at a loom the size of a big screen TV, her hands weaving coloured thread back and forth with amazing skill. The tapestry shimmered like it was three-dimensional – a waterfall scene so real I could see the water moving and clouds drifting across a fabric sky.

Annabeth caught her breath. 'It's beautiful.'

The woman turned. She was even prettier than her fabric. Her long dark hair was braided with threads of gold. She had piercing green eyes and she wore a silky black dress with shapes that seemed to move in the fabric: animal shadows, black upon black, like deer running through a forest at night.

'You appreciate weaving, my dear?' the woman asked.

'Oh, yes, ma'am!' Annabeth said. 'My mother is –'

She stopped herself. You couldn't just go around announcing that your mom was Athena, the goddess who invented the loom. Most people would lock you in a rubber room.

Our hostess just smiled. 'You have good taste, my dear. I'm so glad you've come. My name is C.C.'

The animals in the corner cage started squealing. They must've been guinea pigs, from the sound of them.

We introduced ourselves to C.C. She looked me over with a twinge of disapproval, as if I'd failed some kind of test. Immediately, I felt bad. For some reason, I really wanted to please this lady.

'Oh dear,' she sighed. 'You *do* need my help.'

'Ma'am?' I asked.

C.C. called to the lady in the business suit. 'Hylla, take Annabeth on a tour, will you? Show her what we have available. The clothing will need to change. And the hair, my goodness. We will do a full image consultation after I've spoken with this young gentleman.'

'But . . .' Annabeth's voice sounded hurt. 'What's wrong with my hair?'

C.C. smiled benevolently. 'My dear, you are lovely. Really! But you're not showing off yourself or your talents at all. So much wasted potential!'

'Wasted?'

'Well, surely you're not happy the way you are! My goodness, there's not a single person who is. But don't worry. We can improve anyone here at the spa. Hylla will show you what I mean. You, my dear, need to unlock your true self!'

Annabeth's eyes glowed with longing. I'd never seen her so much at a loss for words. 'But . . . what about Percy?'

'Oh, definitely,' C.C. said, giving me a sad look. 'Percy requires my personal attention. He needs *much* more work than you.'

Normally if somebody had told me that, I would've got angry, but when C.C. said it, I felt sad. I'd disappointed her. I had to figure out how to do better.

The guinea pigs squealed like they were hungry.

'Well . . .' Annabeth said. 'I suppose . . .'

'Right this way, dear,' Hylla said. And Annabeth allowed herself to be led away into the waterfall-laced gardens of the spa.

C.C. took my arm and guided me towards the mirrored wall. 'You see, Percy . . . to unlock your potential, you'll need serious help. The first step is admitting that you're not happy the way you are.'

I fidgeted in front of the mirror. I hated thinking about my appearance – like the first zit that had cropped up on my nose at the beginning of the school year, or the fact that my two front teeth weren't perfectly even, or that my hair never stayed down straight.

C.C.'s voice brought all of these things to mind, as if she were passing me under a microscope. And my clothes were not cool. I knew that.

Who cares? part of me thought. But standing in front of C.C.'s mirror, it was hard to see anything good in myself.

'There, there,' C.C. consoled. 'How about we try . . . this.'

She snapped her fingers and a sky-blue curtain rolled down over the mirror. It shimmered like the fabric on her loom.

'What do you see?' C.C. asked.

I looked at the blue cloth, not sure what she meant. 'I don't –'

Then it changed colours. I saw myself – a reflection, but not a reflection. Shimmering there on the cloth was a cooler version of Percy Jackson – with just the right clothes, a confident smile on my face. My teeth were straight. No zits. A perfect tan. More athletic. Maybe a couple of centimetres taller. It was me, without the faults.

'Whoa,' I managed.

'Do you want that?' C.C. asked. 'Or shall I try a different –'

'No,' I said. 'That's . . . that's amazing. Can you really –'

'I can give you a full makeover,' C.C. promised.

'What's the catch?' I said. 'I have to like . . . eat a special diet?'

'Oh, it's quite easy,' C.C. said. 'Plenty of fresh fruit, a mild exercise programme, and of course . . . this.'

She stepped over to her wet bar and filled a glass with water. Then she ripped open a drink-mix packet and poured in some red powder. The mixture began to glow. When it faded, the drink looked just like a strawberry milkshake.

'One of these, substituted for a regular meal,' C.C. said. 'I guarantee you'll see results immediately.'

'How is that possible?'

She laughed. 'Why question it? I mean, don't you want the perfect you right away?'

Something nagged at the back of my mind. 'Why are there no guys at this spa?'

'Oh, but there are,' C.C. assured me. 'You'll meet them quite soon. Just try the mixture. You'll see.'

I looked at the blue tapestry, at the reflection of me, but not me.

'Now, Percy,' C.C. chided. 'The hardest part of the makeover process is giving up control. You have to decide: do you want to trust *your* judgement about what you should be, or *my* judgement?'

My throat felt dry. I heard myself say, 'Your judgement.'

C.C. smiled and handed me the glass. I lifted it to my lips.

It tasted just like it looked – like a strawberry milkshake. Almost immediately a warm feeling spread through my gut: pleasant at first, then painfully hot, searing, as if the mixture were coming to a boil inside me.

I doubled over and dropped the cup. 'What have you . . . what's happening?'

'Don't worry, Percy,' C.C. said. 'The pain will pass. Look! As I promised. Immediate results.'

Something was horribly wrong.

The curtain dropped away, and in the mirror I saw my hands shrivelling, curling, growing long delicate claws. Fur sprouted on my face, under my shirt, in every uncomfortable place you can imagine. My teeth felt too heavy in my mouth. My clothes were getting too big, or C.C. was getting too tall – no, I was shrinking.

In one awful flash, I sank into a cavern of dark cloth. I was buried in my own shirt. I tried to run but hands grabbed me — hands as big as I was. I tried to scream for help, but all that came out of my mouth was, '*Reeet, reeet, reeet!*'

The giant hands squeezed me around the middle, lifting me into the air. I struggled and kicked with legs and arms that seemed much too stubby, and then I was staring, horrified, into the enormous face of C.C.

'Perfect!' her voice boomed. I squirmed in alarm, but she only tightened her grip around my furry belly. 'See, Percy? You've unlocked your true self!'

She held me up to the mirror, and what I saw made me scream in terror, '*Reeet, reeet, reeet!*' There was C.C., beautiful and smiling, holding a fluffy, bucktoothed creature with tiny claws and white-and-orange fur. When I twisted, so did the furry critter in the mirror. I was . . . I was . . .

'A guinea pig,' C.C. said. 'Lovely, aren't you? Men are pigs, Percy Jackson. I used to turn them into *real* pigs, but they were so smelly and large and difficult to keep. Not much different than they were before, really. Guinea pigs are much more convenient! Now come, and meet the other men.'

'*Reeet!*' I protested, trying to scratch her, but C.C. squeezed me so tight I almost blacked out.

'None of that, little one,' she scolded, 'or I'll feed you to the owls. Go into the cage like a good little pet. Tomorrow, if you behave, you'll be on your way. There is always a classroom in need of a new guinea pig.'

My mind was racing as fast as my tiny little heart. I needed to get back to my clothes, which were lying in a heap on the floor. If I could do that, I could get Riptide out of my pocket and . . . And what? I couldn't uncap the pen. Even if I did, I couldn't hold the sword.

I squirmed helplessly as C.C. brought me over to the guinea pig cage and opened the wire door.

'Meet my discipline problems, Percy,' she warned. 'They'll never make good classroom pets, but they might teach you some manners. Most of them have been in this cage for three hundred years. If you don't want to stay with them permanently, I'd suggest you –'

Annabeth's voice called, 'Miss C.C.?'

C.C. cursed in Ancient Greek. She plopped me into the cage and closed the door. I squealed and clawed at the bars, but it was no good. I watched as C.C. hurriedly kicked my clothes under the loom just as Annabeth came in.

I almost didn't recognize her. She was wearing a sleeveless silk dress like C.C.'s, only white. Her blonde hair was newly washed and combed and braided with gold. Worst of all, she was wearing makeup, which I never thought Annabeth would be caught dead in. I mean, she looked good. Really good. I probably would've been tongue-tied if I could've said anything except *reet, reet, reet*. But there was also something totally wrong about it. It just wasn't Annabeth.

She looked around the room and frowned. 'Where's Percy?'

I squealed up a storm, but she didn't seem to hear me.

C.C. smiled. 'He's having one of our treatments, my dear. Not to worry. You look wonderful! What did you think of your tour?'

Annabeth's eyes brightened. 'Your library is amazing!'

'Yes, indeed,' C.C. said. 'The best knowledge of the past three millennia. Anything you want to study, anything you want to *be*, my dear.'

'An architect?'

'Pah!' C.C. said. 'You, my dear, have the makings of a sorceress. Like me.'

Annabeth took a step back. 'A sorceress?'

'Yes, my dear.' C.C. held up her hand. A flame appeared in her palm and danced across her fingertips. 'My mother is Hecate, the goddess of magic. I know a daughter of Athena when I see one. We are not so different, you and I. We both seek knowledge. We both admire greatness. Neither of us needs to stand in the shadow of men.'

'I-I don't understand.'

Again, I squealed my best, trying to get Annabeth's attention, but she either couldn't hear me or didn't think the noises were important. Meanwhile, the other guinea pigs were emerging from their hutch to check me out. I didn't think it was possible for guinea pigs to look mean, but these did. There were half a dozen, with dirty fur and cracked teeth and beady red eyes. They were covered with shavings and smelled like they really had been in here for three hundred years, without getting their cage cleaned.

'Stay with me,' C.C. was telling Annabeth. 'Study with me. You can join our staff, become a sorceress, learn to bend others to your will. You will become immortal!'

'But –'

'You are too intelligent, my dear,' C.C. said. 'You know better than to trust that silly camp for heroes. How many great female half-blood heroes can you name?'

'Um, Atalanta, Amelia Earhart –'

'Bah! Men get all the glory.' C.C. closed her fist and extinguished the magic flame. 'The only way to power for women is sorcery. Medea, Calypso, now there were powerful women! And me, of course. The greatest of all.'

'You . . . C.C. . . . Circe!'

'Yes, my dear.'

Annabeth backed up, and Circe laughed. 'You need not worry. I mean you no harm.'

'What have you done to Percy?'

'Only helped him realize his true form.'

Annabeth scanned the room. Finally she saw the cage, and me scratching at the bars, all the other guinea pigs crowding around me. Her eyes went wide.

'Forget him,' Circe said. 'Join me and learn the ways of sorcery.'

'But —'

'Your friend will be well cared for. He'll be shipped to a wonderful new home on the mainland. The kindergartners will adore him. Meanwhile, you will be wise and powerful. You will have all you ever wanted.'

Annabeth was still staring at me, but she had a dreamy expression on her face. She looked the same way I had when Circe enchanted me into drinking the guinea pig milkshake. I squealed and scratched, trying to warn her to snap out of it, but I was absolutely powerless.

'Let me think about it,' Annabeth murmured. 'Just . . . give me a minute alone. To say goodbye.'

'Of course, my dear,' Circe cooed. 'One minute. Oh . . . and so you have absolute privacy . . .' She waved her hand and iron bars slammed down over the windows. She swept out of the room and I heard the locks on the door click shut behind her.

The dreamy look melted off Annabeth's face.

She rushed over to my cage. 'All right, which one is you?'

I squealed, but so did all the other guinea pigs. Annabeth looked desperate. She scanned the room and spotted the turn-up of my jeans sticking out from under the loom.

Yes!

She rushed over and rummaged through my pockets.

But instead of bringing out Riptide, she found the bottle of Hermes's multivitamins and started struggling with the cap.

I wanted to scream at her that this wasn't the time for taking supplements! She had to draw the sword!

She popped a lemon chewable in her mouth just as the door flew open and Circe came back in, flanked by two of her business-suited attendants.

'Well,' Circe sighed, 'how fast a minute passes. What is your answer, my dear?'

'This,' Annabeth said, and she drew her bronze knife.

The sorceress stepped back, but her surprise quickly passed. She sneered. 'Really, little girl, a knife against *my* magic? Is that wise?'

Circe looked back at her attendants, who smiled. They raised their hands as if preparing to cast a spell.

Run! I wanted to tell Annabeth, but all I could make were rodent noises. The other guinea pigs squealed in terror and scuttled around the cage. I had the urge to panic and hide, too, but I had to think of something! I couldn't stand to lose Annabeth the way I'd lost Tyson.

'What will Annabeth's makeover be?' Circe mused. 'Something small and ill-tempered. I know . . . a shrew!'

Blue fire coiled from her fingers curling like serpents around Annabeth.

I watched, horror-struck, but nothing happened. Annabeth was still Annabeth, only angrier. She leaped forward and stuck the point of her knife against Circe's neck. 'How about turning me into a panther instead? One that has her claws at your throat!'

'How!' Circe yelped.

Annabeth held up my bottle of vitamins for the sorceress to see.

Circe howled in frustration. 'Curse Hermes and his multivitamins! Those are such a fad! They do *nothing* for you.'

'Turn Percy back to a human or else!' Annabeth said.

'I can't!'

'Then you asked for it.'

Circe's attendants stepped forward, but their mistress said, 'Get back! She's immune to magic until that cursed vitamin wears off.'

Annabeth dragged Circe over to the guinea pig cage, knocked the top off, and poured the rest of the vitamins inside.

'No!' Circe screamed.

I was the first to get a vitamin, but all the other guinea pigs scuttled out, too, and checked out this new food.

The first nibble, and I felt all fiery inside. I gnawed at the vitamin until it stopped looking so huge, and the cage got smaller, and then suddenly, *bang!* The cage exploded. I was sitting on the floor, a human again — somehow back in my regular clothes, thank the gods – with six other guys who all looked disoriented, blinking and shaking wood shavings out of their hair.

'No!' Circe screamed. 'You don't understand! Those are the worst!'

One of the men stood up – a huge guy with a long tangled pitch-black beard and teeth the same colour. He wore mismatched clothes of wool and leather, knee-length boots, and a floppy felt hat. The other men were dressed more simply – in breeches and stained white shirts. All of them were barefoot.

'Argggh!' bellowed the big man. 'What's the witch done t'me!'

'No!' Circe moaned.

Annabeth gasped. 'I recognize you! Edward Teach, son of Ares?'

'Aye, lass,' the big man growled. 'Though most call me Blackbeard! And there's the sorceress what captured us, lads. Run her through, and then I mean to find me a big bowl of celery! Argggggh!'

Circe screamed. She and her attendants ran from the room, chased by the pirates.

Annabeth sheathed her knife and glared at me.

'Thanks . . .' I faltered. 'I'm really sorry –'

Before I could figure out how to apologize for being such an idiot, she tackled me with a hug, then pulled away just as quickly. 'I'm glad you're not a guinea pig.'

'Me, too.' I hoped my face wasn't as red as it felt.

She undid the golden braids in her hair.

'Come on, Seaweed Brain,' she said. 'We have to get away while Circe's distracted.'

We ran down the hillside through the terraces, past screaming spa workers and pirates ransacking the resort. Blackbeard's men broke the tiki torches for the luau, threw herbal wraps into the swimming pool and kicked over tables of sauna towels.

I almost felt bad letting the unruly pirates out, but I guessed they deserved something more entertaining than the exercise wheel after being cooped up in a cage for three centuries.

'Which ship?' Annabeth said as we reached the docks.

I looked around desperately. We couldn't very well take our rowboat. We had to get off the island fast, but what else could we use? A sub? A fighter jet? I couldn't pilot any of those things. And then I saw it.

'There,' I said.

Annabeth blinked. 'But —'

'I can make it work.'

'How?'

I couldn't explain. I just somehow knew an old sailing vessel was the best bet for me. I grabbed Annabeth's hand and pulled her towards the three-mast ship. Painted on its prow was the name that I would only decipher later: *Queen Anne's Revenge*.

'Argggh!' Blackbeard yelled somewhere behind us. 'Those scallywags are a-boarding me vessel! Get 'em, lads!'

'We'll never get going in time!' Annabeth yelled as we climbed aboard.

I looked around at the hopeless maze of sail and ropes. The ship was in great condition for a three-hundred-year-old vessel, but it would still take a crew of fifty several hours to get underway. We didn't have several hours. I could see the pirates running down the stairs, waving tiki torches and sticks of celery.

I closed my eyes and concentrated on the waves lapping against the hull, the ocean currents, the winds all around me. Suddenly, the right word appeared in my mind. 'Mizzenmast!' I yelled.

Annabeth looked at me like I was nuts, but in the next second, the air was filled with whistling sounds of ropes being snapped taut, canvases unfurling and wooden pulleys creaking.

Annabeth ducked as a cable flew over her head and wrapped itself around the bowsprit. 'Percy, how . . .'

I didn't have an answer, but I could feel the ship responding to me as if it were part of my body. I willed the sails to rise as easily as if I were flexing my arm. I willed the rudder to turn.

The *Queen Anne's Revenge* lurched away from the dock, and by the time the pirates arrived at the water's edge, we were already underway, sailing into the Sea of Monsters.

13 ANNABETH TRIES TO SWIM HOME

I'd finally found something I was really good at.

The *Queen Anne's Revenge* responded to my every command. I knew which ropes to hoist, which sails to raise, which direction to steer. We ploughed through the waves at what I figured was about ten knots. I even understood how fast that was. For a sailing ship, pretty darn fast.

It all felt perfect – the wind in my face, the waves breaking over the prow.

But now that we were out of danger, all I could think about was how much I missed Tyson, and how worried I was about Grover.

I couldn't get over how badly I'd messed up on Circe's Island. If it hadn't been for Annabeth, I'd still be a rodent, hiding in a hutch with a bunch of cute furry pirates. I thought about what Circe had said: *See, Percy? You've unlocked your true self!*

I still felt changed. Not just because I had a sudden desire to eat lettuce. I felt jumpy, like the instinct to be a scared little animal was now a part of me. Or maybe it had always been there. That's what really worried me.

We sailed through the night.

Annabeth tried to help me keep lookout, but sailing didn't agree with her. After a few hours' rocking back and forth, her face turned the colour of guacamole and she went below to lie in a hammock.

I watched the horizon. More than once I spotted monsters. A plume of water as tall as a skyscraper spewed into the moonlight. A row of green spines slithered across the waves – something maybe thirty metres long, reptilian. I didn't really want to know.

Once I saw Nereids, the glowing lady spirits of the sea. I tried to wave at them, but they disappeared into the depths, leaving me unsure whether they'd seen me or not.

Sometime after midnight, Annabeth came up on deck. We were just passing a smoking volcano island. The sea bubbled and steamed around the shore.

'One of the forges of Hephaestus,' Annabeth said. 'Where he makes his metal monsters.'

'Like the bronze bulls?'

She nodded. 'Go around. Far around.'

I didn't need to be told twice. We steered clear of the island, and soon it was just a red patch of haze behind us.

I looked at Annabeth. 'The reason you hate Cyclopes so much . . . the story about how Thalia really died. What happened?'

It was hard to see her expression in the dark.

'I guess you deserve to know,' she said finally. 'The night Grover was escorting us to camp, he got confused, took some wrong turns. You remember he told you that once?'

I nodded.

'Well, the worst wrong turn was into a Cyclops's lair in Brooklyn.'

'They've got Cyclopes in Brooklyn?' I asked.

'You wouldn't believe how many, but that's not the point. This Cyclops, he tricked us. He managed to split us up inside this maze of corridors in an old house in Flatbush. And he could sound like anyone, Percy. Just the way Tyson did aboard the *Princess Andromeda*. He lured us, one at time. Thalia thought she was running to save Luke. Luke thought he heard me scream for help. And me . . . I was alone in the dark. I was seven years old. I couldn't even find the exit.'

She brushed the hair out of her face. 'I remember finding the main room. There were bones all over the floor. And there were Thalia and Luke and Grover, tied up and gagged, hanging from the ceiling like smoked hams. The Cyclops was starting a fire in the middle of the floor. I drew my knife, but he heard me. He turned and smiled. He spoke, and somehow he knew my dad's voice. I guess he just plucked it out of my mind. He said, "Now, Annabeth, don't you worry. I love you. You can stay here with me. You can stay forever."'

I shivered. The way she told it — even now, six years later — freaked me out worse than any ghost story I'd ever heard. 'What did you do?'

'I stabbed him in the foot.'

I stared at her. 'Are you kidding? You were seven years old and you stabbed a grown Cyclops in the foot?'

'Oh, he would've killed me. But I surprised him. It gave me just enough time to run to Thalia and cut the ropes on her hands. She took it from there.'

'Yeah, but still . . . that was pretty brave, Annabeth.'

She shook her head. 'We barely got out alive. I still have nightmares, Percy. The way that Cyclops talked in my father's voice. It was his fault we took so long getting to camp. All the monsters who'd been chasing us had time to catch up. That's really why Thalia died. If it hadn't been for that Cyclops, she'd still be alive today.'

We sat on the deck, watching the Heracles constellation rise in the night sky.

'Go below,' Annabeth told me at last. 'You need some rest.'

I nodded. My eyes were heavy. But when I got below and found a hammock, it took me a long time to fall asleep. I kept thinking about Annabeth's story. I wondered, if I were her, would I have had enough courage to go on this quest, to sail straight towards the lair of another Cyclops?

I didn't dream about Grover.

Instead I found myself back in Luke's stateroom aboard the *Princess Andromeda*. The curtains were open. It was night-time outside. The air swirled with shadows. Voices whispered all around me – spirits of the dead.

Beware, they whispered. *Traps. Trickery.*

Kronos's golden sarcophagus glowed faintly – the only source of light in the room.

A cold laugh startled me. It seemed to come from miles below the ship. *You don't have the courage, young one. You can't stop me.*

I knew what I had to do. I had to open that coffin.

I uncapped Riptide. Ghosts whirled around me like a tornado. *Beware!*

My heart pounded. I couldn't make my feet move, but I had to stop Kronos. I had to destroy whatever was in that box.

Then a girl spoke right next to me, 'Well, Seaweed Brain?'

I looked over, expecting to see Annabeth, but the girl wasn't Annabeth. She wore punk-style clothes with silver chains on her wrists. She had spiky black hair, dark eyeliner around her stormy blue eyes and a spray of freckles across her nose. She looked familiar, but I wasn't sure why.

'Well?' she asked. 'Are we going to stop him or not?'

I couldn't answer. I couldn't move.

The girl rolled her eyes. 'Fine. Leave it to me and Aegis.'

She tapped her wrist and her silver chains transformed – flattening and expanding into a huge shield. It was silver and bronze, with the monstrous face of Medusa protruding from the centre. It looked like a death mask, as if the gorgon's real head had been pressed into the metal. I didn't know if that were true, or if the shield could really petrify me, but I looked away. Just being near it made me cold with fear. I got a feeling that in a real fight, the bearer of that shield would be almost impossible to beat. Any sane enemy would turn and run.

The girl drew her sword and advanced on the sarcophagus. The shadowy ghosts parted for her, scattering before the terrible aura of her shield.

'No,' I tried to warn her.

But she didn't listen. She marched straight up to the sarcophagus and pushed aside the golden lid.

For a moment she stood there, gazing down at whatever was in the box.

The coffin began to glow.

'No.' The girl's voice trembled. 'It can't be.'

From the depths of the ocean, Kronos laughed so loudly the whole ship trembled.

'No!' The girl screamed as the sarcophagus engulfed her in a blast of golden light.

'Ah!' I sat bolt upright in my hammock.

Annabeth was shaking me. 'Percy, you were having a nightmare. You need to get up.'

'Wh-what is it?' I rubbed my eyes. 'What's wrong?'

'Land,' she said grimly. 'We're approaching the island of the Sirens.'

I could barely make out the island ahead of us — just a dark spot in the mist.

'I want you to do me a favour,' Annabeth said. 'The Sirens . . . we'll be in range of their singing soon.'

I remembered stories about the Sirens. They sang so sweetly their voices enchanted sailors and lured them to their death.

'No problem,' I assured her. 'We can just stop up our ears. There's a big tub of candle wax below deck —'

'I want to hear them.'

I blinked. 'Why?'

'They say the Sirens sing the truth about what you desire. They tell you things about yourself you didn't even realize. That's what's so enchanting. If you survive . . . you become wiser. I want to hear them. How often will I get that chance?'

Coming from most people, this would've made no sense. But Annabeth being who she was — well, if she could struggle through Ancient Greek architecture books and enjoy documentaries on the History Channel, I guessed the Sirens would appeal to her, too.

She told me her plan. Reluctantly, I helped her get ready.

As soon as the rocky coastline of the island came into view, I ordered one of the ropes to wrap around Annabeth's waist, tying her to the foremast.

'Don't untie me,' she said, 'no matter what happens or how much I plead. I'll want to go straight over the edge and drown myself.'

'Are you trying to tempt me?'

'Ha-ha.'

I promised I'd keep her secure. Then I took two large wads of candle wax, kneaded them into earplugs, and stuffed my ears.

Annabeth nodded sarcastically, letting me know the earplugs were a real fashion statement. I made a face at her and turned to the pilot's wheel.

The silence was eerie. I couldn't hear anything but the rush of blood in my head. As we approached the island, jagged rocks loomed out of the fog. I willed the *Queen Anne's Revenge* to skirt around them. If we sailed any closer, those rocks would shred our hull like blender blades.

I glanced back. At first, Annabeth seemed totally normal. Then she got a puzzled look on her face. Her eyes widened.

She strained against the ropes. She called my name – I could tell just from reading her lips. Her expression was clear: she had to get out. This was life or death. I had to let her out of the ropes *right now*.

She seemed so miserable it was hard not to cut her free.

I forced myself to look away. I urged the *Queen Anne's Revenge* to go faster.

I still couldn't see much of the island – just mist and rocks – but floating in the water were pieces of wood and fibreglass, the wreckage of old ships, even some flotation cushions from aeroplanes.

How could music cause so many lives to veer off course? I mean, sure, there were some Top Forty songs that made me want to take a fiery nosedive, but still . . . What could the Sirens possibly sing about?

For one dangerous moment, I understood Annabeth's curiosity. I was tempted to take out the earplugs, just to get a taste of the song. I could feel the Sirens' voices vibrating in the timbers of the ship, pulsing along with the roar of blood in my ears.

Annabeth was pleading with me. Tears streamed down her cheeks. She strained against the ropes, as if they were holding her back from everything she cared about.

How could you be so cruel? she seemed to be asking me. *I thought you were my friend.*

I glared at the misty island. I wanted to uncap my sword, but there was nothing to fight. How do you fight a song?

I tried hard not to look at Annabeth. I managed it for about five minutes.

That was my big mistake.

When I couldn't stand it any longer, I looked back and found . . . a heap of cut ropes. An empty mast. Annabeth's bronze knife lay on the deck. Somehow, she'd managed to wriggle it into her hand. I'd totally forgotten to disarm her.

I rushed to the side of the boat and saw her paddling

madly for the island, the waves carrying her straight towards the jagged rocks.

I screamed her name, but if she heard me, it didn't do any good. She was entranced, swimming towards her death.

I looked back at the pilot's wheel and yelled, 'Stay!'

Then I jumped over the side.

I sliced into the water and willed the currents to bend around me, making a jet stream that shot me forward.

I came to the surface and spotted Annabeth, but a wave caught her, sweeping her between two razor-sharp fangs of rock.

I had no choice. I plunged after her.

I dived under the wrecked hull of a yacht, wove through a collection of floating metal balls on chains that I realized afterwards were mines. I had to use all my power over water to avoid getting smashed against the rocks or tangled in the nets of barbed wire strung just below the surface.

I jetted between the two rock fangs and found myself in a half-moon-shaped bay. The water was choked with more rocks and ship wreckage and floating mines. The beach was black volcanic sand.

I looked around desperately for Annabeth.

There she was.

Luckily or unluckily, she was a strong swimmer. She'd made it past the mines and the rocks. She was almost to the black beach.

Then the mist cleared and I saw them – the Sirens.

Imagine a flock of vultures the size of people – with dirty black plumage, grey talons and wrinkled pink necks. Now imagine human heads on top of those necks, but the human heads keep changing.

I couldn't hear them, but I could see they were singing. As their mouths moved, their faces morphed into people I knew — my mom, Poseidon, Grover, Tyson, Chiron. All the people I most wanted to see. They smiled reassuringly, inviting me forward. But no matter what shape they took, their mouths were greasy and caked with the remnants of old meals. Like vultures, they'd been eating with their faces, and it didn't look like they'd been feasting on Monster Doughnuts.

Annabeth swam towards them.

I knew I couldn't let her get out of the water. The sea was my only advantage. It had always protected me one way or another. I propelled myself forward and grabbed her ankle.

The moment I touched her, a shock went through my body, and I saw the Sirens the way Annabeth must've been seeing them.

Three people sat on a picnic blanket in Central Park. A feast was spread out before them. I recognized Annabeth's dad from photos she'd shown me — an athletic-looking, sandy-haired guy in his forties. He was holding hands with a beautiful woman who looked a lot like Annabeth. She was dressed casually — in blue jeans and a denim shirt and hiking boots — but something about the woman radiated power. I knew that I was looking at the goddess Athena. Next to them sat a young man . . . Luke.

The whole scene glowed in a warm, buttery light. The three of them were talking and laughing, and when they saw Annabeth, their faces lit up with delight. Annabeth's mom and dad held out their arms invitingly. Luke grinned and gestured for Annabeth to sit next to him — as if he'd never betrayed her, as if he were still her friend.

Behind the trees of Central Park, a city skyline rose. I caught my breath, because it was Manhattan, but *not* Manhattan. It had been totally rebuilt from dazzling white marble, bigger and grander than ever – with golden windows and rooftop gardens. It was better than New York. Better than Mount Olympus.

I knew immediately that Annabeth had designed it all. She was the architect for a whole new world. She had reunited her parents. She had saved Luke. She had done everything she'd ever wanted.

I blinked hard. When I opened my eyes, all I saw were the Sirens – ragged vultures with human faces, ready to feed on another victim.

I pulled Annabeth back into the surf. I couldn't hear her, but I could tell she was screaming. She kicked me in the face, but I held on.

I willed the currents to carry us out into the bay. Annabeth pummelled and kicked me, making it hard to concentrate. She thrashed so much we almost collided with a floating mine. I didn't know what to do. I'd never get back to the ship alive if she kept fighting.

We went under and Annabeth stopped struggling. Her expression became confused. Then our heads broke the surface and she started to fight again.

The water! Sound didn't travel well underwater. If I could submerge her long enough, I could break the spell of the music. Of course, Annabeth wouldn't be able to breathe, but at the moment, that seemed like a minor problem.

I grabbed her around the waist and ordered the waves to push us down.

We shot into the depths – three metres, six metres. I knew I had to be careful because I could withstand a lot more pressure than Annabeth. She fought and struggled for breath as bubbles rose around us.

Bubbles.

I was desperate. I had to keep Annabeth alive. I imagined all the bubbles in the sea – always churning, rising. I imagined them coming together, being pulled towards me.

The sea obeyed. There was a flurry of white, a tickling sensation all around me, and when my vision cleared, Annabeth and I had a huge bubble of air around us. Only our legs stuck into the water.

She gasped and coughed. Her whole body shuddered, but when she looked at me, I knew the spell had been broken.

She started to sob – I mean horrible, heartbroken sobbing. She put her head on my shoulder and I held her.

Fish gathered to look at us – a school of barracudas, some curious marlins.

Scram! I told them.

They swam off, but I could tell they went reluctantly. I swear I understood their intentions. They were about to start rumours flying around the sea about the son of Poseidon and some girl at the bottom of Siren Bay.

'I'll get us back to the ship,' I told her. 'It's okay. Just hang on.'

Annabeth nodded to let me know she was better now, then she murmured something I couldn't hear because of the wax in my ears.

I made the current steer our weird little air submarine through the rocks and barbed wire and back towards the hull of the *Queen Anne's Revenge*, which was maintaining a slow and steady course away from the island.

We stayed underwater, following the ship, until I judged we had moved out of earshot of the Sirens. Then I surfaced and our air bubble popped.

I ordered a rope ladder to drop over the side of the ship, and we climbed aboard.

I kept my earplugs in, just to be sure. We sailed until the island was completely out of sight. Annabeth sat huddled in a blanket on the forward deck. Finally she looked up, dazed and sad, and mouthed, *Safe*.

I took out the earplugs. No singing. The afternoon was quiet except for the sound of the waves against the hull. The fog had burned away to a blue sky, as if the island of the Sirens had never existed.

'You okay?' I asked. The moment I said it, I realized how lame that sounded. Of course she wasn't okay.

'I didn't realize,' she murmured.

'What?'

Her eyes were the same colour as the mist over the Sirens' island. 'How powerful the temptation would be.'

I didn't want to admit that I'd seen what the Sirens had promised her. I felt like a trespasser. But I figured I owed it to Annabeth.

'I saw the way you rebuilt Manhattan,' I told her. 'And Luke and your parents.'

She blushed. 'You saw that?'

'What Luke told you back on the *Princess Andromeda*, about starting the world from scratch . . . that really got to you, huh?'

She pulled her blanket around her. 'My fatal flaw. That's

what the Sirens showed me. My fatal flaw is hubris.'

I blinked. 'That brown stuff they spread on veggie sandwiches?'

She rolled her eyes. 'No, Seaweed Brain. That's *hummus*. Hubris is worse.'

'What could be worse than hummus?'

'Hubris means deadly pride, Percy. Thinking you can do things better than anyone else . . . even the gods.'

'You feel that way?'

She looked down. 'Don't you ever feel like, what if the world really *is* messed up? What if we *could* do it all over again from scratch? No more war. Nobody homeless. No more summer reading homework.'

'I'm listening.'

'I mean, the West represents a lot of the best things mankind ever did – that's why the fire is still burning. That's why Olympus is still around. But sometimes you just see the bad stuff, you know? And you start thinking the way Luke does: "If I could tear this all down, I would do it better." Don't you ever feel that way? Like *you* could do a better job if you ran the world?'

'Um . . . no. Me running the world would kind of be a nightmare.'

'Then you're lucky. Hubris isn't your fatal flaw.'

'What is?'

'I don't know, Percy, but every hero has one. If you don't find it and learn to control it . . . well, they don't call it "fatal" for nothing.'

I thought about that. It didn't exactly cheer me up.

I also noticed Annabeth hadn't said much about the *personal* things she would change – like getting her parents back together, or saving Luke. I understood. I didn't want to admit how many times I'd dreamed of getting my own parents back together.

I pictured my mom, alone in our little apartment on the Upper East Side. I tried to remember the smell of her blue waffles in the kitchen. It seemed so far away.

'So was it worth it?' I asked Annabeth. 'Do you feel . . . wiser?'

She gazed into the distance. 'I'm not sure. But we *have* to save the camp. If we don't stop Luke . . .'

She didn't need to finish. If Luke's way of thinking could even tempt Annabeth, there was no telling how many other half-bloods might join him.

I thought about my dream of the girl and the golden sarcophagus. I wasn't sure what it meant, but I got the feeling I was missing something. Something terrible that Kronos was planning. What had the girl seen when she opened that coffin lid?

Suddenly Annabeth's eyes widened. 'Percy.'

I turned.

Up ahead was another blotch of land – a saddle-shaped island with forested hills and white beaches and green meadows – just like I'd seen in my dreams.

My nautical senses confirmed it. Thirty degrees, thirty-one minutes north, seventy-five degrees, twelve minutes west.

We had reached the home of the Cyclops.

14 WE MEET THE SHEEP OF DOOM

When you think 'monster island', you think craggy rocks and bones scattered on the beach like the island of the Sirens.

The Cyclops's island was nothing like that. I mean, okay, it had a rope bridge across a chasm, which was not a good sign. You might as well put up a billboard that said, SOMETHING EVIL LIVES HERE. But, except for that, the place looked like a Caribbean postcard. It had green fields and tropical fruit trees and white beaches. As we sailed towards the shore, Annabeth breathed in the sweet air. 'The Fleece,' she said.

I nodded. I couldn't see the Fleece yet, but I could feel its power. I could believe it would heal anything, even Thalia's poisoned tree. 'If we take it away, will the island die?'

Annabeth shook her head. 'It'll fade. Go back to what it would be normally, whatever that is.'

I felt a little guilty about ruining this paradise, but I reminded myself we had no choice. Camp Half-Blood was in trouble. And Tyson . . . Tyson would still be with us if it wasn't for this quest.

In the meadow at the base of the ravine, several dozen sheep were milling around. They looked peaceful enough, but they were huge — the size of hippos. Just past them was a path that led up into the hills. At the top of the path, near the edge of the canyon, was the massive oak tree I'd seen in my dreams. Something gold glittered in its branches.

'This is too easy,' I said. 'We could just hike up there and take it.'

Annabeth's eyes narrowed. 'There's supposed to be a guardian. A dragon or . . .'

That's when a deer emerged from the bushes. It trotted into the meadow, probably looking for grass to eat, when the sheep all bleated at once and rushed the animal. It happened so fast that the deer stumbled and was lost in a sea of wool and trampling hooves.

Grass and tufts of fur flew into the air.

A second later the sheep all moved away, back to their regular peaceful wanderings. Where the deer had been was a pile of clean white bones.

Annabeth and I exchanged looks.

'They're like piranhas,' she said.

'Piranhas with wool. How will we –'

'Percy!' Annabeth gasped, grabbing my arm. 'Look.'

She pointed down the beach, to just below the sheep meadow, where a small boat had been run aground . . . the other lifeboat from the CSS *Birmingham*.

We decided there was no way we could get past the man-eating sheep. Annabeth wanted to sneak up the path invisibly and grab the Fleece, but in the end I convinced her that something would go wrong. The sheep would smell her. Another guardian would appear. Something. And if that happened, I'd be too far away to help.

Besides, our first job was to find Grover and whoever had come ashore in that lifeboat – assuming they'd got past the sheep. I was too nervous to say what I was secretly hoping . . . that Tyson might still be alive.

We moored the *Queen Anne's Revenge* on the back side of the island where the cliffs rose straight up a good sixty metres feet. I figured the ship was less likely to be seen there.

The cliffs looked climbable, barely – about as difficult as the lava wall back at camp. At least it was free of sheep. I hoped that Polyphemus did not also keep carnivorous mountain goats.

We rowed a lifeboat to the edge of the rocks and made our way up, very slowly. Annabeth went first because she was the better climber.

We only came close to dying six or seven times, which I thought was pretty good. Once, I lost my grip and I found myself dangling by one hand from a ledge fifteen metres above the rocky surf. But I found another handhold and kept climbing. A minute later Annabeth hit a slippery patch of moss and her foot slipped. Fortunately, she found something else to put it against. Unfortunately, that something was my face.

'Sorry,' she murmured.

'S'okay,' I grunted, though I'd never really wanted to know what Annabeth's sneaker tasted like.

Finally, when my fingers felt like molten lead and my arm muscles were shaking from exhaustion, we hauled ourselves over the top of the cliff and collapsed.

'Ugh,' I said.

'Ouch,' moaned Annabeth.

'Garrr!' bellowed another voice.

If I hadn't been so tired, I would've leaped another sixty metres. I whirled around, but I couldn't see who'd spoken.

Annabeth clamped her hand over my mouth. She pointed.

The ledge we were sitting on was narrower than I'd realized. It dropped off on the opposite side, and that's where the voice was coming from – right below us.

'You're a feisty one!' the deep voice bellowed.

'Challenge me!' Clarisse's voice, no doubt about it. 'Give me back my sword and I'll fight you!'

The monster roared with laughter.

Annabeth and I crept to the edge. We were right above the entrance of the Cyclops's cave. Below us stood Polyphemus and Grover, still in his wedding dress. Clarisse was tied up, hanging upside down over a pot of boiling water. I was half hoping to see Tyson down there, too. Even if he'd been in danger, at least I would've known he was alive. But there was no sign of him.

'Hmm,' Polyphemus pondered. 'Eat loudmouth girl now or wait for wedding feast? What does my bride think?'

He turned to Grover, who backed up and almost tripped over his completed bridal train. 'Oh, um, I'm not hungry right now, dear. Perhaps –'

'Did you say *bride*?' Clarisse demanded. 'Who – Grover?'

Next to me, Annabeth muttered, 'Shut up. She has to shut up.'

Polyphemus glowered. 'What "Grover"?'

'The satyr!' Clarisse yelled.

'Oh!' Grover yelped. 'The poor thing's brain is boiling from that hot water. Pull her down, dear!'

Polyphemus's eyelid narrowed over his baleful milky eye, as if he were trying to see Clarisse more clearly.

The Cyclops was an even more horrible sight than he had been in my dreams. Partly because his rancid smell was now up close and personal. Partly because he was dressed in his wedding outfit – a crude kilt and shoulder-wrap, stitched together from baby-blue tuxedoes, as if he'd skinned an entire wedding party.

'What satyr?' asked Polyphemus. 'Satyrs are good eating. You bring me a satyr?'

'No, you big idiot!' bellowed Clarisse. '*That* satyr! Grover! The one in the wedding dress!'

I wanted to wring Clarisse's neck, but it was too late. All I could do was watch as Polyphemus turned and ripped off Grover's wedding veil – revealing his curly hair, his scruffy adolescent beard, his tiny horns.

Polyphemus breathed heavily, trying to contain his anger. 'I don't see very well,' he growled. 'Not since many years ago when the other hero stabbed me in eye. But YOU'RE – NO – LADY – CYCLOPS!'

The Cyclops grabbed Grover's dress and tore it away. Underneath, the old Grover reappeared in his jeans and T-shirt. He yelped and ducked as the monster swiped over his head.

'Stop!' Grover pleaded. 'Don't eat me raw! I – I have a good recipe!'

I reached for my sword, but Annabeth hissed, 'Wait!'

Polyphemus was hesitating, a boulder in his hand, ready to smash his would-be bride.

'Recipe?' he asked Grover.

'Oh y-yes! You don't want to eat me raw. You'll get E. coli and botulism and all sorts of horrible things. I'll taste much better roasted over a slow fire. With mango chutney! You could go get some mangoes right now, down there in the woods. I'll just wait here.'

The monster pondered this. My heart hammered against my ribs. I figured I'd die if I charged. But I couldn't let the monster kill Grover.

'Roasted satyr with mango chutney,' Polyphemus mused. He looked back at Clarisse, still hanging over the pot of boiling water. 'You a satyr, too?'

'No, you overgrown pile of dung!' she yelled. 'I'm a girl! The daughter of Ares! Now untie me so I can rip your arms off!'

'Rip my arms off,' Polyphemus repeated.

'And stuff them down your throat!'

'You got spunk.'

'Let me down!'

Polyphemus snatched up Grover as if he were a wayward puppy. 'Have to graze sheep now. Wedding postponed until tonight. Then we'll eat satyr for the main course!'

'But . . . you're still getting married?' Grover sounded hurt. 'Who's the bride?'

Polyphemus looked towards the boiling pot.

Clarisse made a strangled sound. 'Oh, no! You can't be serious. I'm not –'

Before Annabeth or I could do anything, Polyphemus plucked her off the rope like she was a ripe apple, and tossed her and Grover deep into the cave. 'Make yourself comfortable! I come back at sundown for big event!'

Then the Cyclops whistled, and a mixed flock of goats and sheep — smaller than the man-eaters — flooded out of the cave and past their master. As they went to pasture, Polyphemus patted some on the back and called them by name — Beltbuster, Tammany, Lockhart and so on.

When the last sheep had waddled out, Polyphemus rolled a boulder in front of the doorway as easily as I would close a refrigerator door, shutting off the sound of Clarisse and Grover screaming inside.

'Mangoes,' Polyphemus grumbled to himself. 'What are mangoes?'

He strolled off down the mountain in his baby-blue groom's outfit, leaving us alone with a pot of boiling water and a six-ton boulder.

We tried for what seemed like hours, but it was no good. The boulder wouldn't move. We yelled into the cracks, tapped on the rock, did everything we could think of to get a signal to Grover, but if he heard us, we couldn't tell.

Even if by some miracle we managed to kill Polyphemus, it wouldn't do us any good. Grover and Clarisse would die inside that sealed cave. The only way to move the rock was to have the Cyclops do it.

In total frustration, I stabbed Riptide against the boulder. Sparks flew, but nothing else happened. A large rock is not the kind of enemy you can fight with a magic sword.

Annabeth and I sat on the ridge in despair and watched the distant baby-blue shape of the Cyclops as he moved among his flocks. He had wisely divided his regular animals from his man-eating sheep, putting each group on either side of the huge crevice that divided the island. The only way across was the rope bridge, and the planks were much too far apart for sheep hooves.

We watched as Polyphemus visited his carnivorous flock on the far side. Unfortunately, they didn't eat him. In fact, they didn't seem to bother him at all. He fed them chunks of mystery meat from a great wicker basket, which only reinforced the feelings I'd been having since Circe turned me into a guinea pig – that maybe it was time I joined Grover and became a vegetarian.

'Trickery,' Annabeth decided. 'We can't beat him by force, so we'll have to use trickery.'

'Okay,' I said. 'What trick?'

'I haven't figured that part out yet.'

'Great.'

'Polyphemus will have to move the rock to let the sheep inside.'

'At sunset,' I said. 'Which is when he'll marry Clarisse and have Grover for dinner. I'm not sure which is grosser.'

'I could get inside,' she said, 'invisibly.'

'What about me?'

'The sheep,' Annabeth mused. She gave me one of those sly looks that always made me wary. 'How much do you like sheep?'

'Just don't let go!' Annabeth said, standing invisibly somewhere off to my right. That was easy for her to say. She wasn't hanging upside down from the belly of a sheep.

Now, I'll admit it wasn't as hard as I'd thought. I'd crawled under a car before to change my mom's oil, and this wasn't too different. The sheep didn't care. Even the Cyclops's smallest sheep were big enough to support my weight, and they had thick wool. I just twirled the stuff into handles for my hands, hooked my feet against the sheep's thigh bones, and presto – I felt like a baby wallaby, riding around against the sheep's chest, trying to keep the wool out of my mouth and my nose.

In case you're wondering, the underside of a sheep doesn't smell that great. Imagine a winter sweater that's been dragged through the mud and left in the laundry hamper for a week. Something like that.

The sun was going down.

No sooner was I in position than the Cyclops roared, 'Oy! Goaties! Sheepies!'

The flock dutifully began trudging back up the slopes towards the cave.

'This is it!' Annabeth whispered. 'I'll be close by. Don't worry.'

I made a silent promise to the gods that if we survived this, I'd tell Annabeth she was a genius. The frightening thing was, I knew the gods would hold me to it.

My sheep taxi started plodding up the hill. After a hundred metres, my hands and feet started to hurt from holding on. I gripped the sheep's wool more tightly, and the animal made a grumbling sound. I didn't blame it. I wouldn't want anybody rock climbing in my hair either. But if I didn't hold on, I was sure I'd fall off right there in front of the monster.

'Hasenpfeffer!' the Cyclops said, patting one of the sheep in front of me. 'Einstein! Widget – eh there, Widget!'

Polyphemus patted my sheep and nearly knocked me to the ground. 'Putting on some extra mutton there?'

Uh-oh, I thought. *Here it comes.*

But Polyphemus just laughed and swatted the sheep's rear end, propelling us forward. 'Go on, fatty! Soon Polyphemus will eat you for breakfast!'

And just like that, I was in the cave.

I could see the last of the sheep coming inside. If Annabeth didn't pull off her distraction soon . . .

The Cyclops was about to roll the stone back into place, when from somewhere outside Annabeth shouted, 'Hello, ugly!'

Polyphemus stiffened. 'Who said that?'

'Nobody!' Annabeth yelled.

That got exactly the reaction she'd been hoping for. The monster's face turned red with rage.

'Nobody!' Polyphemus yelled back. 'I remember you!'

'You're too stupid to remember anybody,' Annabeth taunted. 'Much less Nobody.'

I hoped to the gods she was already moving when she said that, because Polyphemus bellowed furiously, grabbed the nearest boulder (which happened to be his front door) and threw it towards the sound of Annabeth's voice. I heard the rock smash into a thousand fragments.

For a terrible moment, there was silence. Then Annabeth shouted, 'You haven't learned to throw any better, either!'

Polyphemus howled. 'Come here! Let me kill you, Nobody!'

'You can't kill Nobody, you stupid oaf,' she taunted. 'Come find me!'

Polyphemus barrelled down the hill towards her voice.

Now, the 'Nobody' thing wouldn't have made sense to anybody, but Annabeth had explained to me that it was the name Odysseus had used to trick Polyphemus centuries ago, right before he poked the Cyclops's eye out with a large hot stick. Annabeth had figured Polyphemus would still have a grudge about that name, and she was right. In his frenzy to find his old enemy, he forgot about resealing the cave entrance. Apparently, he didn't even stop to consider that Annabeth's voice was female, whereas the first Nobody had been male. On the other hand, he'd wanted to marry Grover, so he couldn't have been all that bright about the whole male/female thing.

I just hoped Annabeth could stay alive and keep distracting him long enough for me to find Grover and Clarisse.

I dropped off my ride, patted Widget on the head, and apologized. I searched the main room, but there was no sign of Grover or Clarisse. I pushed through the crowd of sheep and goats towards the back of the cave.

Even though I'd dreamed about this place, I had a hard time finding my way through the maze. I ran down corridors littered with bones, past rooms full of sheepskin rugs and life-size cement sheep that I recognized as the work of Medusa. There were collections of sheep T-shirts; large tubs of lanolin cream; and woolly coats, socks and hats with rams' horns. Finally, I found the spinning room, where Grover was huddled in the corner, trying to cut Clarisse's bonds with a pair of safety scissors.

'It's no good,' Clarisse said. 'This rope is like iron!'

'Just a few more minutes!'

'Grover,' she cried, exasperated. 'You've been working at it for hours!'

And then they saw me.

'*Percy?*' Clarisse said. 'You're supposed to be blown up!'

'Good to see you, too. Now hold still while I –'

'Perrrrrcy!' Grover bleated and tackled me with a goat-hug. 'You heard me! You came!'

'Yeah, buddy,' I said. 'Of course I came.'

'Where's Annabeth?'

'Outside,' I said. 'But there's no time to talk. Clarisse, hold still.'

I uncapped Riptide and sliced off her ropes. She stood stiffly, rubbing her wrists. She glared at me for a moment, then looked at the ground and mumbled, 'Thanks.'

'You're welcome,' I said. 'Now, was anyone else on board your lifeboat?'

Clarisse looked surprised. 'No. Just me. Everybody else aboard the *Birmingham* . . . well, I didn't even know you guys made it out.'

I looked down, trying not to believe that my last hope of seeing Tyson alive had just been crushed. 'Okay. Come on, then. We have to help –'

An explosion echoed through the cave, followed by a scream that told me we might be too late. It was Annabeth crying out in fear.

15 NOBODY GETS THE FLEECE

'I got Nobody!' Polyphemus gloated.

We crept to the cave entrance and saw the Cyclops, grinning wickedly, holding up empty air. The monster shook his fist, and a baseball cap fluttered to the ground. There was Annabeth, hanging upside down by her legs.

'Hah!' the Cyclops said. 'Nasty invisible girl! Already got feisty one for wife. Means you gotta be roasted with mango chutney!'

Annabeth struggled, but she looked dazed. She had a nasty cut on her forehead. Her eyes were glassy.

'I'll rush him,' I whispered to Clarisse. 'Our ship is around the back of the island. You and Grover —'

'No way,' they said at the same time. Clarisse had armed herself with a highly collectible ram's-horn spear from the Cyclops's cave. Grover had found a sheep's thigh bone, which he didn't look too happy about, but he was gripping it like a club, ready to attack.

'We'll take him together,' Clarisse growled.

'Yeah,' Grover said. Then he blinked, like he couldn't believe he'd just agreed with Clarisse about something.

'All right,' I said. 'Attack plan Macedonia.'

They nodded. We'd all taken the same training courses at Camp Half-Blood. They knew what I was talking about. They would sneak around either side and attack the Cyclops from the flanks while I held his attention in the front. Probably what this meant was that we'd *all* die instead of just me, but I was grateful for the help.

I hefted my sword and shouted, 'Hey, Ugly!'

The giant whirled towards me. '*Another* one? Who are you?'

'Put down my friend. *I*'m the one who insulted you.'

'*You* are Nobody?'

'That's right, you smelly bucket of nose drool!' It didn't sound quite as good as Annabeth's insults, but it was all I could think of. 'I'm Nobody and I'm proud of it! Now, put her down and get over here. I want to stab your eye out again.'

'RAAAR!' he bellowed.

The good news: he dropped Annabeth. The bad news: he dropped her head first onto the rocks, where she lay motionless as a rag doll.

The other bad news: Polyphemus barrelled towards me, five hundred smelly kilograms of Cyclops that I would have to fight with a very small sword.

'For Pan!' Grover rushed in from the right. He threw his sheep bone, which bounced harmlessly off the monster's forehead. Clarisse ran in from the left and set her spear against the ground just in time for the Cyclops to step on it. He wailed in pain, and Clarisse dived out of the way to avoid getting trampled. But the Cyclops just plucked out the shaft like a large splinter and kept advancing on me.

I moved in with Riptide.

The monster made a grab for me. I rolled aside and stabbed him in the thigh.

I was hoping to see him disintegrate, but this monster was much too big and powerful.

'Get Annabeth!' I yelled at Grover.

He rushed over, grabbed her invisibility cap, and picked her up while Clarisse and I tried to keep Polyphemus distracted.

I have to admit, Clarisse was brave. She charged the Cyclops again and again. He pounded the ground, stomped at her, grabbed at her, but she was too quick. And as soon as she made an attack, I followed up by stabbing the monster in the toe or the ankle or the hand.

But we couldn't keep this up forever. Eventually we would tire or the monster would get in a lucky shot. It would only take one hit to kill us.

Out of the corner of my eye, I saw Grover carrying Annabeth across the rope bridge. It wouldn't have been my first choice, given the man-eating sheep on the other side, but at the moment that looked better than *this* side of the chasm, and it gave me an idea.

'Fall back!' I told Clarisse.

She rolled away as the Cyclops's fist smashed the olive tree beside her.

We ran for the bridge, Polyphemus right behind us. He was cut up and hobbling from so many wounds, but all we'd done was slow him down and make him mad.

'Grind you into sheep chow!' he promised. 'A thousand curses on Nobody!'

'Faster!' I told Clarisse.

We tore down the hill. The bridge was our only chance. Grover had just made it to the other side and was setting

Annabeth down. We had to make it across, too, before the giant caught us.

'Grover!' I yelled. 'Get Annabeth's knife!'

His eyes widened when he saw the Cyclops behind us, but he nodded like he understood. As Clarisse and I scrambled across the bridge, Grover began sawing at the ropes.

The first strand went *snap!*

Polyphemus bounded after us, making the bridge sway wildly.

The ropes were now half cut. Clarisse and I dived for solid ground, landing beside Grover. I made a wild slash with my sword and cut the remaining ropes.

The bridge fell away into the chasm, and the Cyclops howled . . . with delight, because he was standing right next to us.

'Failed!' he yelled gleefully. 'Nobody failed!'

Clarisse and Grover tried to charge him, but the monster swatted them aside like flies.

My anger swelled. I couldn't believe I'd come this far, lost Tyson, suffered through so much, only to fail – stopped by a big stupid monster in a baby-blue tuxedo kilt. Nobody was going to swat down my friends like that! I mean . . . *nobody*, not Nobody. Ah, you know what I mean.

Strength coursed through my body. I raised my sword and attacked, forgetting that I was hopelessly outmatched. I jabbed the Cyclops in the belly. When he doubled over I smacked him in the nose with the hilt of my sword. I slashed and kicked and bashed until the next thing I knew, Polyphemus was sprawled on his back, dazed and groaning, and I was standing above him, the tip of my sword hovering over his eye.

'Uhhhhhhhh,' Polyphemus moaned.

'Percy!' Grover gasped. 'How did you –'

'Please, noooo!' the Cyclops moaned, pitifully staring up at me. His nose was bleeding. A tear welled in the corner of his half-blind eye. 'M-m-my sheepies need me. Only trying to protect my sheep!'

He began to sob.

I had won. All I had to do was stab – one quick strike.

'Kill him!' Clarisse yelled. 'What are you waiting for?'

The Cyclops sounded so heartbroken, just like . . . like Tyson.

'He's a Cyclops!' Grover warned. 'Don't trust him!'

I knew he was right. I knew Annabeth would've said the same thing.

But Polyphemus sobbed . . . and for the first time it sank in that *he* was a son of Poseidon, too. Like Tyson. Like me. How could I just kill him in cold blood?

'We only want the Fleece,' I told the monster. 'Will you agree to let us take it?'

'No!' Clarisse shouted. 'Kill him!'

The monster sniffed. 'My beautiful Fleece. Prize of my collection. Take it, cruel human. Take it and go in peace.'

'I'm going to step back slowly,' I told the monster. 'One false move . . .'

Polyphemus nodded like he understood.

I stepped back . . . and as fast as a cobra, Polyphemus smacked me to the edge of the cliff.

'Foolish mortal!' he bellowed, rising to his feet. 'Take my Fleece? Ha! I eat you first.'

He opened his enormous mouth, and I knew that his rotten molars were the last things I would ever see.

Then something went *whoosh* over my head and *thump!*

A rock the size of a basketball sailed into Polyphemus's throat – a beautiful three-pointer, nothing but net. The Cyclops choked, trying to swallow the unexpected pill. He staggered backwards, but there was no place to stagger. His heel slipped, the edge of the cliff crumbled, and the great Polyphemus made chicken-wing motions that did nothing to help him fly as he tumbled into the chasm.

I turned.

Halfway down the path to the beach, standing completely unharmed in the midst of a flock of killer sheep, was an old friend.

'Bad Polyphemus,' Tyson said. 'Not all Cyclopes as nice as we look.'

Tyson gave us the short version: Rainbow the hippocampus – who'd apparently been following us ever since the Long Island Sound, waiting for Tyson to play with him – had found Tyson sinking beneath the wreckage of the CSS *Birmingham* and pulled him to safety. He and Tyson had been searching the Sea of Monsters ever since, trying to find us, until Tyson caught the scent of sheep and found this island.

I wanted to hug the big oaf, except he was standing in the middle of killer sheep. 'Tyson, thank the gods. Annabeth is hurt!'

'You thank the gods she is hurt?' he asked, puzzled.

'No!' I knelt beside Annabeth and was worried sick by what I saw. The gash on her forehead was worse than I'd realized. Her hairline was sticky with blood. Her skin was pale and clammy.

Grover and I exchanged nervous looks. Then an idea came to me. 'Tyson, the Fleece. Can you get it for me?'

'Which one?' Tyson said, looking around at the hundreds of sheep.

'In the tree!' I said. 'The gold one!'

'Oh. Pretty. Yes.'

Tyson lumbered over, careful not to step on the sheep. If any of us had tried to approach the Fleece, we would've been eaten alive, but I guess Tyson smelled like Polyphemus, because the flock didn't bother him at all. They just cuddled up to him and bleated affectionately, as though they expected to get sheep treats from the big wicker basket. Tyson reached up and lifted the Fleece off its branch. Immediately the leaves on the oak tree turned yellow. Tyson started wading back towards me, but I yelled, 'No time! Throw it!'

The gold ram skin sailed through the air like a glittering shag frisbee. I caught it with a grunt. It was heavier than I'd expected – about thirty kilograms of precious gold wool.

I spread it over Annabeth, covering everything but her face, and prayed silently to all the gods I could think of, even the ones I didn't like.

Please. Please.

The colour returned to her face. Her eyelids fluttered open. The cut on her forehead began to close. She saw Grover and said weakly, 'You're not . . . married?'

Grover grinned. 'No. My friends talked me out of it.'

'Annabeth,' I said, 'just lay still.'

But, despite our protests she sat up, and I noticed that the cut on her face was almost completely healed. She looked a lot better. In fact, she shimmered with health, as if someone had injected her with glitter.

Meanwhile, Tyson was starting to have trouble with the sheep. 'Down!' he told them as they tried to climb him, looking for food. A few were sniffing in our direction. 'No, sheepies. This way! Come here!'

They heeded him, but it was obvious they were hungry, and they were starting to realize Tyson didn't have any treats for them. They wouldn't hold out forever with so much fresh meat nearby.

'We have to go,' I said. 'Our ship is . . .' The *Queen Anne's Revenge* was a very long way away. The shortest route was across the chasm, and we'd just destroyed the only bridge. The only other possibility was through the sheep.

'Tyson,' I called, 'can you lead the flock as far away as possible?'

'The sheep want food.'

'I know! They want people food! Just lead them away from the path. Give us time to get to the beach. Then join us there.'

Tyson looked doubtful, but he whistled. 'Come, sheepies! Um, people food this way!'

He jogged off into the meadow, the sheep in pursuit.

'Keep the Fleece around you,' I told Annabeth. 'Just in case you're not fully healed yet. Can you stand?'

She tried, but her face turned pale again. 'Ohh. *Not* fully healed.'

Clarisse dropped next to her and felt her chest, which made Annabeth gasp.

'Ribs broken,' Clarisse said. 'They're mending, but definitely broken.'

'How can you tell?' I asked.

Clarisse glared at me. 'Because I've broken a few, runt! I'll have to carry her.'

Before I could argue, Clarisse picked up Annabeth like a sack of flour and lugged her down to the beach. Grover and I followed.

As soon as we got to the edge of the water, I concentrated on the *Queen Anne's Revenge*. I willed it to raise anchor and come to me. After a few anxious minutes, I saw the ship rounding the tip of the island.

'Incoming!' Tyson yelled. He was bounding down the path to join us, the sheep about fifty metres behind, bleating in frustration as their Cyclops friend ran away without feeding them.

'They probably won't follow us into the water,' I told the others. 'All we have to do is swim for the ship.'

'With Annabeth like this?' Clarisse protested.

'We can do it,' I insisted. I was starting to feel confident again. I was back in my home turf – the sea. 'Once we get to the ship, we're home free.'

We almost made it, too.

We were just wading past the entrance to the ravine, when we heard a tremendous roar and saw Polyphemus, scraped up and bruised but still very much alive, his baby-blue wedding outfit in tatters, splashing towards us with a boulder in each hand.

'You'd think he'd run out of rocks,' I muttered.

'Swim for it!' Grover said.

He and Clarisse plunged into the surf. Annabeth hung on to Clarisse's neck and tried to paddle with one hand, the wet Fleece weighing her down.

But the monster's attention wasn't on the Fleece.

'You, young Cyclops!' Polyphemus roared. 'Traitor to your kind!'

Tyson froze.

'Don't listen to him!' I pleaded. 'Come on.'

I pulled Tyson's arm, but I might as well have been pulling a mountain. He turned and faced the older Cyclops. 'I am not a traitor.'

'You serve mortals!' Polyphemus shouted. 'Thieving humans!'

Polyphemus threw his first boulder. Tyson swatted it aside with his fist.

'Not a traitor,' Tyson said. 'And you are *not* my kind.'

'Death or victory!' Polyphemus charged into the surf, but his foot was still wounded. He immediately stumbled and fell on his face. That would've been funny, except he started to get up again, spitting salt water and growling.

'Percy!' Clarisse yelled. 'Come on!'

They were almost to the ship with the Fleece. If I could just keep the monster distracted a little longer . . .

'Go,' Tyson told me. 'I will hold Big Ugly.'

'No! He'll kill you.' I'd already lost Tyson once. I wasn't going to lose him again. 'We'll fight him together.'

'Together,' Tyson agreed.

I drew my sword.

Polyphemus advanced carefully, limping worse than ever. But there was nothing wrong with his throwing arm. He chucked his second boulder. I dived to one side, but I still would've been squashed if Tyson's fist hadn't blasted the rock to rubble.

I willed the sea to rise. A six-metre wave surged up, lifting me on its crest. I rode towards the Cyclops and kicked him in the eye, leaping over his head as the water blasted him onto the beach.

'Destroy you!' Polyphemus spluttered. 'Fleece stealer!'

'*You* stole the Fleece!' I yelled. 'You've been using it to lure satyrs to their deaths!'

'So? Satyrs good eating!'

'The Fleece should be used to heal! It belongs to the children of the gods!'

'*I* am a child of the gods!' Polyphemus swiped at me, but I sidestepped. 'Father Poseidon, curse this thief!' He was blinking hard now, like he could barely see, and I realized he was targeting by the sound of my voice.

'Poseidon won't curse me,' I said, backing up as the Cyclops grabbed air. 'I'm his son, too. He won't play favourites.'

Polyphemus roared. He ripped an olive tree out of the side of the cliff and smashed it where I'd been standing a moment before. 'Humans not the same! Nasty, tricky, lying!'

Grover was helping Annabeth aboard the ship. Clarisse was waving frantically at me, telling me to come on.

Tyson worked his way around Polyphemus, trying to get behind him.

'Young one!' the older Cyclops called. 'Where are you? Help me!'

Tyson stopped.

'You weren't raised right!' Polyphemus wailed, shaking his olive tree club. 'Poor orphaned brother! Help me!'

No one moved. No sound but the ocean and my own heartbeat. Then Tyson stepped forward, raising his hands defensively. 'Don't fight, Cyclops brother. Put down the –'

Polyphemus spun towards his voice.

'Tyson!' I shouted.

The tree struck him with such force it would've flattened me into a Percy pizza with extra olives. Tyson flew backwards, ploughing a trench in the sand. Polyphemus charged after him, but I shouted, 'No!' and lunged as far as I could with Riptide. I'd hoped to sting Polyphemus in the back of the thigh, but I managed to leap a little bit higher.

'Blaaaaah!' Polyphemus bleated just like his sheep, and swung at me with his tree.

I dived, but still got raked across the back by a dozen jagged branches. I was bleeding and bruised and exhausted. The guinea pig inside me wanted to bolt. But I swallowed down my fear.

Polyphemus swung the tree again, but this time I was ready. I grabbed a branch as it passed, ignoring the pain in my hands as I was jerked skywards, and let the Cyclops lift me into the air. At the top of the arc I let go and fell straight against the giant's face – landing with both feet on his already damaged eye.

Polyphemus yowled in pain. Tyson tackled him, pulling him down. I landed next to them – sword in hand, within striking distance of the monster's heart. But I locked eyes with Tyson, and I knew I couldn't do it. It just wasn't right.

'Let him go,' I told Tyson. 'Run.'

With one last mighty effort, Tyson pushed the cursing older Cyclops away, and we ran for the surf.

'I will smash you!' Polyphemus yelled, doubling over in pain. His enormous hands cupped over his eye.

Tyson and I plunged into the waves.

'Where are you?' Polyphemus screamed. He picked up his tree club and threw it into the water. It splashed off to our right.

I summoned up a current to carry us, and we started gaining speed. I was beginning to think we might make it to the ship, when Clarisse shouted from the deck, 'Yeah, Jackson! In your face, Cyclops!'

Shut up, I wanted to yell.

'Rarrr!' Polyphemus picked up a boulder. He threw it towards the sound of Clarisse's voice, but it fell short, narrowly missing Tyson and me.

'Yeah, yeah!' Clarisse taunted. 'You throw like a wimp! Teach you to try marrying me, you idiot!'

'Clarisse!' I yelled, unable to stand it. 'Shut up!'

Too late. Polyphemus threw another boulder, and this time I watched helplessly as it sailed over my head and crashed through the hull of the *Queen Anne's Revenge*.

You wouldn't believe how fast a ship can sink. The *Queen Anne's Revenge* creaked and groaned and listed forward like it was going down a playground slide.

I cursed, willing the sea to push us faster, but the ship's masts were already going under.

'Dive!' I told Tyson. And as another rock sailed over our heads, we plunged underwater.

My friends were sinking fast, trying to swim, without luck, in the bubbly trail of the ship's wreckage.

Not many people realize that when a ship goes down, it acts like a sinkhole, pulling down everything around it. Clarisse was a strong swimmer, but even she wasn't making any progress. Grover frantically kicked with his hooves. Annabeth was hanging on to the Fleece, which flashed in the water like a wave of new pennies.

I swam towards them, knowing that I might not have the strength to pull my friends out. Worse, pieces of timber were swirling around them; none of my power with water would help if I got whacked on the head by a beam.

We need help, I thought.

Yes. Tyson's voice, loud and clear in my head.

I looked over at him, startled. I'd heard Nereids and other water spirits speak to me underwater before, but it never occurred to me . . . Tyson was a son of Poseidon. We could communicate with each other.

Rainbow, Tyson said.

I nodded, then closed my eyes and concentrated, adding my voice to Tyson's: *RAINBOW! We need you!*

Immediately, shapes shimmered in the darkness below – three horses with fish tails, galloping upwards faster than dolphins. Rainbow and his friends glanced in our direction and seemed to read our thoughts. They whisked into the wreckage, and a moment later burst upwards in a cloud of bubbles — Grover, Annabeth and Clarisse each clinging to the neck of a hippocampus.

Rainbow, the largest, had Clarisse. He raced over to us and allowed Tyson to grab hold of his mane. His friend who bore Annabeth did the same for me.

We broke the surface of the water and raced away from Polyphemus's island. Behind us, I could hear the Cyclops roaring in triumph, 'I did it! I finally sank Nobody!'

I hoped he never found out he was wrong.

We skimmed across the sea as the island shrank to a dot and then disappeared.

'Did it,' Annabeth muttered in exhaustion. 'We . . .'

She slumped against the neck of the hippocampus and instantly fell asleep.

I didn't know how far the hippocampi could take us. I didn't know where we were going. I just propped up Annabeth so she wouldn't fall off, covered her in the Golden Fleece that we'd been through so much to get, and said a silent prayer of thanks.

Which reminded me . . . I still owed the gods a debt.

'You're a genius,' I told Annabeth quietly.

Then I put my head against the Fleece, and before I knew it I was asleep, too.

WE GET A SURPRISE ON MIAMI BEACH

'Percy, wake up.'

Salt water splashed my face. Annabeth was shaking my shoulder.

In the distance, the sun was setting behind a city skyline. I could see a beachside highway lined with palm trees, storefronts glowing with red-and-blue neon, a harbour filled with sailboats and cruise ships.

'Miami, I think,' Annabeth said. 'But the hippocampi are acting funny.'

Sure enough, our fishy friends had slowed down and were whinnying and swimming in circles, sniffing the water. They didn't look happy. One of them sneezed. I could tell what they were thinking.

'This is as far as they'll take us,' I said. 'Too many humans. Too much pollution. We'll have to swim to shore on our own.'

None of us was very psyched about that, but we thanked Rainbow and his friends for the ride. Tyson cried a little. He unfastened the makeshift saddle pack he'd made, which contained his tool kit and a couple of other things he'd salvaged from the *Birmingham* wreck. He hugged Rainbow around the neck, gave him a soggy mango he'd picked up on the island and said goodbye.

Once the hippocampi's white manes disappeared into the

sea, we swam for shore. The waves pushed us forward, and in no time we were back in the mortal world. We wandered along the cruise line docks, pushing through crowds of people arriving for vacations. Porters bustled around with carts of luggage. Taxi drivers yelled at each other in Spanish and tried to cut in line for customers. If anybody noticed us – five kids dripping wet and looking like they'd just had a fight with a monster – they didn't let on.

Now that we were back among mortals, Tyson's single eye had blurred from the Mist. Grover had put on his cap and sneakers. Even the Fleece had transformed from a sheepskin to a red-and-gold high school letter jacket with a large glittery Omega on the pocket.

Annabeth ran to the nearest newspaper box and checked the date on the *Miami Herald*. She cursed. 'June eighteenth! We've been away from camp ten days!'

'That's impossible!' Clarisse said.

But I knew it wasn't. Time travelled differently in monstrous places.

'Thalia's tree must be almost dead,' Grover wailed. 'We have to get the Fleece back *tonight*.'

Clarisse slumped down on the pavement. 'How are we supposed to do that?' Her voice trembled. 'We're hundreds of miles away. No money. No ride. This is just like the Oracle said. It's *your* fault, Jackson! If you hadn't interfered –'

'Percy's fault?!' Annabeth exploded. 'Clarisse, how can you say that? You are the biggest –'

'Stop it!' I said.

Clarisse put her head in her hands. Annabeth stomped her foot in frustration.

The thing was: I'd almost forgotten this quest was supposed to be Clarisse's. For a scary moment, I saw things from her point of view. How would I feel if a bunch of other heroes had butted in and made me look bad?

I thought about what I'd overheard in the boiler room of the CSS *Birmingham* — Ares yelling at Clarisse, warning her that she'd better not fail. Ares couldn't care less about the camp, but if Clarisse made him look bad . . .

'Clarisse,' I said, 'what did the Oracle tell you exactly?'

She looked up. I thought she was going to tell me off, but instead she took a deep breath and recited her prophecy:

> *'You shall sail the iron ship with warriors of bone,*
> *You shall find what you seek and make it your own,*
> *But despair for your life entombed within stone,*
> *And fail without friends, to fly home alone.'*

'Ouch,' Grover mumbled.

'No,' I said. 'No . . . wait a minute. I've got it.'

I searched my pockets for money, and found nothing but a golden drachma. 'Does anybody have any cash?'

Annabeth and Grover shook their heads morosely. Clarisse pulled a wet Confederate dollar from her pocket and sighed.

'Cash?' Tyson asked hesitantly. 'Like . . . green paper?'

I looked at him. 'Yeah.'

'Like the kind in duffel bags?'

'Yeah, but we lost those bags days a-g-g —'

I stuttered to a halt as Tyson rummaged in his saddle pack and pulled out the airtight bag full of cash that Hermes had included in our supplies.

'Tyson!' I said. 'How did you −'

'Thought it was a feed bag for Rainbow,' he said. 'Found it floating in sea, but only paper inside. Sorry.'

He handed me the cash. Fives and tens, at least three hundred dollars.

I ran to the kerb and grabbed a taxi that was just letting out a family of cruise passengers. 'Clarisse,' I yelled. 'Come on. You're going to the airport. Annabeth, give her the Fleece.'

I'm not sure which of them looked more stunned as I took the Fleece letter jacket from Annabeth, tucked the cash into its pocket, and put it in Clarisse's arms.

Clarisse said, 'You'd let me −'

'It's your quest,' I said. 'We only have enough money for one flight. Besides, I can't travel by air. Zeus would blast me into a million pieces. That's what the prophecy meant: you'd fail without friends, meaning you'd need our help, but you'd have to fly home alone. You have to get the Fleece back safely.'

I could see her mind working − suspicious at first, wondering what trick I was playing, then finally deciding I meant what I said.

She jumped in the cab. 'You can count on me. I won't fail.'

'Not failing would be good.'

The cab peeled out in a cloud of exhaust. The Fleece was on its way.

'Percy,' Annabeth said, 'that was so −'

'Generous?' Grover offered.

'*Insane*,' Annabeth corrected. 'You're betting the lives of everybody at camp that Clarisse will get the Fleece safely back by tonight?'

'It's her quest,' I said. 'She deserves a chance.'

'Percy is nice,' Tyson said.

'Percy is *too* nice,' Annabeth grumbled, but I couldn't help thinking that maybe, just maybe, she was a little impressed. I'd surprised her, anyway. And that wasn't easy to do.

'Come on,' I told my friends. 'Let's find another way home.'

That's when I turned and found a sword's point at my throat.

'Hey, cuz,' said Luke. 'Welcome back to the States.'

His bear-man thugs appeared on either side of us. One grabbed Annabeth and Grover by their T-shirt collars. The other tried to grab Tyson, but Tyson knocked him into a pile of luggage and roared at Luke.

'Percy,' Luke said calmly, 'tell your giant to back down or I'll have Oreius bash your friends' heads together.'

Oreius grinned and raised Annabeth and Grover off the ground, kicking and screaming.

'What do you want, Luke?' I growled.

He smiled, the scar rippling on the side of his face.

He gestured towards the end of the dock, and I noticed what should've been obvious. The biggest boat in port was the *Princess Andromeda*.

'Why, Percy,' Luke said, 'I want to extend my hospitality, of course.'

The bear-man twins herded us aboard the *Princess Andromeda*. They threw us down on the aft deck in front of a swimming pool with sparkling fountains that sprayed into the air. A dozen of Luke's assorted goons — snake people,

Laistrygonians, demigods in battle armour – had gathered to watch us get some 'hospitality'.

'And so, the Fleece,' Luke mused. 'Where is it?'

He looked us over, prodding my shirt with the tip of his sword, poking Grover's jeans.

'Hey!' Grover yelled. 'That's real goat fur under there!'

'Sorry, old friend.' Luke smiled. 'Just give me the Fleece and I'll leave you to return to your, ah, little nature quest.'

'Blaa-ha-ha!' Grover protested. 'Some old friend!'

'Maybe you didn't hear me.' Luke's voice was dangerously calm. 'Where – is – the – Fleece?'

'Not here,' I said. I probably shouldn't have told him anything, but it felt good to throw the truth in his face. 'We sent it on ahead of us. You messed up.'

Luke's eyes narrowed. 'You're lying. You couldn't have . . .' His face reddened as a horrible possibility occurred to him. 'Clarisse?'

I nodded.

'You trusted . . . you gave . . .'

'Yeah.'

'Agrius!'

The bear-man flinched. 'Y-yes?'

'Get below and prepare my steed. Bring it to the deck. I need to fly to Miami Airport, fast!'

'But, boss –'

'Do it!' Luke screamed. 'Or I'll feed you to the drakon!'

The bear-man gulped and lumbered down the stairs. Luke paced in front of the swimming pool, cursing in Ancient Greek, gripping his sword so tight his knuckles turned white.

The rest of Luke's crew looked uneasy. Maybe they'd never seen their boss so unhinged before.

I started thinking . . . If I could use Luke's anger, get him to talk so everybody could hear how crazy his plans were . . .

I looked at the swimming pool, at the fountains spraying mist into the air, making a rainbow in the sunset. And suddenly I had an idea.

'You've been toying with us all along,' I said. 'You wanted us to bring you the Fleece and save you the trouble of getting it.'

Luke scowled. 'Of course, you idiot! And you've messed everything up!'

'Traitor!' I dug my last gold drachma out of my pocket and threw it at Luke. As I expected, he dodged it easily. The coin sailed into the spray of rainbow-coloured water.

I hoped my prayer would be accepted in silence. I thought with all my heart: *O goddess, accept my offering.*

'You tricked all of us!' I yelled at Luke. 'Even DIONYSUS at CAMP HALF-BLOOD!'

Behind Luke, the fountain began to shimmer, but I needed everyone's attention on me, so I uncapped Riptide.

Luke just sneered. 'This is no time for heroics, Percy. Drop your puny little sword, or I'll have you killed sooner rather than later.'

'Who poisoned Thalia's tree, Luke?'

'I did, of course,' he snarled. 'I already told you that. I used elder python venom, straight from the depths of Tartarus.'

'Chiron had nothing to do with it?'

'Ha! You know he would never do that. The old fool wouldn't have the guts.'

'You call it guts? Betraying your friends? Endangering the whole camp?'

Luke raised his sword. 'You don't understand the half of it. I was going to let you take the Fleece . . . once I was done with it.'

That made me hesitate. Why would he let me take the Fleece? He must've been lying. But I couldn't afford to lose his attention.

'You were going to heal Kronos,' I said.

'Yes! The Fleece's magic would've sped his mending process by tenfold. But you haven't stopped us, Percy. You've only slowed us down a little.'

'And so you poisoned the tree, you betrayed Thalia, you set us up — all to help Kronos destroy the gods.'

Luke gritted his teeth. 'You know that! Why do you keep asking me?'

'Because I want everybody in the audience to hear you.'

'*What* audience?'

Then his eyes narrowed. He looked behind him and his goons did the same. They gasped and stumbled back.

Above the pool, shimmering in the rainbow mist, was an Iris-message vision of Dionysus, Tantalus and the whole camp in the dining pavilion. They sat in stunned silence, watching us.

'Well,' said Dionysus drily, 'some unplanned dinner entertainment.'

'Mr D, you heard him,' I said. 'You all heard Luke. The poisoning of the tree wasn't Chiron's fault.'

Mr D sighed. 'I suppose not.'

'The Iris-message could be a trick,' Tantalus suggested, but his attention was mostly on his cheeseburger, which he was trying to corner with both hands.

'I fear not,' Mr D said, looking with distaste at Tantalus. 'It appears I shall have to reinstate Chiron as activities director. I suppose I do miss the old horse's pinochle games.'

Tantalus grabbed the cheeseburger. It didn't bolt away from him. He lifted it from the plate and stared at it in amazement, as if it were the largest diamond in the world. 'I got it!' he cackled.

'We are no longer in need of your services, Tantalus,' Mr D announced.

Tantalus looked stunned. 'What? But —'

'You may return to the Underworld. You are dismissed.'

'No! But — Noooooooooooo!'

As he dissolved into mist, his fingers clutched at the cheeseburger, trying to bring it to his mouth. But it was too late. He disappeared and the cheeseburger fell back onto its plate. The campers exploded into cheering.

Luke bellowed with rage. He slashed his sword through the fountain and the Iris-message dissolved, but the deed was done.

I was feeling pretty good about myself, until Luke turned and gave me a murderous look.

'Kronos was right, Percy. You're an unreliable weapon. You need to be replaced.'

I wasn't sure what he meant, but I didn't have time to think about it. One of his men blew a brass whistle, and the deck doors flew open. A dozen more warriors poured out, making a circle around us, the brass tips of their spears bristling.

Luke smiled at me. 'You'll never leave this boat alive.'

'One on one,' I challenged Luke. 'What are you afraid of?'

Luke curled his lip. The soldiers who were about to kill us hesitated, waiting for his order.

Before he could say anything, Agrius, the bear-man, burst onto the deck leading a flying horse. It was the first pure-black pegasus I'd ever seen, with wings like a giant raven. The pegasus mare bucked and whinnied. I could understand her thoughts. She was calling Agrius and Luke some names so bad Chiron would've washed her muzzle out with saddle soap.

'Sir!' Agrius called, dodging a pegasus hoof. 'Your steed is ready!'

Luke kept his eyes on me.

'I told you last summer, Percy,' he said. 'You can't bait me into a fight.'

'And you keep avoiding one,' I noticed. 'Scared your warriors will see you get whipped?'

Luke glanced at his men, and he saw I'd trapped him. If he backed down now, he would look weak. If he fought me, he'd lose valuable time chasing after Clarisse. For my part, the best I could hope for was to distract him, giving my friends a chance to escape. If anybody could think of a plan to get them out of there, Annabeth could. On the downside, I knew how good Luke was at sword-fighting.

'I'll kill you quickly,' he decided, and raised his weapon. Backbiter was a foot longer than my own sword. Its blade glinted with an evil grey-and-gold light where the human steel had been melded with celestial bronze. I could almost feel the blade fighting against itself, like two opposing magnets bound together. I didn't know how the blade had been made, but I sensed a tragedy. Someone had died in the process. Luke whistled to one of his men, who threw him a round leather-and-bronze shield.

He grinned at me wickedly.

'Luke,' Annabeth said, 'at least give him a shield.'

'Sorry, Annabeth,' he said. 'You bring your own equipment to this party.'

The shield was a problem. Fighting two-handed with just a sword gives you more power, but fighting one-handed with a shield gives you better defence and versatility. There are more moves, more options, more ways to kill. I thought back to Chiron, who'd told me to stay at camp no matter what, and learn to fight. Now I was going to pay for not listening to him.

Luke lunged and almost killed me on the first try. His sword went under my arm, slashing through my shirt and grazing my ribs.

I jumped back, then counter-attacked with Riptide, but Luke slammed my blade away with his shield.

'My, Percy,' Luke chided. 'You're out of practice.'

He came at me again with a swipe to the head. I parried, returned with a thrust. He sidestepped easily.

The cut on my ribs stung. My heart was racing. When Luke lunged again, I jumped backwards into the swimming pool and felt a surge of strength. I spun underwater, creating a funnel cloud, and blasted out of the deep end, straight at Luke's face.

The force of the water knocked him down, spluttering and blinded. But before I could strike, he rolled aside and was on his feet again.

I attacked and sliced off the edge of his shield, but that didn't even faze him. He dropped to a crouch and jabbed at my legs. Suddenly my thigh was on fire, with a pain so intense I collapsed. My jeans were ripped above the knee. I was hurt. I didn't know how badly. Luke hacked downwards and I rolled behind a deckchair. I tried to stand, but my leg wouldn't take the weight.

'Perrrrrcy!' Grover bleated.

I rolled again as Luke's sword slashed the deckchair in half, metal pipes and all.

I clawed towards the swimming pool, trying hard not to black out. I'd never make it. Luke knew it, too. He advanced slowly, smiling. The edge of his sword was tinged with red.

'One thing I want you to watch before you die, Percy.' He looked at the bear-man Oreius, who was still holding Annabeth and Grover by the necks. 'You can eat your dinner now, Oreius. Bon appétit.'

'He-he! He-he!' The bear-man lifted my friends and bared his teeth.

That's when all Hades broke loose.

Whish!

A red-feathered arrow sprouted from Oreius's mouth. With a surprised look on his hairy face, he crumpled to the deck.

'Brother!' Agrius wailed. He let the pegasus's reins go

slack just long enough for the black steed to kick him in the head and fly away free over Miami Bay.

For a split second, Luke's guards were too stunned to do anything except watch the bear twins' bodies dissolve into smoke.

Then there was a wild chorus of war cries and hooves thundering against metal. A dozen centaurs charged out of the main stairwell.

'Ponies!' Tyson cried with delight.

My mind had trouble processing everything I saw. Chiron was among the crowd, but his relatives were almost nothing like him. There were centaurs with black Arabian stallion bodies, others with gold palomino coats, others with orange-and-white spots like paint horses. Some wore brightly coloured T-shirts with Day-Glo letters that said PARTY PONIES: SOUTH FLORIDA CHAPTER. Some were armed with bows, some with baseball bats, some with paintball guns. One had his face painted like a Comanche warrior and was waving a large orange Styrofoam hand making a big Number 1. Another was bare-chested and painted entirely green. A third had googly-eye glasses with the eyeballs bouncing around on Slinky coils, and one of those baseball caps with soda-can-and-straw attachments on either side.

They exploded onto the deck with such ferocity and colour that for a moment even Luke was stunned. I couldn't tell whether they had come to celebrate or attack.

Apparently both. As Luke was raising his sword to rally his troops, a centaur shot a custom-made arrow with a leather boxing glove on the end. It smacked Luke in the face and sent him crashing into the swimming pool.

His warriors scattered. I couldn't blame them. Facing the hooves of a rearing stallion is scary enough, but when it's a centaur, armed with a bow and whooping it up in a soda-drinking hat, even the bravest warrior would retreat.

'Come get some!' yelled one of the party ponies.

They let loose with their paintball guns. A wave of blue and yellow exploded against Luke's warriors, blinding them and splattering them from head to toe. They tried to run, only to slip and fall.

Chiron galloped towards Annabeth and Grover, neatly plucked them off the deck, and deposited them on his back.

I tried to get up, but my wounded leg still felt like it was on fire.

Luke was crawling out of the pool.

'Attack, you fools!' he ordered his troops. Somewhere down below deck, a large alarm bell thrummed.

I knew any second we would be swamped by Luke's reinforcements. Already, his warriors were getting over their surprise, coming at the centaurs with swords and spears drawn.

Tyson slapped half a dozen of them aside, knocking them over the guardrail into Miami Bay. But more warriors were coming up the stairs.

'Withdraw, brethren!' Chiron said.

'You won't get away with this, horse man!' Luke shouted. He raised his sword, but got smacked in the face with another boxing glove arrow, and sat down hard in a deckchair.

A palomino centaur hoisted me onto his back. 'Dude, get your big friend!'

'Tyson!' I yelled. 'Come on!'

Tyson dropped the two warriors he was about to tie into a knot and jogged after us. He jumped on the centaur's back.

'Dude!' the centaur groaned, almost buckling under Tyson's weight. 'Do the words "low-carb diet" mean anything to you?'

Luke's warriors were organizing themselves into a phalanx. But by the time they were ready to advance, the centaurs had galloped to the edge of the deck and fearlessly jumped the guardrail, as if it were a steeplechase and not ten storeys above the ground. I was sure we were going to die. We plummeted towards the docks, but the centaurs hit the tarmac with hardly a jolt and galloped off, whooping and yelling taunts at the *Princess Andromeda* as we raced into the streets of downtown Miami.

I have no idea what the Miamians thought as we galloped by.

Streets and buildings began to blur as the centaurs picked up speed. It felt as if space were compacting – as if each centaur step took us miles and miles. In no time, we'd left the city behind. We raced through marshy fields of high grass and ponds and stunted trees.

Finally, we found ourselves in a trailer park at the edge of a lake. The trailers were all horse trailers, tricked out with televisions and mini-refrigerators and mosquito netting. We were in a centaur camp.

'Dude!' said a party pony as he unloaded his gear. 'Did you see that bear guy? He was all like, "Whoa, I have an arrow in my mouth!"'

The centaur with the googly-eye glasses laughed. 'That was awesome! Head slam!'

The two centaurs charged at each other full-force and knocked heads, then went staggering off in different directions with crazy grins on their faces.

Chiron sighed. He set Annabeth and Grover down on a picnic blanket next to me. 'I really wish my cousins wouldn't slam their heads together. They don't have the brain cells to spare.'

'Chiron,' I said, still stunned by the fact that he was here. 'You saved us.'

He gave me a dry smile. 'Well now, I couldn't very well let you die, especially since you've cleared my name.'

'But how did you know where we were?' Annabeth asked.

'Advanced planning, my dear. I figured you would wash up near Miami if you made it out of the Sea of Monsters alive. Almost everything strange washes up near Miami.'

'Gee, thanks,' Grover mumbled.

'No, no,' Chiron said. 'I didn't mean . . . Oh, never mind. I *am* glad to see you, my young satyr. The point is, I was able to eavesdrop on Percy's Iris-message and trace the signal. Iris and I have been friends for centuries. I asked her to alert me to any important communications in this area. It then took no effort to convince my cousins to ride to your aid. As you see, centaurs can travel quite fast when we wish to. Distance for us is not the same as distance for humans.'

I looked over at the campfire, where three party ponies were teaching Tyson to operate a paintball gun. I hoped they knew what they were getting into.

'So what now?' I asked Chiron. 'We just let Luke sail away? He's got Kronos aboard that ship. Or parts of him, anyway.'

Chiron knelt, carefully folding his front legs underneath him. He opened the medicine pouch on his belt and started to treat my wounds. 'I'm afraid, Percy, that today has been something of a draw. We didn't have the strength of numbers to take that ship. Luke was not organized enough to pursue us. Nobody won.'

'But we got the Fleece!' Annabeth said. 'Clarisse is on her way back to camp with it right now.'

Chiron nodded, though he still looked uneasy. 'You are all true heroes. And as soon as we get Percy fixed up, you must return to Half-Blood Hill. The centaurs shall carry you.'

'You're coming, too?' I asked.

'Oh yes, Percy. I'll be relieved to get home. My brethren here simply do not appreciate Dean Martin's music. Besides, I must have some words with Mr D. There's the rest of the summer to plan. So much training to do. And I want to see . . . I'm curious about the Fleece.'

I didn't know exactly what he meant, but it made me worried about what Luke had said: *I was going to let you take the Fleece . . . once I was done with it.*

Had he just been lying? I'd learned with Kronos there was usually a plan within a plan. The titan lord wasn't called the Crooked One for nothing. He had ways of getting people to do what he wanted without them ever realizing his true intentions.

Over by the campfire, Tyson let loose with his paintball gun. A blue projectile splattered against one of the centaurs, hurling him backwards into the lake. The centaur came up grinning, covered in swamp muck and blue paint, and gave Tyson two thumbs up.

'Annabeth,' Chiron said, 'perhaps you and Grover would go supervise Tyson and my cousins before they, ah, teach each other too many bad habits?'

Annabeth met his eyes. Some kind of understanding passed between them.

'Sure, Chiron,' Annabeth said. 'Come on, goat boy.'

'But I don't like paintball.'

'Yes, you do.' She hoisted Grover to his hooves and led him off towards the campfire.

Chiron finished bandaging my leg. 'Percy, I had a talk with Annabeth on the way here. A talk about the prophecy.'

Uh-oh, I thought.

'It wasn't her fault,' I said. 'I made her tell me.'

His eyes flickered with irritation. I was sure he was going to chew me out, but then his look turned to weariness. 'I suppose I could not expect to keep it secret forever.'

'So *am* I the one in the prophecy?'

Chiron tucked his bandages back into his pouch. 'I wish I knew, Percy. You're not yet sixteen. For now we must simply train you as best we can, and leave the future to the Fates.'

The Fates. I hadn't thought about those old ladies in a long time, but as soon as Chiron mentioned them, something clicked.

'That's what it meant,' I said.

Chiron frowned. 'That's what *what* meant?'

'Last summer. The omen from the Fates, when I saw

them snip somebody's life string. I thought it meant I was going to die right away, but it's worse than that. It's got something to do with your prophecy. The death they foretold – it's going to happen when I'm sixteen.'

Chiron's tail whisked nervously in the grass. 'My boy, you can't be sure of that. We don't even know if the prophecy is about you.'

'But there isn't any other half-blood child of the Big Three!'

'That we know of.'

'And Kronos is rising. He's going to destroy Mount Olympus!'

'He will try,' Chiron agreed. 'And Western Civilization along with it, if we don't stop him. But we *will* stop him. You will not be alone in that fight.'

I knew he was trying to make me feel better, but I remembered what Annabeth had told me. It would come down to one hero. One decision that would save or destroy the West. And I felt sure the Fates had been giving me some kind of warning about that. Something terrible was going to happen, either to me or to somebody I was close to.

'I'm just a *kid*, Chiron,' I said miserably. 'What good is one lousy hero against something like Kronos?'

Chiron managed a smile. '"What good is one lousy hero?" Joshua Lawrence Chamberlain said something like that to me once, just before he single-handedly changed the course of your Civil War.'

He pulled an arrow from his quiver and turned the razor-sharp tip so it glinted in the firelight. 'Celestial bronze, Percy. An immortal weapon. What would happen if you shot this at a human?'

'Nothing,' I said. 'It would pass right through.'

'That's right,' he said. 'Humans don't exist on the same level as the immortals. They can't even be hurt by our weapons. But you, Percy – you are part god, part human. You live in both worlds. You can be harmed by both, and you can affect both. *That's* what makes heroes so special. You carry the hopes of humanity into the realm of the eternal. Monsters never die. They are reborn from the chaos and barbarism that is always bubbling underneath civilization, the very stuff that makes Kronos stronger. They must be defeated again and again, kept at bay. Heroes embody that struggle. You fight the battles humanity must win, every generation, in order to stay human. Do you understand?'

'I . . . I don't know.'

'You must try, Percy. Because whether or not you are the child of the prophecy, Kronos thinks you might be. And, after today, he will finally despair of turning you to his side. That *is* the only reason he hasn't killed you yet, you know. As soon as he's sure he can't use you, he will destroy you.'

'You talk like you know him.'

Chiron pursed his lips. 'I *do* know him.'

I stared at him. I sometimes forgot just how old Chiron was. 'Is that why Mr D blamed you when the tree was poisoned? Why you said some people don't trust you?'

'Indeed.'

'But Chiron . . . I mean, come on! Why would they think you'd ever betray the camp for Kronos?'

Chiron's eyes were deep brown, full of thousands of years of sadness. 'Percy, remember your training. Remember your study of mythology. What is my connection to the titan lord?'

I tried to think, but I'd always got my mythology mixed up. Even now, when it was so real, so important to my own life, I had trouble keeping all the names and facts straight. I shook my head. 'You, uh, owe Kronos a favour or something? He spared your life?'

'Percy,' Chiron said, his voice impossibly soft. 'The titan Kronos is my father.'

19 THE CHARIOT RACE ENDS WITH A BANG

We arrived in Long Island just after Clarisse, thanks to the centaurs' travel powers. I rode on Chiron's back, but we didn't talk much, especially not about Kronos. I knew it had been difficult for Chiron to tell me. I didn't want to push him with more questions. I mean, I've met plenty of embarrassing parents, but Kronos, the evil titan lord who wanted to destroy Western Civilization? Not the kind of dad you invited to school for career day.

When we got to camp, the centaurs were anxious to meet Dionysus. They'd heard he threw some really wild parties, but they were disappointed. The wine god was in no mood to celebrate as the whole camp gathered at the top of Half-Blood Hill.

The camp had been through a hard two weeks. The arts and crafts cabin had burned to the ground from an attack by a *Draco Aionius* (which as near as I could figure was Latin for 'really-big-lizard-with-breath-that-blows-stuff-up'). The Big House's rooms were overflowing with wounded. The kids in the Apollo cabin, who were the best healers, had been working overtime performing first aid. Everybody looked weary and battered as we crowded around Thalia's tree.

The moment Clarisse draped the Golden Fleece over the lowest bough, the moonlight seemed to brighten, turning from grey to liquid silver. A cool breeze rustled in the branches and rippled through the grass, all the way into the valley. Everything came into sharper focus – the glow of the fireflies down in the woods, the smell of the strawberry fields, the sound of the waves on the beach.

Gradually, the needles on the pine tree started turning from brown to green.

Everybody cheered. It was happening slowly, but there could be no doubt – the Fleece's magic was seeping into the tree, filling it with new power and expelling the poison.

Chiron ordered a twenty-four/seven guard duty on the hilltop, at least until he could find an appropriate monster to protect the Fleece. He said he'd place an ad in *Olympus Weekly* right away.

In the meantime, Clarisse was carried on her cabin mates' shoulders down to the amphitheatre, where she was honoured with a laurel wreath and a lot of celebrating around the campfire.

Nobody gave Annabeth or me a second look. It was as if we'd never left. In a way, I guess that was the best thank-you anyone could give us, because if they admitted we'd snuck out of camp to do the quest, they'd have to expel us. And, really, I didn't want any more attention. It felt good to be just one of the campers for once.

Later that night, as we were roasting marshmallows and listening to the Stoll brothers tell us a ghost story about an evil king who was eaten alive by demonic breakfast pastries, Clarisse shoved me from behind and whispered in my ear, 'Just because you were cool one time, Jackson, don't think you're off the hook with Ares. I'm still waiting for the right opportunity to pulverize you.'

I gave her a grudging smile.

'What?' she demanded.

'Nothing,' I said. 'Just good to be home.'

The next morning, after the party ponies headed back to Florida, Chiron made a surprise announcement: the chariot races would go ahead as scheduled. We'd all figured they were history now that Tantalus was gone, but completing them did feel like the right thing to do, especially now that Chiron was back and the camp was safe.

Tyson wasn't too keen on the idea of getting back in a chariot after our first experience, but he was happy to let me team up with Annabeth. I would drive, Annabeth would defend, and Tyson would act as our pit crew. While I worked with the horses, Tyson fixed up Athena's chariot and added a whole bunch of special modifications.

We spent the next two days training like crazy. Annabeth and I agreed that if we won, the prize of no chores for the rest of the month would be split between our two cabins. Since Athena had more campers, they would get most of the time off, which was fine by me. I didn't care about the prize. I just wanted to win.

The night before the race, I stayed late at the stables. I was talking to our horses, giving them one final brushing, when somebody right behind me said, 'Fine animals, horses. Wish I'd thought of them.'

A middle-aged guy in a postal carrier outfit was leaning against the stable door. He was slim, with curly black hair under his white pith helmet, and he had a mailbag slung over his shoulder.

'Hermes?' I stammered.

'Hello, Percy. Didn't recognize me without my jogging clothes?'

'Uh . . .' I wasn't sure whether I was supposed to kneel or buy stamps from him or what. Then it occurred to me why he must be here. 'Oh, listen, Lord Hermes, about Luke . . .'

The god arched his eyebrows.

'Uh, we saw him, all right,' I said, 'but –'

'You weren't able to talk sense into him?'

'Well, we kind of tried to kill each other in a duel to the death.'

'I see. You tried the diplomatic approach.'

'I'm really sorry. I mean, you gave us those awesome gifts and everything. And I know you wanted Luke to come back. But . . . he's turned bad. *Really* bad. He said he feels like you abandoned him.'

I waited for Hermes to get angry. I figured he'd turn me into a hamster or something, and I did *not* want to spend any more time as a rodent.

Instead, he just sighed. 'Do you ever feel your father abandoned *you*, Percy?'

Oh, man.

I wanted to say, 'Only a few hundred times a day.' I hadn't spoken to Poseidon since last summer. I'd never even been to his underwater palace. And then there was the whole thing with Tyson – no warning, no explanation. Just *boom*, you have a brother. You'd think that deserved a little heads-up phone call or something.

The more I thought about it, the angrier I got. I realized I *did* want recognition for the quest I'd completed, but not from the other campers. I wanted my dad to say something. To notice me.

Hermes readjusted the mailbag on his shoulder. 'Percy, the hardest part about being a god is that you must often act indirectly, especially when it comes to your own children. If we were to intervene every time our children had a problem . . . well, that would only create more problems and more resentment. But I believe if you give it some thought, you will see that Poseidon *has* been paying attention to you. He has answered your prayers. I can only hope that some day, Luke may realize the same about me. Whether you feel like you succeeded or not, you reminded Luke who he was. You spoke to him.'

'I tried to kill him.'

Hermes shrugged. 'Families are messy. Immortal families are eternally messy. Sometimes the best we can do is to remind each other that we're related, for better or worse . . . and try to keep the maiming and killing to a minimum.'

It didn't sound like much of a recipe for the perfect family. Then again, as I thought about my quest, I realized maybe Hermes was right. Poseidon had sent the hippocampi to help us. He'd given me powers over the sea that I'd never known about before. And there was Tyson. Had Poseidon brought us together on purpose? How many times had Tyson saved my life this summer?

In the distance, the conch horn sounded, signalling curfew.

'You should get to bed,' Hermes said. 'I've helped you get into quite enough trouble this summer already. I really only came to make this delivery.'

'A delivery?'

'I *am* the messenger of the gods, Percy.' He took an electronic signature pad from his mailbag and handed it to me. 'Sign there, please.'

I picked up the stylus before realizing it was entwined with a pair of tiny green snakes. 'Ah!' I dropped the pad.

Ouch, said George.

Really, Percy, Martha scolded. *Would you want to be dropped on the floor of a horse stable?*

'Oh, uh, sorry.' I didn't much like touching snakes, but I picked up the pad and the stylus again. Martha and George wriggled under my fingers, forming a kind of pencil grip like the ones my special ed teacher made me use in second grade.

Did you bring me a rat? George asked.

'No . . .' I said. 'Uh, we didn't find any.'

What about a guinea pig?

George! Martha chided. *Don't tease the boy.*

I signed my name and gave the pad back to Hermes.

In exchange, he handed me a sea-blue envelope.

My fingers trembled. Even before I opened it, I could tell it was from my father. I could sense his power in the cool blue paper, as if the envelope itself had been folded out of an ocean wave.

'Good luck tomorrow,' Hermes said. 'Fine team of horses you have there, though you'll excuse me if I root for the Hermes cabin.'

And don't be too discouraged when you read it, dear, Martha told me. *He* does *have your interests at heart.*

'What do you mean?' I asked.

Don't mind her, George said. *And next time, remember, snakes work for tips.*

'Enough, you two,' Hermes said. 'Goodbye, Percy. For now.'

Small white wings sprouted from his pith helmet. He began to glow, and I knew enough about the gods to avert my eyes before he revealed his true divine form. With a brilliant white flash he was gone, and I was alone with the horses.

I stared at the blue envelope in my hands. It was addressed in strong but elegant handwriting that I'd seen once before, on a package Poseidon had sent me last summer.

Percy Jackson
c/o Camp Half-Blood
Farm Road 3.141
Long Island, New York 11954

An actual letter from my father. Maybe he would tell me I'd done a good job getting the Fleece. He'd explain about Tyson, or apologize for not talking to me sooner. There were so many things that I wanted that letter to say.

I opened the envelope and unfolded the paper.

Two simple words were printed in the middle of the page:

Brace yourself.

The next morning, everybody was buzzing about the chariot race, though they kept glancing nervously towards the sky like they expected to see Stymphalian birds gathering. None did. It was a beautiful summer day with blue sky and plenty of sunshine. The camp had started to look the way it should look: the meadows were green and lush; the white columns gleamed on the Greek buildings; dryads played happily in the woods.

And I was miserable. I'd been lying awake all night, thinking about Poseidon's warning.

Brace yourself.

I mean, he goes to the trouble of writing a letter, and he writes two words?

Martha the snake had told me not to feel disappointed. Maybe Poseidon had a reason for being so vague. Maybe he didn't know exactly what he was warning me about, but he sensed something big was about to happen – something that could completely knock me off my feet unless I was prepared. It was hard, but I tried to turn my thoughts to the race.

As Annabeth and I drove onto the track, I couldn't help admiring the work Tyson had done on the Athena chariot. The carriage gleamed with bronze reinforcements. The wheels were realigned with magical suspension so we glided along with hardly a bump. The rigging for the horses was so perfectly balanced that the team turned at the slightest tug of the reins.

Tyson had also made us two javelins, each with three buttons on the shaft. The first button primed the javelin to explode on impact, releasing razor wire that would tangle and shred an opponent's wheels. The second button produced a blunt (but still very painful) bronze spearhead designed to knock a driver out of his carriage. The third button brought up a grappling hook that could be used to lock on to an enemy's chariot or push it away.

I figured we were in pretty good shape for the race, but Tyson still warned me to be careful. The other chariot teams had plenty of tricks up their togas.

'Here,' he said, just before the race began.

He handed me a wristwatch. There wasn't anything special about it – just a white-and-silver clock face, a black leather strap – but as soon as I saw it I realized that this was what I'd seen him tinkering on all summer.

I didn't usually like to wear watches. Who cared what time it was? But I couldn't say no to Tyson.

'Thanks, man.' I put it on and found it was surprisingly light and comfortable. I could hardly tell I was wearing it.

'Didn't finish in time for the trip,' Tyson mumbled. 'Sorry, sorry.'

'Hey, man. No big deal.'

'If you need protection in race,' he advised, 'hit the button.'

'Ah, okay.' I didn't see how keeping time was going to help a whole lot, but I was touched that Tyson was concerned. I promised him I'd remember the watch. 'And, hey, um, Tyson . . .'

He looked at me.

'I wanted to say, well . . .' I tried to figure out how to apologize for getting embarrassed about him before the quest, for telling everyone he wasn't my real brother. It wasn't easy to find the words.

'I know what you will tell me,' Tyson said, looking ashamed. 'Poseidon did care for me after all.'

'Uh, well –'

'He sent you to help me. Just what I asked for.'

I blinked. 'You asked Poseidon for . . . me?'

'For a friend,' Tyson said, twisting his shirt in his hands. 'Young Cyclopes grow up alone on the streets, learn to make things out of scraps. Learn to survive.'

'But that's so cruel!'

He shook his head earnestly. 'Makes us appreciate blessings, not be greedy and mean and fat like Polyphemus. But I got scared. Monsters chased me so much, clawed me sometimes –'

'The scars on your back?'

A tear welled in his eye. 'Sphinx on Seventy-second Street. Big bully. I prayed to Daddy for help. Soon the people at Meriwether found me. Met you. Biggest blessing ever. Sorry I said Poseidon was mean. He sent me a brother.'

I stared at the watch that Tyson had made me.

'Percy!' Annabeth called. 'Come on!'

Chiron was at the starting line, ready to blow the conch.

'Tyson . . .' I said.

'Go,' Tyson said. 'You will win!'

'I – yeah, okay, big guy. We'll win this one for you.' I climbed on board the chariot and got into position just as Chiron blew the starting signal.

The horses knew what to do. We shot down the track so fast I would've fallen out if my arms hadn't been wrapped in the leather reins. Annabeth held on tight to the rail. The wheels glided beautifully. We took the first turn a full chariot-length ahead of Clarisse, who was busy trying to fight off a javelin attack from the Stoll brothers in the Hermes chariot.

'We've got 'em!' I yelled, but I spoke too soon.

'Incoming!' Annabeth yelled. She threw her first javelin

in grappling-hook mode, knocking away a lead-weighted net that would have entangled us both. Apollo's chariot had come up on our flank. Before Annabeth could rearm herself, the Apollo warrior threw a javelin into our right wheel. The javelin shattered, but not before snapping some of our spokes. Our chariot lurched and wobbled. I was sure the wheel would collapse altogether, but we somehow kept going.

I urged the horses to keep up the speed. We were now neck and neck with Apollo. Hephaestus was coming up close behind. Ares and Hermes were falling behind, riding side by side as Clarisse went sword-on-javelin with Connor Stoll.

If we took one more hit to our wheel, I knew we would capsize.

'You're mine!' the driver from Apollo yelled. He was a first-year camper. I didn't remember his name, but he sure was confident.

'Yeah, right!' Annabeth yelled back.

She picked up her second javelin – a real risk considering we still had one full lap to go – and threw it at the Apollo driver.

Her aim was perfect. The javelin grew a heavy spear point just as it caught the driver in the chest, knocking him against his teammate and sending them both toppling out of their chariot in a backwards somersault. The horses felt the reins go slack and went crazy, riding straight for the crowd. Campers scrambled for cover as the horses leaped the corner of the stands and the golden chariot flipped over. The horses galloped back towards their stable, dragging the upside-down chariot behind them.

I held our own chariot together through the second turn, despite the groaning of the right wheel. We passed the starting line and thundered into our final lap.

The axle creaked and moaned. The wobbling wheel was making us lose speed, even though the horses were responding to my every command, running like a well-oiled machine.

The Hephaestus team was still gaining.

Beckendorf grinned as he pressed a button on his command console. Steel cables shot out of the front of his mechanical horses, wrapping around our back rail. Our chariot shuddered as Beckendorf's winch system started working – pulling us backwards while Beckendorf pulled himself forward.

Annabeth cursed and drew her knife. She hacked at the cables but they were too thick.

'Can't cut them!' she yelled.

The Hephaestus chariot was now dangerously close, their horses about to trample us underfoot.

'Switch with me!' I told Annabeth. 'Take the reins!'

'But –'

'Trust me!'

She pulled herself to the front and grabbed the reins. I turned, trying hard to keep my footing, and uncapped Riptide.

I slashed down and the cables snapped like kite string. We lurched forward, but Beckendorf's driver just swung his chariot to our left and pulled up next to us. Beckendorf drew his sword. He slashed at Annabeth and I parried the blade away.

We were coming up on the last turn. We'd never make

it. I needed to disable the Hephaestus chariot and get it out of the way, but I had to protect Annabeth, too. Just because Beckendorf was a nice guy didn't mean he wouldn't send us both to the infirmary if we let our guard down.

We were neck and neck now, Clarisse coming up from behind, making up for lost time.

'See ya, Percy!' Beckendorf yelled. 'Here's a little parting gift!'

He threw a leather pouch into our chariot. It stuck to the floor immediately and began billowing green smoke.

'Greek fire!' Annabeth yelled.

I cursed. I'd heard stories about what Greek fire could do. I figured we had maybe ten seconds before it exploded.

'Get rid of it!' Annabeth shouted, but I couldn't. Hephaestus's chariot was still alongside, waiting until the last second to make sure their little present blew up. Beckendorf was keeping me busy with his sword. If I let my guard down long enough to deal with the Greek fire, Annabeth would get sliced and we'd crash anyway. I tried to kick the leather pouch away with my foot, but I couldn't. It was stuck fast.

Then I remembered the watch.

I didn't know how it could help, but I managed to punch the stopwatch button. Instantly, the watch changed. It expanded, the metal rim spiralling outwards like an old-fashioned camera shutter, a leather strap wrapping around my forearm until I was holding a round war shield a metre wide, the inside soft leather, the outside polished bronze engraved with designs I didn't have time to examine.

All I knew: Tyson had come through. I raised the shield

and Beckendorf's sword clanged against it. His blade shattered.

'What?' he shouted. 'How –'

He didn't have time to say more because I knocked him in the chest with my new shield and sent him flying out of his chariot, tumbling in the dirt.

I was about to use Riptide to slash at the driver when Annabeth yelled, 'Percy!'

The Greek fire was shooting sparks. I shoved the tip of my sword under the leather pouch and flipped it up like a spatula. The firebomb dislodged and flew into the Hephaestus chariot at the driver's feet. He yelped.

In a split second the driver made the right choice: he dived out of the chariot, which careened away and exploded in green flames. The metal horses seemed to short-circuit. They turned and dragged the burning wreckage back towards Clarisse and the Stoll brothers, who had to swerve to avoid it.

Annabeth pulled the reins for the last turn. I held on, sure we would capsize, but somehow she brought us through and spurred the horses across the finish line. The crowd roared.

Once the chariot stopped, our friends mobbed us. They started chanting our names, but Annabeth yelled over the noise, 'Hold up! Listen! It wasn't just us!'

The crowd didn't want to be quiet, but Annabeth made herself heard: 'We couldn't have done it without somebody else! We couldn't have won this race or got the Fleece or saved Grover or anything! We owe our lives to Tyson, Percy's . . .'

'Brother!' I said, loud enough for everybody to hear. 'Tyson, my baby brother.'

Tyson blushed. The crowd cheered. Annabeth planted a kiss on my cheek. The roaring got a lot louder after that. The entire Athena cabin lifted me and Annabeth and Tyson onto their shoulders and carried us towards the winner's platform, where Chiron was waiting to bestow the laurel wreaths.

THE FLEECE WORKS ITS MAGIC TOO WELL

That afternoon was one of the happiest I'd ever spent at camp, which maybe goes to show, you never know when your world is about to be rocked to pieces.

Grover announced that he'd be able to spend the rest of the summer with us before resuming his quest for Pan. His bosses at the Council of Cloven Elders were so impressed that he hadn't got himself killed and had cleared the way for future searchers, that they granted him a two-month furlough and a new set of reed pipes. The only bad news: Grover insisted on playing those pipes all afternoon long, and his musical skills hadn't improved much. He played 'YMCA', and the strawberry plants started going crazy, wrapping around our feet like they were trying to strangle us. I guess I couldn't blame them.

Grover told me he could dissolve the empathy link between us, now that we were face to face, but I told him I'd just as soon keep it if that was okay with him. He put down his reed pipes and stared at me. 'But, if I get in trouble again, you'll be in danger, Percy! You could die!'

'If you get in trouble again, I want to know about it. And I'll come help you again, G-man. I wouldn't have it any other way.'

In the end he agreed not to break the link. He went

back to playing 'YMCA' for the strawberry plants. I didn't need an empathy link with the plants to know how they felt about it.

Later on during archery class, Chiron pulled me aside and told me he'd fixed my problems with Meriwether Prep. The school no longer blamed me for destroying their gymnasium. The police were no longer looking for me.

'How did you manage that?' I asked.

Chiron's eyes twinkled. 'I merely suggested that the mortals had seen something different on that day – a furnace explosion that was not your fault.'

'You just said that and they bought it?'

'I manipulated the Mist. Some day, when you're ready, I'll show you how it's done.'

'You mean, I can go back to Meriwether next year?'

Chiron raised his eyebrows. 'Oh, no, they've still expelled you. Your headmaster, Mr Bonsai, said you had – how did he put it? – un-groovy karma that disrupted the school's educational aura. But you're not in any legal trouble, which was a relief to your mother. Oh, and speaking of your mother . . .'

He unclipped his cell phone from his quiver and handed it to me. 'It's high time you called her.'

The worst part was the beginning – the 'Percy-Jackson-what-were-you-thinking-do-you-have-any-idea-how-worried-I-was-sneaking-off-to-camp-without-permission-going-on-dangerous-quests-and-scaring-me-half-to-death' part.

But finally she paused to catch her breath. 'Oh, I'm just glad you're safe!'

That's the great thing about my mom. She's no good at staying angry. She tries, but it just isn't in her nature.

'I'm sorry, Mom,' I told her. 'I won't scare you again.'

'Don't promise me that, Percy. You know very well it will only get worse.' She tried to sound casual about it, but I could tell she was pretty shaken up.

I wanted to say something to make her feel better, but I knew she was right. Being a half-blood, I would always be doing things that scared her. And, as I got older, the dangers would just get greater.

'I could come home for a while,' I offered.

'No, no. Stay at camp. Train. Do what you need to do. But you *will* come home for the next school year?'

'Yeah, of course. Uh, if there's any school that will take me.'

'Oh, we'll find something, dear,' my mother sighed. 'Some place where they don't know us yet.'

As for Tyson, the campers treated him like a hero. I would've been happy to have him as my cabin mate forever, but that evening, as we were sitting on a sand dune overlooking the Long Island Sound, he made an announcement that completely took me by surprise.

'Dream came from Daddy last night,' he said. 'He wants me to visit.'

I wondered if he was kidding, but Tyson really didn't know how to kid. 'Poseidon sent you a dream message?'

Tyson nodded. 'Wants me to go underwater for the rest of the summer. Learn to work at Cyclopes' forges. He called it an inter — an intern —'

'An internship?'

'Yes.'

I let that sink in. I'll admit, I felt a little jealous. Poseidon had never invited *me* underwater. But then I thought, Tyson was *going*? Just like that?

'When would you leave?' I asked.

'Now.'

'Now. Like . . . *now* now?'

'Now.'

I stared out at the waves in the Long Island Sound. The water was glistening red in the sunset.

'I'm happy for you, big guy,' I managed. 'Seriously.'

'Hard to leave my new brother,' he said with a tremble in his voice. 'But I want to make things. Weapons for the camp. You will need them.'

Unfortunately, I knew he was right. The Fleece hadn't solved all the camp's problems. Luke was still out there, gathering an army aboard the *Princess Andromeda*. Kronos was still re-forming in his golden coffin. Eventually, we would have to fight them.

'You'll make the best weapons ever,' I told Tyson. I held up my watch proudly. 'I bet they'll tell good time, too.'

Tyson sniffled. 'Brothers help each other.'

'You're my brother,' I said. 'No doubt about it.'

He patted me on the back so hard he almost knocked me down the sand dune. Then he wiped a tear from his cheek and stood to go. 'Use the shield well.'

'I will, big guy.'

'Save your life some day.'

The way he said it, so matter-of-fact, I wondered if that Cyclops eye of his could see into the future.

He headed down to the beach and whistled. Rainbow, the hippocampus, burst out of the waves. I watched the two of them ride off together into the realm of Poseidon.

Once they were gone, I looked down at my new wristwatch. I pressed the button and the shield spiralled out to full size. Hammered into the bronze were pictures in Ancient Greek style, scenes from our adventures this summer. There was Annabeth slaying a Laistrygonian dodgeball player, me fighting the bronze bulls on Half-Blood Hill, Tyson riding Rainbow towards the *Princess Andromeda*, the CSS *Birmingham* blasting its cannons at Charybdis. I ran my hand across a picture of Tyson battling the Hydra as he held aloft a box of Monster Doughnuts.

I couldn't help feeling sad. I knew Tyson would have an awesome time under the ocean. But I'd miss everything about him – his fascination with horses, the way he could fix chariots or crumple metal with his bare hands, or tie bad guys into knots. I'd even miss him snoring like an earthquake in the next bunk all night.

'Hey, Percy.'

I turned.

Annabeth and Grover were standing at the top of the sand dune. I guess maybe I had some sand in my eyes, because I was blinking a lot.

'Tyson . . .' I told them. 'He had to . . .'

'We know,' Annabeth said softly. 'Chiron told us.'

'Cyclopes' forges.' Grover shuddered. 'I hear the cafeteria food there is terrible! Like, no enchiladas *at all*.'

Annabeth held out her hand. 'Come on, Seaweed Brain. Time for dinner.'

We walked back towards the dining pavilion together, just the three of us, like old times.

A storm raged that night, but it parted around Camp Half-Blood as storms usually did. Lightning flashed against the horizon, waves pounded the shore, but not a drop fell in our valley. We were protected again thanks to the Fleece, sealed inside our magical borders.

Still, my dreams were restless. I heard Kronos taunting me from the depths of Tartarus: *Polyphemus sits blindly in his cave, young hero, believing he has won a great victory. Are you any less deluded?* The titan's cold laughter filled the darkness.

Then my dream changed. I was following Tyson to the bottom of the sea, into the court of Poseidon. It was a radiant hall filled with blue light, the floor cobbled with pearls. And there, on a throne of coral, sat my father, dressed like a simple fisherman in khaki shorts and a sun-bleached T-shirt. I looked up into his tanned, weathered face, his deep green eyes, and he spoke two words: *Brace yourself.*

I woke with a start.

There was a banging on the door. Grover flew inside without waiting for permission. 'Percy!' he stammered. 'Annabeth . . . on the hill . . . she . . .'

The look in his eyes told me something was terribly wrong. Annabeth had been on guard duty that night, protecting the Fleece. If something had happened –

I ripped off the covers, my blood like ice water in my veins. I threw on some clothes while Grover tried to make a complete sentence, but he was too stunned, too out of breath. 'She's lying there . . . just lying there . . .'

I ran outside and raced across the central yard, Grover

right behind me. Dawn was just breaking, but the whole camp seemed to be stirring. Word was spreading. Something huge had happened. A few campers were already making their way towards the hill, satyrs and nymphs and heroes in a weird mix of armour and pyjamas.

I heard the clop of horse hooves, and Chiron galloped up behind us, looking grim.

'Is it true?' he asked Grover.

Grover could only nod, his expression dazed.

I tried to ask what was going on, but Chiron grabbed me by the arm and effortlessly lifted me onto his back. Together we thundered up Half-Blood Hill, where a small crowd had started to gather.

I expected to see the Fleece missing from the pine tree, but it was still there, glittering in the first light of dawn. The storm had broken and the sky was blood-red.

'Curse the Titan Lord,' Chiron said. 'He's tricked us again, given himself another chance to control the prophecy.'

'What do you mean?' I asked.

'The Fleece,' he said. 'The Fleece did its work too well.'

We galloped forward, everyone moving out of our way. There at the base of the tree, a girl was lying unconscious. Another girl in Greek armour was kneeling next to her.

Blood roared in my ears. I couldn't think straight. Annabeth had been attacked? But why was the Fleece still there?

The tree itself looked perfectly fine, whole and healthy, suffused with the essence of the Golden Fleece.

'It healed the tree,' Chiron said, his voice ragged. 'And poison was not the only thing it purged.'

Then I realized Annabeth wasn't the one lying on the

ground. She was the one in armour, kneeling next to the unconscious girl. When Annabeth saw us, she ran to Chiron. 'It . . . she . . . just suddenly there . . .'

Her eyes were streaming with tears, but I still didn't understand. I was too freaked out to make sense of it all. I leaped off Chiron's back and ran towards the unconscious girl. Chiron said, 'Percy, wait!'

I knelt by her side. She had short black hair and freckles across her nose. She was built like a long-distance runner, lithe and strong, and she wore clothes that were somewhere between punk and Goth – a black T-shirt, black tattered jeans, and a leather jacket with badges from a bunch of bands I'd never heard of.

She wasn't a camper. I didn't recognize her from any of the cabins. And yet I had the strangest feeling I'd seen her before . . .

'It's true,' Grover said, panting from his run up the hill. 'I can't believe . . .'

Nobody else came close to the girl.

I put my hand on her forehead. Her skin was cold, but my fingertips tingled as if they were burning.

'She needs nectar and ambrosia,' I said. She was clearly a half-blood, whether she was a camper or not. I could sense that just from one touch. I didn't understand why everyone was acting so scared.

I took her by the shoulders and lifted her into a sitting position, resting her head on my shoulder.

'Come on!' I yelled to the others. 'What's wrong with you people? Let's get her to the Big House.'

No one moved, not even Chiron. They were all too stunned.

Then the girl took a shaky breath. She coughed and opened her eyes.

Her irises were startlingly blue – electric blue.

The girl stared at me in bewilderment, shivering and wild-eyed. 'Who –'

'I'm Percy,' I said. 'You're safe now.'

'Strangest dream . . .'

'It's okay.'

'Dying.'

'No,' I assured her. 'You're okay. What's your name?'

That's when I knew. Even before she said it.

The girl's blue eyes stared into mine, and I understood what the Golden Fleece quest had been about. The poisoning of the tree. Everything. Kronos had done it to bring another chess piece into play – *another chance to control the prophecy*.

Even Chiron, Annabeth and Grover, who should've been celebrating this moment, were too shocked, thinking about what it might mean for the future. And I was holding someone who was destined to be my best friend, or possibly my worst enemy.

'I am Thalia,' the girl said. 'Daughter of Zeus.'

CHIRON'S GUIDE

TO WHO'S WHO IN
GREEK
MYTHOLOGY

ARES
(Air'-eez)
GOD OF WAR

Distinguishing Features:
Biker leathers, Harley Davidson, sunglasses and a stinking attitude.

Now:
Can be found riding his Harley around the suburbs of LA. One of those gods who could pick a fight in an empty room.

Then:
Back in the day, this son of Zeus and Hera used to be inseparable from his shield and helmet. Fought on the side of the Trojans during the war of Troy, but, frankly, has been involved in every minor skirmish since Goldilocks told the three bears that their beds were a little uncomfy.

ZEUS
(Zoos)
GOD OF THE SKY

Distinguishing Features:
Pin-striped suit, neatly trimmed grey beard, stormy eyes and a very large, dangerous lightning bolt.

Now:
On stormy days, he can be found brooding in his throne room in Mount Olympus, over the Empire State Building in New York. Sometimes he travels the world in disguise, so be nice to everyone! You never know when the next person you meet might be packing the master bolt.

Then:
In the old days, Zeus ruled over his unruly family of Olympians while they bickered and fought and got jealous of each other. Not much different to today, really. Zeus always had an eye for beautiful women, which often got him in trouble with his wife, Hera. A less-than-stellar father figure, Zeus once tossed Hera's son Hephaestus off the top of Mount Olympus because the baby was too ugly!

POSEIDON
(Po-sy'-dun)
GOD OF THE SEA

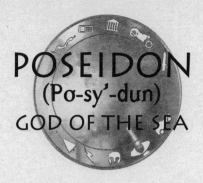

Distinguishing Features:
Hawaiian shirt, shorts, flip-flops and a three-pointed trident.

Now:
Poseidon walks the beaches of Florida, occasionally stopping to chat with fishermen or take pictures for tourists. If he's in a bad mood, he stirs up a hurricane.

Then:
Poseidon was always a moody guy. On his good days, he did cool stuff like create horses out of sea foam. On his bad days, he caused minor problems like destroying cities with earthquakes or sinking entire fleets of ships. But, hey, a god has the right to throw a temper tantrum, doesn't he?

HADES
(Hay'-deez)
GOD OF THE UNDERWORLD

Distinguishing Features:
Evil smile, helm of darkness (which makes him invisible, so you can't see the evil smile), black robes sewn from the souls of the damned. He sits on a throne of bones.

Now:
Hades rarely leaves his palace in the Underworld, probably because of traffic congestion on the Fields of Asphodel freeway. He oversees a booming population among the dead and has all sorts of employment trouble with his ghouls and spectres. This keeps him in a foul mood most of the time.

Then:
Hades is best known for the romantic way he won his wife, Persephone. He kidnapped her. Really, though, how would *you* like to marry someone who lives in a dark cave filled with zombies all year round?

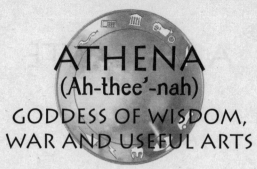

ATHENA
(Ah-thee'-nah)
GODDESS OF WISDOM,
WAR AND USEFUL ARTS

Distinguishing Features:
Dark hair, striking grey eyes, casual yet fashionable clothes, (except when she's going into battle; then it's full body armour). Athena is always accompanied by at least one owl, her sacred (and, fortunately, housebroken) animal.

Now:
You're likely to spot Athena at an American university, sitting in on lectures about military history or technology. She favours people who invent useful things, and will sometimes appear to reward them with magical gifts or bits of useful advice (like next week's lottery numbers). So start working on that revolutionary new bread slicer!

Then:
Athena was one of the most active goddesses in human affairs. She helped out Odysseus, sponsored the entire city of Athens, and made sure the Greeks won the Trojan War. On the downside, she's proud and has a big temper. Just ask Arachne, who got turned into a spider for daring to compare her weaving skills to Athena's. So whatever you do, DO NOT claim that you fix toilets better than Athena. There's no telling what she'll turn you into.

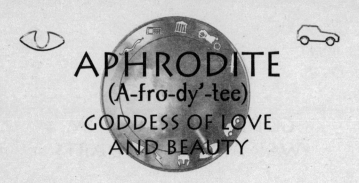

APHRODITE
(A-fro-dy'-tee)
GODDESS OF LOVE
AND BEAUTY

Distinguishing Features:
She's really, really pretty.

Now:
She's more beautiful than Angelina Jolie.

Then:
She's more beautiful than Helen of Troy.

HERMES
(Her'-meez)
GOD OF THE ROADWAYS, TRAVELLERS, MERCHANTS AND THIEVES

Distinguishing Features:
Jogger's clothes and winged athletic shoes, a mobile phone that turns into the caduceus, his symbol of power – a winged staff with two snakes, George and Martha, entwined round it.

Now:
Hermes is a hard person to find, because he's always on the run. When he's not delivering messages for the gods, he's running a telecommunications company, an express delivery service and every other type of business you can imagine that involves travel. Did you have a question about his activities as god of thieves? Leave a message. He'll get back to you in a few millennia.

Then:
Hermes got started young as a troublemaker. When he was one day old, he sneaked out of his crib and stole some cattle from his brother, Apollo. Apollo probably would've blasted the young tyke to bits, but fortunately Hermes appeased him with a new musical instrument he created called the lyre. Apollo liked it so much he forgot all about the cows. The lyre made Apollo very popular with the ladies, which was more than he could say about the cattle.

DIONYSUS
(Dy-oh-ny'-sus)
GOD OF WINE

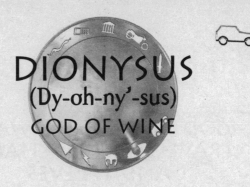

Distinguishing Features:
Leopard-skin shirt, walking shorts, purple socks and sandals, the general pasty demeanour of someone who has been up partying far too late.

Now:
Dionysus has been sentenced to one hundred years of 'rehab' as director of Camp Half-Blood. The only thing the god of wine can drink these days is Diet Coke, which doesn't make him happy. He can usually be found playing pinochle with a group of terrified satyrs on the front porch of the Big House. If you want to join the game, be prepared to bet large.

Then:
Dionysus invented wine, which so impressed his father Zeus that he promoted Dionysus to god. The guy who invented prune juice, by contrast, got sentenced to the Fields of Punishment. Dionysus mostly spent his time partying it up in Ancient Greece, but once a crew of sailors tried to kill him, thinking the god was too incapacitated to fight back. Dionysus turned them into dolphins and sent them over the side. The moral of this story: do not mess with a god, even a drunk one.

POLYPHEMUS
(Poly-fee'-mus)
ELDER CYCLOPS

Distinguishing Features:
One large eye in the centre of his head, sheep breath, fashionable caveman outfit, bad dental hygiene.

Now:
The giant Polyphemus hangs out in a cave on a deserted island, where he herds sheep and enjoys simple pastoral pleasures, like eating the occasional Greek hero who happens to sail by.

Then:
The giant Polyphemus hung out in a cave on a deserted island, where he herded sheep and enjoyed simple pastoral pleasures, like eating the occasional Greek hero who happened to sail by. (Some monsters never learn.)

CIRCE
(Sear'-see)
ENCHANTRESS

Distinguishing Features:
Great hairdo, beautiful robes, enchanting singing voice, deadly wand hidden up her sleeve.

Now:
Circe runs a fashionable spa and resort on an island in the Sea of Monsters. Stop by if you'd like a makeover, but be warned, you might not leave the same person, or even the same species.

Then:
Circe loved to entertain sailors. She would welcome them warmly, feed them well, then turn them into pigs. Odysseus put a stop to this practice by eating a magic herb, then holding the sorceress at knife-point until she released his polymorphed crewmates. Circe promptly fell in love with Odysseus. Go figure.

SIRENS
(Sy'-rens)
MONSTERS

Distinguishing Features:
Ugly bodies, faces like vultures, beautiful singing voices. (Hey, that sounds like my elementary school choir teacher . . .)

Now:
The Sirens inhabit the Sea of Monsters, where they lure sailors to their deaths by singing sweet songs, something like 80s Oldies radio, only worse.

Then:
Back in the day, the Sirens were a real threat to the Greek shipping industry. Then a smart guy named Odysseus discovered that you could plug your ears with wax and sail right past the Sirens without hearing a thing. Strangely, Odysseus is usually remembered for his other accomplishments, not as the inventor of ear wax.

PERCY'S SUMMER CAMP REPORT

Dear Percy Jackson,

Below is your progress report for the summer, which will be sent home to your parents. We are happy to report that your marks are passable, so you will not be fed to the harpies at the present time. Please review and sign for our records.

Sincerely,
Chiron, Activities Director
Dionysus, Camp Director

Activity	Grade	Comments
Monster Maiming	A	Percy shows great aptitude at lopping off limbs.
Defence	B	Percy almost got killed several times this summer. Good job! He needs to concentrate on minding his surroundings and not getting bitten by poisonous scorpions.
Swordfighting	A+	Percy's sword skills are excellent. However, it would be better if he could fight without dousing himself in salt water first.
Team Spirit	C	Percy gets in occasional fights with his fellow campers. We would like him to remember that Clarisse's head does not belong in the barbecue pit.

Greek Speak	C	Percy is making progress with Ancient Greek. Unfortunately, on his final exam he translated 'The great Achilles took the field' as 'My grandfather's hamburger is nasty'. Keep trying.
Chariot Racing	A	In Percy's last race, he not only won but left most of the other chariots in flames. Well done!
Foot Racing	C-	Needs improvement. Percy is still slower than the nymphs, and this is while they are in tree form.
Archery	C-	Needs improvement. On the bright side, Percy is firing fewer stray arrows. He has not shot any of his fellow campers in weeks.
Javelin Throwing	B	Percy has been practising! His last throw almost hit the target. True, he knocked a bronze bull's head off, but that is easily fixed.
Rock Climbing	A	Percy excels at rock climbing. Perhaps it's because he does not enjoy falling in the lava below.

Signed: _Percy Jackson_

HOMEWORK OR FIGHTING MONSTERS?

TOUGH CHOICE . . .

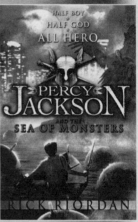

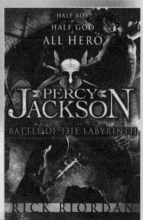

Puffin by Post

Percy Jackson and the Sea of Monsters – Rick Riordan

If you have enjoyed this book and want to read more,
then check out these other great Puffin titles.
You can order any of the following books direct with Puffin by Post:

Percy Jackson and the Lightning Thief • Rick Riordan • 9780141319131	£5.99
'One of the books of the year . . . Vastly entertaining' – *Independent*	

Percy Jackson and the Titan's Curse • Rick Riordan • 9780141321264	£5.99
'A smart idea brilliantly realized' – *Independent*	

Percy Jackson and the Battle of the Labyrinth • Rick Riordan • 9780141382913	£9.99
Percy Jackson faces his most dangerous quest yet, in this fourth brilliant adventure!	

The Pig Scrolls • Paul Shipton • 9780141316369	£5.99
'The most inspired comedy to come along since the Artemis Fowl series. A triumph' – *The Times*	

Questors • Joan Lennon • 9780141319162	£5.99
'Positively wizard-like levels of inventiveness' – *Scotsman*	

Just contact:

Puffin Books, C/o Bookpost, PO Box 29,
Douglas, Isle of Man, IM99 1BQ
Credit cards accepted. For further details:
Telephone: 01624 677237
Fax: 01624 670923

You can email your orders to: bookshop@enterprise.net
Or order online at: www.bookpost.co.uk

Free delivery in the UK.
Overseas customers must add £2 per book.

Prices and availability are subject to change.

Visit puffin.co.uk to find out about the latest titles, read extracts and
exclusive author interviews, and enter exciting competitions.
You can also browse thousands of Puffin books online.